T0128469

# MILLION DOLLAR SECRETS

LAMESHIA MELODIC

authorHOUSE®

*AuthorHouse™*
*1663 Liberty Drive*
*Bloomington, IN 47403*
*www.authorhouse.com*
*Phone: 833-262-8899*

*Email requests to: authorlameshia@gmail.com*
*©So Melodic Enterprises*
*(316)-993-0219*

*Published by AuthorHouse    04/05/2023*

*ISBN: 979-8-8230-0518-0 (sc)*
*ISBN: 979-8-8230-0517-3 (e)*

*Library of Congress Control Number: 2023906289*

*Print information available on the last page.*

*Any people depicted in stock imagery provided by Getty Images are models, and such images are being used for illustrative purposes only. Certain stock imagery © Getty Images.*

*This book is printed on acid-free paper.*

*This is a work of fiction. All of the characters, names, incidents, organizations, and dialogue in this novel are either the products of the author's imagination or are used fictitiously.*

# DEDICATION

This book is dedicated to my heartbeats
with a message to "Dream Big!"

### To...
My Son ~ Donovan, The Apple of Mommy's eye
My Baby Sisters ~ Patience Ivy & LaTrisha Ivy
My Baby Brother ~ AJ Jones Jr.
My Mommy ~ Faith Mallory
My Daddy ~ Andre Shaw
**I love you all,**
**Meshia**

~In Loving Memory of Dennis E. Shaw SR., James
S. McGill Sr. and Lonyne "Baby" Shaw-Tucker~

# ACKNOWLEDGEMENTS

**To My Son**: I love you so much! When I think of you, I am often speechless and that means a lot coming from your Mommy who is always full of words. You mean the world to me and everything I do is for you! Please remember in all that you do aim high there are NO limits- not even the sky! You are my greatest accomplishment. Love you bunches Tireni Donovan!

**To All of My Family & Friends:** I love you ALL more than you know! Thanks for all of your love, support, protection, encouragement, and constant sacrifices. There is no one but God who could ever love you more than I do! I Love you today, forever, and always!

# CHAPTER 1

**"W**e 'bout to set you foo's! You should know betta than to sit down at this table" Terrel shouted as he slammed his card down on the table. "You already know bruh!" Ta'Ron encouraged him as he stood up and leaned across the table to give him dap. Terrel, well "T" as we all called him, was always so animated. There was never a dull moment when he was around. He should have been a comedian. He is the only person I know who can crack a joke about anything and anyone at any time and it is always hilarious. He was the type of guy you always wanted around. He could tell you a joke about a loaf of bread and have you on the floor in tears. I was sure he would be famous by now and we would be traveling all around to see him do his thang. Unfortunately, that has not happened, but hey it is not too late, I hope. I sure hate things turned out the way they did for him.

We have all known one another for a very long time. We grew up in the same neighborhood, went to high school together and we are still close to this day. Wherever you found me you could be certain to find the crew. Ta'Ron, Cassandra aka "Cassie", T, Donovan, Devin, and Ronald, better known as "Ronnie." We were inseparable. We were always seven deep as we called it. Back in the days people use to joke around and call us *"Seventh Heaven"*, after that television sitcom, but we didn't mind. Cassie and I were criticized for being the only two girls hanging out with five boys and believe me the rumors spread quickly about us sleeping around with all of them. We did not pay any attention to their foolishness, we knew they were just jealous, and I didn't blame them. Everyone in my crew was fine, hell we still are, and had something going for themselves! We had been through a lot together and it didn't matter what people thought, we vowed that we would be friends for life, and here we are in our early thirties, and we have kept that promise.

T grew up just a few doors down from me as a child. He lived with his grandmother because his father left his mother and started a new family and never looked back, which was hard for his mother to handle after sixteen years of marriage. She started doing drugs and running the streets, going in and out of jail and the whole nine. So, to keep T and his siblings out of the system his Grandma, who everybody calls "Mama Shirley," took them in. Mama Shirley was sweet but strict. She didn't want T to become a *statistic* as she would always say. Our neighborhood was full of decent people. It was a mixed neighborhood. All races, and all backgrounds. Mama Shirley and Mr. Sam, "Pop" as we called him, had lived in that neighborhood years before mom and dad moved there. Pop was a retired army vet. He had been in the army for years. We never knew how many years because his story would change every time, he told it. They were already up in age when T moved in, but they were determined to show them a decent life. We used to tease T all the time about them being too strict, but all in all we knew why they were doing it.

T and I became good friends instantly. I was outside sitting on the porch when he first moved in. It didn't take long at all for them to get all of their things moved into the house. Mama Shirley yelled down the street at me, "Tierra-Michelle, come here baby I want you to meet my grandson!" "Yes ma'am" I shouted back as I begin to walk down to her house. He was tall and dark with light brown eyes, a cutie pie. "Tierra-Michelle this is my Grandson Terrel, he is going to be living with Pop and I now" she said. I stretched out my arm to shake his hand and to say nice to meet you; however, he decided to grab me and hug me and pinch my cheeks as if I was his long-lost cousin. "Quit being so silly all of the time boy!" Mama Shirley yelled at him as she pulled us a part. By this time, I was already laughing. And had a look of confusion on my face, I'm sure. "Are those your real eyes?" I asked him. "Are those your real feet?" he replied giggling and pointing down at my sandals. I looked down to see what was so funny and noticed it looked like I had been kicking a bucket of flour around with my bare feet. Just a few moments prior to him coming we had gone for a swim, and I had showered and forgot to lotion. I was so embarrassed. I wanted to get an attitude, but I couldn't because he was laughing so hard, he made me laugh. "Don't just throw your things around boy what's wrong with you?" Pop shouted as he swung open the front door. Oh, hi Tarra, Pop could never say my name and would call me something different every time. "Hey Pop" I replied. "Sorry baby but Terrel has to come in and learn where to put his things he will be out later." "Yes sir, see you later T" I exclaimed.

"How you gonna just give me a nickname when you just met me?" "The same way you can hug me pinch my cheeks and clown on my feet when we first met" I said sarcastically. "Ha ha ok I got you, T it is Miss. Tierra- Michelle" he said. And from that moment on we have been friends.

It didn't take long at all for the rest of the crew to accept T. He was a hot mess. Girls at school could not get over his light brown eyes and they would fight over him, and he would often get in fights with other guys because they were jealous. He maintained good grades, but his sarcasm would get him in trouble so much that he could hardly stay in class. I was so happy to hear that he was actually going to graduate with us. A few years after T moved in with his grandparents, Pop died, and T had to become the man around the house. It wasn't about money because Pop had left Mama Shirley a nice amount of money and they had already invested a lot while he was living. But he had to do a lot of things around the house which cut into his hangout time. He had to be with his younger siblings a lot and had to run errands for his grandma all the time. Mama Shirley took it hard. They had been high school sweethearts and married for forty-five years. He was almost sixty-five when he died. She wasn't as happy as she always was. She was the type of lady who tried to feed all the neighborhood kids and even tried to make us eat popsicles as teens. We never turned her down. All the added pressure really took a toll on T after high school he decided not to go away to college like we had all planned, but to stay back with Mama Shirley to make sure her and his siblings were ok. While we are all off to college having the time of our life T made some new friends, and they were straight trouble. Rumor had it that he was hanging out with

"Spice" and his crew, a group of degenerate fools who had rap sheets longer than Rapunzel's hair.

He started dating a girl from our neighborhood named Cheyenne Adams who was nothing but a headache with feet. Right after high school she got pregnant and wanted T to treat her like Paris Hilton or somebody. She was a pretty girl but nasty as she wanted to be. She took pride in being the girl that all the boys wanted, and most of them had. Her mother was Native American, and her dad was white. She had really pretty skin and teeth and truth be told a cute shape too, but she was just dirty as hell. She would make moves on people's boyfriends, fathers, and husbands right in front of their faces and laugh about it, and T of all people had gotten this hussy pregnant. When Summer was born T was so excited, she was the most beautiful baby I had ever seen. He would do anything for her. Cheyenne pretended to be in love with T because she knew that he loved that baby, and she could use her to get anything she wanted. She still was a bonified slut. Sleeping with anybody she thought had money. But we couldn't convince T of that. He loved that Girl and was determined that they would be the family that he never had. He proposed to her and everything. I was hot but if he was happy what could we do. He would run around saying "You can't help who you love Tierra-Michelle!" The hell you can't I thought to myself but didn't say a word.

During the middle of our sophomore year in college T came to visit us and we tried to talk him into enrolling in school. We heard he was hanging out with the wrong crowds and constantly getting into fights over Cheyenne. But T declined he said he was making good money in the factory and had great benefits and a family and that was all he needed. Mama Shirley wanted him to join the army like Pop, but T wasn't interested at all. We had a good visit and hated to see him go. He left a day earlier than planned because he said he missed Summer so bad and couldn't wait to see her, he had never been away from her prior to this trip. So, he packed up and went home and promised to back for homecoming weekend. He did return for homecoming with the news that he and Cheyenne had broken up and that she was now living with his running buddy "Spice." And how he heard that he was abusive to Cheyenne, so he took Summer, and she was with Mama Shirley while he was visiting us. I didn't bother saying I told you so, I just reminded him that it was homecoming weekend, and that there was a campus full of single ladies to help get his mind off of her. We had so much fun that weekend. The seven of us back together again. Ta'Ron and I were still together as we had been all of our lives, and life as we knew it was good.

School was ending and we were preparing to go home for the summer. I couldn't believe we were already going to be juniors in college. Everyone was chasing their dreams. We made it home and thought that we would plan a few trips for the summer instead of working. Afterall, we had worked all school year long and now it was vacation time. T agreed to go with us since Mama Shirley assured him Summer would be fine. So, we loaded up and headed to Miami, party town. This was the first time we had been to Miami; we were from Georgia and Georgia is what we knew. We arrived in Miami and got settled into our rooms, Ronnie has cousins there and they came to show us around the town. We had so much fun, we ate, we drank, we danced, we drank, we partied, and did I mention we drank. The whole trip is almost a blur because we drank so much. Three days into our weeklong vacation Mama Shirley calls and said that Cheyenne and Spice had come over kicked in the door, pushed her down and taken Summer right out of her arms. "O hell to the naw" I heard T yell and slam the phone down, "Take me home now, they got me messed up" He was yelling and pacing the floor back and forth. Donovan and Devin kept trying to calm him down, he finally told us what was going on and no one complained that the trip was cut short, we loaded up the car and back to Georgia we went. When we got there everything Mama Shirley had described was true. My dad had sent someone over to fix her door and everybody in the neighborhood was taking turns watching out for her house. "You gone run up in my Grandma house, touch her and take my daughter, yal crazy than a mother f…" "Watch your mouth!" Mama Shirley interrupted him. Once he found out she was ok, he grabbed his keys and stormed out the door. Ronnie, Ta'Ron Devin, and Donovan went with him. They were out all night, and they couldn't find them anywhere. When we saw them the next morning T just kept saying "He can have that hoe, just give me my baby!" over and over he would repeat that same phrase. I felt so bad there was nothing we could say that would make him feel better.

Two days had past and still no sign of Cheyenne or Spice and T was uncontrollable. He was snapping at everybody, threatening the whole neighborhood, cussing out the police and all. Finally, after five days of nothing Cousin Rhonda called me saying that she heard Cheyenne had been murdered and they think Spice did it. I didn't want to tell T for several reasons, one because I knew it would send him in a panic to find Summer and two because Cousin Rhonda was nosey as hell, and she didn't always get the story right. Sure, enough we turned on the news and heard about a woman's body that had been found on the side of the road with gunshot wounds to the head and chest, but they didn't say a name. Some idiot called T and told him before I got a chance, and he went nuts. "Calm down T" we all kept saying, "We don't know if it's her yet." But he was not trying to hear it. When it was finally confirmed that the twenty-one-year-old woman's body that was found on the side of the road by a jogger, was Cheyenne Adams you could see the fire in his eyes. He cried so hard until he lost his breath. We tried to comfort him but there were no possible words that could be spoken. As I looked around at everybody in the room, all eyes were filled with tears, and no one said a word.

They had released an Amber alert for two-year-old Summer Danae Griffin. This was unbelievable. I couldn't believe all of this was really happening. Seven days had passed since it all started and still no one had a clue where Spice and Summer were. Spice was a big-time drug dealer. He had no heart, and he didn't play with his money. Word on the street is that Cheyenne was running dope for him, and money and product kept coming up missing. Some speculate she was using the drugs herself while others were saying she had started messing with Reno an OG on the other side of town. Either way, Spice didn't care, and he came to kidnap Summer hoping to get his money and or product back from Cheyenne, when that didn't happen, he shot her in cold blood and dumped her body on the side of the road like roadkill and ran off with Summer.

T hadn't slept in days we all took shifts on sitting with him, buying beer and liquor just to take some of the sting away. During this ordeal Donovan and Devin's grandfather passed and so they had to go to Mississippi for the funeral, Ronnie and Cassie went with them for support. Ta'Ron and I stayed back to make sure Terrel had someone by his side and the twins understood completely. Tips were flooding in from all over but no real leads, mostly "I heard, and I think" type of tips. Finally, some girl called T saying she overheard Spice and his friends saying that he was hiding at some girl's house and that she knew for a fact that they were there because her friend took them some food so that they didn't have to leave the house. The girl gave no name only the address. Why in the world would she call him directly? Ta'Ron wouldn't let me go and I was pissed. He said he didn't know what was going on over there and that me getting hurt wasn't an option. T said he didn't care if it was a setup, he wanted his baby and would get her back if he had to by himself, and that the police were taking too long. They rushed off to the location. They stopped answering my calls and I got worried, I couldn't sit still, T was one of my best friends and Ta'Ron was my first and only true love. I couldn't handle it if anything happened to either one of them. Hours had passed and finally I got a frantic call from Ta'Ron. I remember it like it was yesterday. He was crying and yelling and talking all fast. He kept saying to get Mama Shirley and meet him at Memorial Hospital, that T had been shot. I tried not to get hysterical and tried to remain calm so that I could pass on the message. He wouldn't give me any details, or if he did, I was too out of it to hear them.

We got to Memorial Hospital and there were police

everywhere. Ta'Ron was sitting in the waiting room with his right fist balled up, punching it into his left hand biting his bottom lip rocking back and forth' with blood all over his clothes. "Baby are you alright, what happen?" I screamed as I ran toward him. But before I could get to him, I was intercepted by two police officers who said no one could talk to him until they finished getting his statement. "I don't give a damn about a statement, what is going on, how is T, what happen?" I yelled as they stood in between us. The Nurse came over to Mama Shirley an asked her to complete some paperwork and asked if she had insurance. I had never seen Mama Shirley act out of character, she was always so well-mannered and polite, but I guess she had had enough as well. She snatched the clipboard from the nurse and lifted it up as if she was gonna slap her with it and said "I got your insurance right here heffa, at least tell me his condition before you ask me for money. I am a widow of a United States Army vet, hell yea we got insurance!" The nurse apologized quicker than I had ever seen, and I realized I had to remain calm and help Mama Shirley through this. They finally came back and told us that we could see him for a second that he was going to be fine. The doctor said that one of the bullets just missed his heart and exited out of his left side and that the other bullet was in his shoulder blade and had to be surgically removed, but that all had went well. We asked when he would get to leave. And that's when the police officers came in and read T his rights as if we weren't in the middle of a visit. "Under arrest for what?" I kept asking, I was already mad because they wouldn't let me talk to Ta'Ron and wouldn't let him come in and visit T with us. "Somebody betta start talking, what happen, was Summer even there, hello?" "Ma'am please calm down, we have Summer, and she is fine, once the Doctor releases her, she will be released to her grandmother's custody." One officer said. "Thank you, Jesus," we all started to cry. T laid there not saying anything, with tears just rolling down his face. Another officer continued with the Miranda rights, for the murder of Spencer "Spice" Barnes… they cuffed him to the bed and let us know that there would be a uniformed officer at his hospital room door until his checkout time and then he would be escorted to county jail, and that they had taken Ta'Ron in as well. I lost it, I broke down in tears how could they even consider taking him after what that man had put him through over the past several days? "The Hell you will, my daddy is a lawyer, and he will make sure this is fixed!" I hollered as I exited the room.

It was true my father was Marcus Jackson, one of the most successful African American attorneys in the country. He was very popular in our community for winning cases and taking on bigwigs alone. He made partner at his firm after only one year of practicing law. He is jokingly referred to by his peers as "Action Jackson." We'll just wait and see how Action Jackson feels when he hears about this. He and my mother had been married for twenty-two years at that time and I am an only child. My mom was very successful as well she is a Psychologist and has her own business and often counseled for free at after school programs in rough neighborhoods. People often said I was spoiled, and they were right, I knew anything I asked my daddy for was mine, and this time would be no different. When I got home, I told my daddy everything that happened, and he got right on top of things. "Don't worry about it Sugga, Daddy's got this" he assured me. And one thing I could always count on was my daddy's word.

Donovan, Cassie, Devin, and Ronnie had returned from Mississippi speechless. I felt bad for not calling them immediately and letting them know what happen. But truth is that I didn't really have all the facts myself and I didn't want add stress to the Wright family, as they were already suffering a loss of, they're own. Luckily my friends understood and didn't waste time trying to see what they could do to help. Everyone in the neighborhood pulled together. This was the first time anything like this had ever happen in our nice, quiet, area. Summer didn't want for anything; she was spoiled rotten by the entire block.

Ta'Ron was finally released, and daddy brought him home. He didn't say much just looked miserable and kept saying "I'm cool." I tried not to pressure him much, but we had no answers, no one knew what really happen at that house but him, T and Spice. Under the advice of my father, I was told not to interrogate him and that he had already advised him not to speak about what happen, not even to us. That all the facts would come out in the trial as they are supposed to, and by doing it this way, he cannot ruin the case for himself or for T as daddy was representing them both. I didn't agree but I knew I didn't want to ruin anything and that my daddy knew how to win a case. We tried not to talk about it much even when T was out on bail, we just allowed him his time with Summer and tried to act as if none of this had ever happen, even though we all knew it did. The trial took forever, summertime was over, and we had to return back to campus to start our junior year of college. Ta'Ron had to go back early as he was the starting point guard for our college basketball team and was there on scholarship. Ta'Ron has always been very athletic. In high school he was All American this, MVP for that, and of course we were homecoming king and queen! He ran track and played basketball and he was excellent in both. Daddy made us promise that we would focus on being college students and let him do his job and we promised.

Occasionally we went back for court and by the end of first semester the trial still wasn't over. Daddy was able to get the charges for second degree murder dropped down to involuntary manslaughter for T, and all the charges for Ta'Ron as an accomplice were completely dropped. We came to every court date no matter what was going on at school. Ta'Ron and the twins sometimes missed one here and there because they were traveling with the team. By the time it was spring break they had finally wrapped up the case and we were ready to hear what the judge had to say. We arrived at court early that morning. Daddy already told me that he would have to do sometime but that he would get the sentence reduced. Unfortunately, like daddy said they found him guilty but at least it wasn't murder. The judge sentenced him to nine years. I was so angry; he had never been in any real trouble, and this was crazy. My daddy assured me that if he did what he was supposed to do, he could get his time reduced, and he did, down to five years. However, T was a new man in prison, and he didn't take anything from anybody, and he caught another case for beating up a guard who kept commenting on how pretty his eyes were. While in prison he just kept getting in trouble and so he ended up serving a little over seven years.

When I heard T was finally coming home, I told

everyone that we had to do it up big for him. He asked that we didn't plan anything for the first weekend he got out because he wanted to spend as much time as possible with his now almost ten-year-old daughter. Mama Shirley had taken care of her just like she did T and his siblings. She was spoiled rotten, and she knew it. She was still as beautiful as ever and she was very talented as well. She could sing, play piano, and she was athletic. We made sure she saw her daddy on every visitation day he had. One of us would always go see him and whoever went knew to take Summer with them and Mama Shirley too if she felt up to it. We all made sure he was good and taken care of, he was like a brother to us, especially Ta'Ron. He sent money weekly and packages and accepted hundreds of dollars' worth of collect calls. Even as the years went by and He was drafted into the NBA he still made it a point to make sure he was "squared away" as he would call it, especially if he couldn't make it to see him. T was always so grateful and though we talked a lot on the phone and wrote many letters he never really talked about what happen ever again. His main focus was Summer, and I felt bad for anyone who tried to stand in his way. We agreed that we wouldn't plan anything the first weekend or so, but I planned a huge Bar-B-Q and pool party at our new house after that. I had been working as a realtor, though I definitely didn't have to work, and I had found this beautiful dream house and we bought it and moved in it a few months ago. So, I had been waiting on any excuse at all to host an event there. This was perfect. We did it big Ta'Ron and the fellas were in charge of the drinks and music and Cassie, and I decorated and got the food and invitations. With Ta'Ron being in the NBA we were going to have A list guests over and I knew everything had to be perfect.

Back when we were younger, we always use to play spades, and dominoes. And neither one of those games were for the faint at heart, where we come from. Our parents and their friends use to have gatherings and play spades and drink and talk trash all night long. We quickly picked up their habits and all of us were a force to be reckoned with. The twins Devin and Donovan were usually partners and Ta'Ron and T were partners, they were good. If we went somewhere else, they would have people getting up from the table all night long. Me and Cassie could play too. We fooled plenty of people. We were fine and we looked sweet and innocent, but you put a deck of cards in front of us and we'd show you who we really were. Ronnie was always the floater. He could play well but he would always be walking around trying to get into some girl's face or manage the music, and when you played cards with us you had be able to pay full attention or else. Right away I knew we would have to get some cards going, I didn't care what celebrity showed up, this was my buddy T and I wanted to make sure he enjoyed every moment of it of his party.

It wasn't long before people started showing up, players, their wives, our neighbors, childhood friends, a few of my co-workers, and a so on. Everything turned out great. It was good to have "Seventh Heaven" back together again. It didn't take long at all for T to start cracking on every guest in the house, and everybody was laughing like we always did. Ta'Ron and T were playing Donovan and Devin in the first game of spades, and it just felt like old times. I was excited. It felt so good to look around and see everybody smiling again. "Who you gonna set a lot has changed partna!" Donovan said as he placed his next card down. Smack talking was a must in a real game of spades. Whether you had a hand or not you gotta act like you are running the show. But just like old times they had people getting up from the table left and right. Cassie and I catered to everyone's needs- refilling drinks keeping the food stocked and everybody kept walking around telling me how much they were enjoying themselves.

Time had escaped me; everyone was having such a great time I didn't realize how late it had gotten. Cousin Rhonda quickly reminded me. "Girl I'm old. It's three o'clock in the morning and yal got me out here about to fall asleep in the pool, let me carry my butt home!" We laughed as I escorted her into the house to gather her things, people followed suit and called it a night as well. After about another hour it was only the seven of us left as usual and two girls Ronnie and Devin met at the party of course. "Thank yal so much, this was the bomb, I need to get on home, I want to cook my little princess breakfast in the morning!" T said. One of the girls offered to drop him off as she had not been drinking all night. Soon everybody left and I kissed the love of my life good night and went to bed as well.

# CHAPTER 2

Ta'Ron and I had been together since our childhood. He is the only real boyfriend I have ever had. In grade school I hated him because he picked on me just about every single day. He was just bad! He was always cute but it's hard to like someone who is constantly mean to you. I remember me going home and telling my mom that this little boy in my class was always messing with me and that I was going to beat him up. My mom is so funny, she was even madder than me. She said, "you wear his little butt out before I have to come up there and do it myself!" Then she continued to ramble as she walked out of my bedroom, and you could still hear her down the hallway. She must've been really mad because I could hear daddy asking her what was wrong and she began to just go off! Daddy kept asking her to slow down and calm down, but she was enraged at the idea that someone had done something to her baby! This was the first time I saw my mother go off! She was really reserved; this was awesome to me because not only did I just get permission from her to fight but she even offered to help! My dad was giggling as he entered my room and sat next to me on the bed. He asked me what all of the fuss was about, and I proceeded with telling him the same story I shared with mom. He laughed even harder. "Before you and your mother shut the whole town down, let me explain something to you baby." He said. "Little boys do that sort of thing to pretty little girls like yourself because they like you and don't know how to get your attention and tell you!" What in the world was daddy talking about. Was he gonna fight with me and mama or not, that's all I could remember thinking. He continued "Now you hear me good Tierra-Michelle, it's cute as a kid but real men never hit women or girls, nor do they talk crazy to them! So, if this little joker starts to go too far and you have already told him to stop and talked to the teacher then you show him what the Jackson's are made of!" That a boy dad now you're talking I thought to myself. "Your mom and I will talk to your teacher to make sure she knows what's going on so that she can talk to his parents, we'll handle this sweetie…. What's this knuckle heads name anyway?" Ta'Ron, I said as daddy pulled my door closed as he told me to wash up for dinner. "Ta'Ron huh?" Yes, sir I shouted Ta'Ron Hunter!

The next morning my parents did exactly what they said they would do, and they talked to my teacher, and she talked to Ta'Ron and his parents. Everything cooled down for a while and then he started throwing paper at me and cracking little jokes, which I didn't mind because all of my comebacks were better. And one day he was back to his old self again. Pulling my pigtails and pinching me, so forth and so on. I guess I just got fed up with his crap and I punched him straight in his face and his nose started to bleed. He was so shocked. Well, I knew for sure the fight would be on then, so I just kept swinging, and swinging and swinging, as I yelled "I'm a Jackson little boy I'm a Jackson!" All that swinging for nothing, he didn't even try to hit me back.

I wore his little butt out just like mama had told me two weeks prior, and I made sure he knew I was a Jackson just like daddy said too! After that day Ta'Ron never tried me like that again. Shoot come to think of it he barely even touches my hair now, and we are married! After that day he started just to be as normal as he could be, even giving me invitations to his birthday parties and such but I was still mad and never attended. As the years went on, we entered junior high, and we went to the same school again. One day I was at my locker, and he walked by, got up in my face and kissed me right on the lips and I punched his tail again! "What is wrong with you girl, dang!" he shouted. I started to feel pretty bad it was just a kiss, but I thought he wanted revenge from the butt whooping I gave him years ago. "I don't know where your lips have been and you didn't ask me for a kiss, that's what's wrong with me!" I said. "Well excuse me Princess I'm sorry!" he said sarcastically, and with an attitude I replied, "hmmm you're excused!" I slammed my locker shut and walked off to class.

A few weeks later he sat next to me in chemistry class and started to talk to me, and he was actually funny and cool. He teased me by calling me mean and we just laughed. We had to partner up in class for the next assignment. And as you may have already guessed this nut chose me. Just because we said sorry and chatted a little bit didn't mean I was trying to become his friend. But we were partners and since this project was a huge part of our grade, we let it all go and worked hard. We spent a lot of time together after school, working on the best way to present our project and we actually did a great job. We earned an "A," I guess you can say that's when we realized that we had "chemistry!" So, we continued to hang out and he finally asked me for a kiss one day on the walk home from school and this time I said yes! As time went along, he asked me to be his girlfriend and I said sure! After all he was cute and a good kisser, well I had never kissed anyone else, but I was sure he was good. We dated all through junior high and into high school. We were inseparable. I was a cheerleader and on the volleyball team (which didn't mean much at our school because everyone who tried out for volleyball made it), and he was an all-around athlete. He played basketball, football, and ran track and was very intelligent and fine!

Everybody said we were so perfect together. Turns out daddy was right, all that hair pulling was because Ta'Ron really did like me. Ta'Ron treated me well. He was such a gentleman and so sweet and creative. He would joke and say it was because I could beat him up, or he was scared of my dad and because I was so spoiled that he didn't have a choice, but I didn't mind. Who cared if I was spoiled, I wanted what I wanted when I wanted it and if it wasn't given to me, I'd get it myself. I like to think of it more as creative bargaining rather than being spoiled but O well. We really did have a good relationship. He kept me laughing all the time and would always find some new way to make me feel special.

I loved Ta'Ron and I knew he loved me. We already planned our entire lives together; He would be in the NBA because though he was talented in many sports' basketball was his favorite. He was fast and he could shoot from anywhere on the court and "swish" there it is! I would be a stay-at-home wife until my singing career took off and I would work in a big office somewhere if I ever got bored or he needed my help. Cheering for the basketball team was easy because my baby was a part of it. And we had it all together. But life has a funny way of changing things around. There was this girl who was always up in his face. Brining him gifts for no reason at all, and always having a "question" for him. I could tell right off that she was a sleaze, but he acted as if he was so lost and that she was just cool. Please I wasn't having it. After a while he finally began to see what she really wanted, and he asked her to back off and she told him that she always gets what she wants.

I had to check her one time too many, so the second time I slapped the taste out of her mouth! One warning is all you get. Her name was LaQuisha Gordon, ugh just sounds trifflin', and she was. LaQuisha was an average looking chick. Not ugly at all but nowhere close to me that's for damn sure. She didn't really have much going for herself and I think she saw my man as a meal ticket. One evening the twins heard about this house party on the other side of town and asked if we all wanted to go. Cassie and I had already had tickets for a concert, and we had been waiting on this night all month. We told them that we wouldn't go but they could go ahead. We went to the concert and had a blast, but when it was over, we decided to drop on by the house party. We got there and it wasn't what I thought it would be. There were clusters of teens here and there sort of doing their own thing. On the inside of the house there were more kids eating and dancing. Cassie and I decided to find the guys, but to our surprise they weren't hard to find at all. R Kelly's "Bump & Grind" was playing and there they were all smiles in the middle of the dance floor while the girls were rubbing their butts all up against them, really? I didn't want to make a scene, so I stood there waiting on the song to be over, but Cassie wasn't as calm, and she snatched Donovan right up and proceeded to give him a piece of her mind. Immediately Ta'Ron pushes the girl away from him and she flies into me. As I am about to move her out the way to get to him, I look up and see that it's Quisha and since she had already declared that she always gets what she wants I gave it to her right there in those people's house. I tried to beat the tramp out of her. Then I charged for him. We broke up for a while because of that and I wasn't for sure If I would ever forgive him, but I did, but not until I got a little revenge of my own.

I had never even thought about boys really. Ta'Ron was all I had ever known, and I wasn't trying to get him. I had no Idea how to get another boyfriend, because this one just came to me. But once the rumors were out about what actually happen that night, I had my share of offers. There were a lot of handsome guys at my school but one in particular that was on our football and baseball team. He was Puerto Rican and fine! He was tall with beautiful caramel colored skin and the blackest hair I had ever seen. He had beautiful white teeth and a perfectly sculpted body. He had huge arms and the best set of thighs and calves ever. He was so sweet, and I adored his accent. We started hanging out and I actually enjoyed our time together. Juan Hernandez was perfect. He was kind of smothering at times, but I knew it was because he really liked me, so I didn't give him a hard time. He met me at my locker after every class, and if I thought Ta'Ron was watching or someone was around that I knew would tell, I planted the best kiss ever on Juan. He asked me to homecoming and although I knew he played on the team with Ta'Ron I said yes. I felt bad because Juan was a great guy and I actually started to like him a lot, but I was in love with Mr. Hunter, and I knew it. I did go to my sophomore homecoming with Juan and had a great time too. He was so attentive and if I would think it in my mind, he already had it or was on his way to get it. I didn't want to hurt him, but I knew I had to cut it off soon before I fell hard for him.

As time went on Devin came to me and pleaded with me to work it out with Ta'Ron, because it was weird on our group friendship. "Come on Tierra-Michelle talk to Sniper, he is miserable, and he regrets everything he did, even still talking to Quisha after all of this went down. He doesn't even like her. You see how long that lasted!" Devin said convincingly. I knew he was right, and I really wanted to talk to him, but I was mad and hurt, he had even started to date her for about a week. And that really made me mad. He said he dumped her because he didn't really like her and wanted me back, but rumor has it that she slept with some other guy at another school, and I'm certain that had something to do with it. Whatever the case I wasn't gonna just dump Juan because he found out for himself that she was no good. "Man, forget Sniper," I said in a nasty tone, "Sniper" was a nickname that Ta'Ron adopted from the basketball team because they said he never or rarely misses a shot, which was true. "If he was truly sorry and loved me, he would come to me himself" I continued. "O come on now girl that man all but stalked you and you made sure to ignore him and didn't listen to him" Devin reminded me. It's true and I did it on purpose, he deserved it and I am not sorry about it. But I did miss him.

He finally came to talk to me, and we decided to take it slow and see how things went. I was honest with Juan, and it was as if I could see his heart break. Why couldn't I just tell Ta'Ron it was over, and I had a new boyfriend? Truth is I loved him and that was that. Time did heal the wounds of my heart and we were back to normal again and it felt so good. And we vowed that we would be faithful from there on out. I couldn't believe we had even broken up, but I was glad that we were back together. He wasn't perfect but he was always good to me. We finished High school as a couple, we were even homecoming king and queen, and we dated all throughout College as well. I can't imagine life without him. With everything that had happen with T, Ta'Ron had given me a promise ring in college and promised to marry me once we graduated, because my dad wanted me to get my degree first. He was scared of losing me the way T lost Cheyenne and for a brief moment Summer. I gladly accepted the promise ring and made sure all the ladies knew he was mine. Our relationship had grown stronger over the years, especially senior year in college.

Senior year is always so busy because from day one you are working toward one thing and one thing only and that is graduation. Mr. Charles Hunter, Ta'Rons father had become ill all of the sudden. He started being hospitalized for long periods of time and the doctors could not figure out what was wrong with him. As soon as they thought they had it figured out they would find out that was not it and try again. He started to lose lots of blood and his body was getting so weak. This was really hard for Ta'Ron because Mr. Charles showed up to all his home games and was always cheering from the stands. So, when it was game time and he could not be there, it took a toll on him. But he did what he always knew how to do. He shot the ball and "swish". I would often try to cheer him up and though his mother and siblings would come to the games it was just not the same. Finally, the doctors figured it out and said that a blood transplant and a bit of bone marrow would get him back to normal. That was the best news for Ta'Ron, and it showed that day on the court. He made 60 of the 101 points of the game!

I was so happy that my baby was back. I knew this was hard for him, but I found myself not always having the right words to say. He decided he would surprise his dad and make a bone marrow donation to get things going. And so, he did. He set up all the appointments and made his donation. I thought that was a wonderful idea and I knew Mr. & Mrs. Hunter would be excited. Once he had everything in place, we went back home on a weekend visit and shared the great news, and they were thrilled. We told them that the doctors would contact him for the next step. We went back to school, and we were enjoying being there and making plans for our future, It's one thing to talk about it in Jr. high and high school but we were just months away from becoming responsible adults, and we had to make sure we had everything in order. So, to remain levelheaded we often had date nights and went out to do something alone, because we were always with the others. And it worked out great. I loved our special time together, no family no friends, no school no basketball just the two of us.

One Friday evening we went to dinner and a movie, and we had laughed so hard that my stomach muscles were tight. On the way to the car, we turned our cell phones back on and he had a lot of missed calls. He had had his phone on silent all day and didn't realize it. He had a missed call from the infamous Memorial Hospital back home and my heart dropped to my feet! They didn't leave a detailed message just that he needs to contact them immediately. Well, it was late in the evening and the doctors were surely gone so he called home. His mom answered the phone, and he asked if his dad was ok and she assured him that he was, he told her that he had received a call from the hospital and that it scared him. She again reassured him that Mr. Charles was just fine that he was just waiting on the next step. He calmed down and said he would just call them first thing Monday morning. Although he tried to act like he wasn't thinking about it, all weekend he would make a reference to that call and say something like "That's weird, I wonder what they want if dad is ok!" I tried to remind him that it could be numerous things, and that he had nothing at all to worry about. First thing Monday morning he called Memorial, and I was there by his side as usual. The lady on the phone told him that the samples that he had given for his dad could not be used and that they wanted him to go to see his doctor here as soon as possible to give another sample. He kept asking questions, but she kept referring him to his doctor. He called his doctor as instructed and there were no immediate appointments. It would be a week before they would be able to see him. He signed up for the first available appointment which was the following Wednesday but during school hours. He didn't care he was determined to find out what was going on and why he had to give more samples. When we arrived, he was very anxious to know what was going on and asked me to go in the back with him. It seemed like it took forever for the doctor to call his name, when they finally did, we headed to the nurse's station where they weighed him and asked a series of questions, then they took us back to a room where we waited, and waited on the doctor to come in. When he finally came in, he greeted us, but at this time Ta'Ron was aggravated and just wanted to get to the reason why he was there.

The doctor flipped back and forth through his chart and then took a seat on a small elementary school sized chair with wheels on the bottom and scooted over next to the patient table Ta'Ron was sitting on. "What is going on sir?" Ta'Ron said. The doctor replied in a sympathetic tone "Son your blood is…. your blood well" Ta'Ron interrupted "come on DOC!" "Mr. Hunter the blood and bone marrow samples you provided cannot be used for your father's transplant!' "Ok was it not enough or what's the problem? He added. The doctor continued "Well we want to take more samples to be sure sir but as it looks right now, your blood or marrow doesn't match your fathers at all! I'm sorry son!" Ta'Ron has a look of confusion on his face as did I, so I stood up to rub his back and asked, what does that mean?" The doctor looked at me and back at Ta'Ron as if he wanted approval to answer my question. And Ta'Ron nodded his head yes and the doctor proceeded. "Well, if we take another sample and they say the same thing it means that you……. that you have……. well like I said we don't' know for certain, but it would mean that there is no way possible that Mr. Charles Hunter is your biological father! I am so sorry but that is the reason for this blood test sir." Whoa I had no clue what to say! We were seniors in College, and this is the only father he has ever known, this has to be a mistake. "Yal scared me man, this is a simple mix up take all the blood you need sir. I look just like my dad, I'm athletic just like him, and we do almost everything just alike. Go ahead and get what you need and if possible, rush this to the lab sir because my dad is sick, and he needs me." Ta'Ron responded calmly. The doctor said that he would and then preceded to drawing blood samples only, and we were advised that we could leave and that he would hear from their office within a matter of days. The doctors hadn't yet told Mr. or Mrs. Hunter yet because they didn't want to raise a fuss and wanted to double check first. That was a long ride home. I didn't bring it up because I didn't want to upset him plus, I was praying that this was all a huge mix up.

Yes, we have been through a lot together and I had to be by his side through all of this. When we pulled up on campus he sat in the car and grabbed his phone. He started to dial and before I could ask who he was calling he was already saying hello. He told his mother what the doctor had said and told her that he gave more blood. I could hear her excited voice on the other end of the phone. "That show is a mix up, that is your daddy baby, don't you worry one bit!" Once he heard that, he said yes ma'am and I love you and got off the phone. He was back to his old self within minutes, and I was happy about that. And a week later he got a call and the doctor said that the blood matched! Whew! What a relief. I was so scared for a moment. I hated to see my baby in pain, and this was a bit too much for him. His dad was able to get the procedures done and heal up in time to come to the championship game.

There was so much excitement in the air we had a lot to celebrate and be thankful for. Life as we knew it was good! We won the championship game ninety- six to sixty-three! What a way to end our senior year. We graduated and Ta'Ron was a part of the NBA draft and signed a contract with the Atlanta Hawks and we were excited. We were from Georgia, so this was no problem at all, after all we grew up rooting for them. This was good because he was able to stay home, close to his family and so was I. After he signed his contract, we went to a celebration dinner party that our family and friends had given him in honor of his new NBA contract. The place was decorated so beautifully. When you first entered there were these large, gorgeous chandeliers that were hanging from the ceiling. Each of them looked like they cost a million bucks each. The floors were amazingly beautiful hardwood, and the décor was phenomenal! The place was packed full of people. Some faces I had never even seen before. Everybody was there in their best suits and dresses. It was a great party. Everybody got up and said nice things about him, including his old High school coach, Coach Tucker who presented him with an unofficial Atlanta Hawks jersey that had Sniper written on the back! The food was great, and the DJ knew exactly how to keep the party going. We laughed, danced, ate, cried, and just had a great time. When it was time for him to give his speech, he was at a loss for words. He asked me to come forward and sing a song! I was totally not prepared for that. But this was his day, so I did. And the only thing I could think of at the time was "Hero" by Mariah Carey, so I let it rip and soon every eye in the party was filled with tears, including mine. He joined me back on the stage and we thanked everybody for their love and support. He gave a heartfelt speech to his parents that sent another wave of tears throughout the building; even the servers were wiping their eyes. It was a beautiful night. He helped me down off the stage and fell down the stairs while still holding the microphone, and I quickly tried to help him up. And he began to laugh in the mic and say, "O I'm trippin'" We all started laughing as we tried helping him up, up it was as if he wanted to stay down there. He kept talking through the mic saying how lucky he was to have me in his life and how much he loved me. As if I hadn't cried enough for the evening, I really let the tears roll. He reached his hand into his pant pocket and pulled out a small box, and he opened it and there sitting inside it was a beautiful diamond ring. Is he doing what I think he's doing on his special day? That day he spoke the most beautiful words to me, he said *"Tierra-Michelle, I have loved you since I first laid eyes on you in elementary school. You have always been the most beautiful woman I have ever seen. Everything about you makes me feel like a better man. You know what to say what not to say and you have a killer right hook too! There has never been a time in my life when you have not been there, and I want that feeling to last forever. And just like in grade school when I pulled your pigtails because I didn't know how to get your attention, today I acted as if I stumbled down the stage steps hoping to get your attention for the very last time. Baby, will you graduate from being my princess to being my queen? Will you marry me and continue to make me the happiest man alive?"* "YES!" I screamed as he placed the ring on my finger. What a surprise! I can't believe he just proposed to me, and in such an unselfish way. This was his moment, yet he made sure to include me in it.

The crowd rushed us both to congratulate us on our new engagement. I was in such a shock I really didn't know how to respond. As Ronnie placed my promise ring that Ta'Ron removed from my finger as he was proposing, in my hand, I was reminded that he had kept his promise to marry me after we graduated, and I started to cry all over again.

Cassie came to wipe my eyes and tell me to pull it together as cameras were snapping all around and I didn't want to be seen crying in all of the pictures. So, what was originally a contract signing party had also become an impromptu engagement party.

Time started to fly by pretty fast. I was so happy that my baby had been drafted and that we were engaged but it seemed like we had gotten so busy that we didn't get to spend much time with one another. I was planning our wedding and he was in camp, and it all just became a headache. He allowed me to plan the wedding and I had no limits. However, between family and friends demanding that their ideas be used, I could no longer tell who the bride was. One day he came back home, and I told him we should just elope, but I didn't want to do it in Vegas because that's where everybody went who eloped. So, we decided to go to Hawaii, just the two of us and have an intimate wedding ceremony on the beach and then stay there for a honeymoon and that's exactly what we did. I was so happy that we just got away for a bit. To our surprise our family and friends were cool with it. I thought that my dad would be upset because I was his only child, but he wasn't, plus later we had a huge reception back home and there we still had the traditional wedding party, and my daddy was still able to walk me down the aisle. So, in the end it worked out for everybody. And here we are now the happily married couple, and we have accomplished everything we said we would accomplish when we were teens. I feel so blessed and honored. I think that of all of my accomplishments thus far, being a wife outshines them all.

# CHAPTER 3

**T**uesdays are always a good day for me because normally I work half a day at HG&T Reality showing houses and making deals. I love my job! It's not exactly what I went to school for, but I love getting families into their dream homes. I work for everyone, whether their budget is for an eighty-thousand-dollar family style home or a million-dollar mansion, my job is to give them what they are looking for and not impose my own ideas on them. I love turning over that first pair of keys to the new homeowners. It is such a wonderful experience, and it doesn't hurt that it pays well either. Sometimes I really get wrapped up in my work. I try to think outside the box to make sure I find the family I am working for that perfect house. I often leave a nice welcoming gift inside the new home, giving them something I know they will enjoy, based on conversations that we have had previously just to see that extra sparkle in their eye when they know that the house actually belongs to them. I have been at the top of my reality firm since the day I started, and I will remain there until the day I leave.

I have always been a pretty competitive person. Ever since I can remember I would stop at nothing to win, except cheating. If I couldn't beat you fair and square, we'd just have to keep on playing until I did! But I was always creative and somehow, I would come up with some off the wall idea, stuff people couldn't even dream of, and I would not only win, but leave mouths open in astonishment. Truth is sometimes I would surprise myself, wondering where I got the idea from. That quality has taken me far in this business. I actually started with HG&T as their receptionist, and I actually loved it. They sell and professionally manage residential and commercial properties all over the United States, so I was able to travel for training and certifications, and with Ta'Ron being in the NBA, if he was to ever get traded the chances of me being able to transfer is pretty high. The job was simple but very busy. I did the normal job any receptionist would do. I answered phones; sent and received faxes, and packages, set appointments, set up meetings and training seminars, responded to email inquiries and helped with the planning of office events. I didn't mind being the errand girl at all! They have an absolutely gorgeous ten story office building with an excellent view of the city. It looked like something straight from a movie. Fountains and ponds surrounded the outside and the inside was very beautiful and detailed. Even the cup holder that the pens sit in looks like it cost a fortune, and I had my own office. I received all the perks the realtors received expect the commissions. I got along great with everybody, and the hours were perfect for a newlywed!

One day we were at our annual company picnic hanging out and having a great time. This was always a major event. The Mayor would stop by and all the other city officials as HG&T had a great reputation with the community. I was there alone because the Hawks were on the road. I didn't mind at all; I have always been a "people person" and I have always known how to carry on a great conversation in any setting. I mingled around with everybody. This particular day I felt like a tour guide. Everybody was asking questions and I seemed to know all the answers to them. They were just rolling off my tongue without me even thinking about it. I was selling the building the food and everything. I wasn't doing it on purpose, it was just coming out. I'm sure it's because I had been asked so many questions while answering the phones and filing paperwork that it was just second nature at this point. And my response to all the décor and food that was at the party was not an expert response, rather my personal opinion that I made sound factual. I didn't realize the "big wigs" were behind me the whole time. The big boss Michael Hoggis (the "H" in HG&T) asked me if I ever thought about getting licensed and actually being a realtor rather than working behind the desk. He said that if I ever wanted to, they would put up the money for all of my licensing and certifications, because he believed with my natural sells ability and "charisma" that I would do great. I had thought about it once before but never in depth. But when I talked to my hubby, he was all for it and so I called Mr. Hoggis and let him know that I was interested, and the rest as they say is history. I closed my first deal a few months after being licensed, and I have not stopped yet.

I get a lot of referrals from clients that I have helped in the past, and that's what really keeps me alive. Plus, I love networking, any excuse to go to a party or function will do. I go to everything I can, and I pass out my cards and I actually get a lot of responses. Some people are not quite ready to buy and are only requesting information, but I don't throw them to the side like most of my colleagues.

I have found that eventually they will be ready and if I create a relationship with them, they will call me when they are. I do also have the advantage of being the wife of a millionaire so his friends/teammates and other professionals he is associated with, have had a lot to do with my success as well. I have sold more than a dozen mansions and vacation homes just to them alone. I love it because here we are in our early thirties both millionaires. And I am not only a millionaire because of him, but because I have closed some amazing deals both residential and commercial and I tell you the commissions have been amazing. I love what I do, it's better than sitting at home all day, plus I don't feel so bad when I go on my random shopping sprees when I know it's my money I'm blowing too!

I usually work a full schedule except on Tuesdays. My husband allows me to have this day all to myself. No cooking, no cleaning, no "busy work" just a day to do whatever I feel like doing. I am even exempt from attending any games that fall on Tuesday, which I never miss although I know what he said; I want to be there for him. So, I am looking forward to today! This is my day to hang out with the two most important women in my life, Mommy and Cassie! After working a few hours, I routinely meet Mommy for brunch. We like to go try different places and just have time with it only being us two. Sometimes if she doesn't have any afternoon appointments we go shopping or just riding around town with the top down on her cherry red Jaguar and just be the divas that we are. Then later on in the evening I hook up with Cassie for some fun girlfriend time and there are no limits to what we might try. My husband is so sensitive to my needs. Mommy being a psychologist suggested this a while ago that we allow one another a little time to themselves so that we didn't get burned out from wearing our different hats in life that we never had time to have fun and have other friendships. She said this would help us to keep the fire burning in our marriage, and she should know, because not only is she a licensed psychologist but she had been married only to daddy and they are still very much in love. So, we tried it and love the idea. He gets his half a day too which sometime changes depending on his schedule, but I don't mind adjusting, as long as I get some quality time alone with him as well.

Today Mommy and I are going to La Che`rie' a new French restaurant on the west side of town. I can barely wait to get there. I have heard great things about this place. I have never really had French food that I know of, and I am interested in trying it and having a great time with "Shelly", as everyone called my mother. My dad is not into all the fine dining, he says it's a waste of money. He will go just to satisfy mom, but he is just fine eating at your area Applebee's or BBQ joint! We always try to make it fun and adventurous, and mommy doesn't mind all of my crazy ideas. So, knowing that Pairs is the fashion capitol of the world, I decided we should dress like them, in stunning dresses and the oversized hats, big sunglasses gloves and a small clutch purse. She agreed and added that we should try to learn a few words or at least work on our French accent! This ought to be fun. It seemed like it took forever for noon to come. Not that I wasn't enjoying my time at work, but I really look forward to Tuesdays.

I finally wrapped everything up at work and headed to the ladies' room on the first floor to change into my

"French" gear on my way out the door. I didn't take long at all to get into character. I decided I would try to imitate the accent rather than trying to learn a few words that I knew I would butcher. So, while I was in the bathroom mirror making sure I looked the part, women started to walk in and complement my outfit as well as my hair and makeup! That really pumped me up. I called mommy on her cell phone to make sure she was headed over already because sometimes her appointments lasted longer than expected. And if it was a high paying client she wasn't going to leave until they were done venting. However, she was pretty good about it when it came to me. She said that she would beat me there and that she would go ahead and get us a table. On my way out the bathroom I dropped my clutch bag because I was trying to balance all of the other things I had in my hand, and someone reached down and said, "I'll get that for you ma'am!" I was thrilled because I knew that if I bent down to get it, I would drop the rest of the things I was holding. I looked up at him as he was straightening up from bending over to grab my bag, and I removed my shades so that I could thank him properly. "Thank you so much sir" I said. "Tierra, Tierra-Michelle" he said with a huge grin on his face. At first, I did not recognize him. And then he said, "O come on it hasn't been that long, you still look amazing!" I caught my breath from all the rushing I had just done and looked at him again. "Juan Hernandez, you have got to be kidding me!" Wow after all these years he was still as fine as he was in high school only, he looked better. "WOW, look at you I can't believe my eyes, it's been years, how are you" I asked. "I am doing well; I am moving back to the area after being in Philly since we graduated. I stopped by to get some information because we are looking into buying a house, and HG&T is where it's at! What are you doing in here?" I tried to hurry and gather my thoughts, but my eyes were fixed on his three-piece Armani suit that was tailored to the "t" to fit his still beautifully sculpted body. "Um ok sorry uh, excuse the dress, I...., I work here, but I am meeting my mother for brunch, and we decided to get a little festive" I chuckled. "Festive indeed" he said as he looked me up and down and licked his lips like he was LL Cool J himself. Woo it just got hot as hell in here all the sudden. Or did I just get hot and bothered because I ran into Juan? Jesus, please help me! This man is looking and smelling like a million bucks, and I have never desired to be with another man in my life but for the past thirty seconds my thoughts were so not on the cross! "This old thing, why thank you!" I don't know why I just lied this dress wasn't old at all. I had just bought it for this Tuesday's French brunch with Mommy. "O wow it was so good to see you, but my mother is waiting for me for brunch, I feel so rude I would love to chat with you and catch up sometime but I gotta run now. I hope you don't think that I am being rude, it's just..." He interrupted me, "Don't be ridiculous, go and have a great time, I'm sure I will see you again, like I said I just relocated, and I am looking for a place" he reminded me. I reached into my clutch, and I handed him my business card and told him to call me sometime. And I jetted out that door like I was Wilma Rudolph!

Once I got into the car I calmed down and started driving to the restaurant. I knew this was going to be a fun day. Even during business hours this place stayed busy, so I wanted to hurry to make sure that I didn't cause us to lose our reservation. When I arrived Mommy waved me to our table, which faced the window and had an amazing view. The place was even more beautiful than I imagined. I greeted her and we sat down and began to talk about how lovely the place was and complimented on another on our attire. We picked up the menu and mommy stated that she already found what she wanted to try and that I should pick something different so that we can try a couple of things and I agreed. I started looking over the menu to see what sounded good, as I scanned the menu Mommy asked, "what are you grinning about?" I told her I wasn't smiling that I was just excited to be here, but secretly I was thinking about Juan and didn't realize that it was showing on the outside. "I didn't say smiling, I said grinning, and who grins at a menu, un huh…. Ok Tierra Michelle…." "Shelly!" I interrupted her and we both started to laugh "Can you just call the waiter over? I am ready to order." She chuckled and said ok, and I was relieved to get out of that conversation. The waiter came to the table and introduced himself "Good afternoon, ladies my name is Corbin, and I will be taking care of you today have you decided on your meal?" We responded yes in unison and proceeded to order brunch. "Corbin, I'm going to have the Brochette D'Agneau a la Greque, please." Mother excitedly ordered, and she pronounced the words rather well, I thought. I then turned on my accent that I had been practicing and ordered my meal. "And I'll have the Truitesaute` Sauce Amere, Sir Corbin" He smiled "Very impressive ladies and excellent choices as well, we will have that right out for you!" Mommy and I laughed as he walked away and high fived letting one another know that we had done well. Brunch came out and it looked beautiful, the plate was well garnished, it looked like something out of a magazine. We had one of the staff members take our picture with Corbin and he seemed to really enjoy it. We ate our brunch and just really enjoyed one another's time. I sat there thinking that I have the best mother in the world and God didn't even make me share her with a sibling, I am a lucky woman! We didn't rush that brunch, we sat for hours laughing and reminiscing and just being grateful to have one another. I must admit that occasionally my mind went back to bumping into Juan and how I couldn't wait to tell Cassie, that I had seen him and give her all the details. It has been years since I have seen this man, why was I feeling giddy like a little schoolgirl over a brief encounter with an ex, and I have an amazing husband who takes good care of me.

I know I am a married woman but after all it's not like we did anything, so why do I feel so guilty? Mom and I left a nice size tip on the table, which is our favorite thing to do, especially when we had great service. We hugged and got into the car, and I immediately turned on my Bluetooth and called Cassie!

# La Che`rie

Lunch & Dinner Daily, 11 a.m. to 10 p.m. | Sunday Brunch 9 a.m. to 2 p.m. | Serving Atlanta Georgia and surrounding area

## Hors d' Oeuvres

**ASSIETTE DE FRUITS ET FONDUE DE BRIE**
Wedge of baked Brie with ripe melon and berries 7

**CHAUSSON DU FROMAGE DE CHÈVRE**
Goat cheese tart 6

**PALOURDES AU GRATIN**
Baked clams with garlic butter and bread crumbs 9

**LES ASPERGES VERTES À LA HOLLANDAISE**
Tender green asparagus with a hollandaise sauce 7

**LES ESCARGOTS AU BEURRE**
Snails served in the shell with butter, tomatoes and garlic 9

**MOULES À LA MARINÈRE**
Mussels cooked in white wine, butter, parsley, and shallots 10

**QUICHE LORRAINE**
Fresh baked quiche with scrambled bacon and gruyere 8

## Soupe et Salades

**SOUPE DU JOUR**
Ask your server for our chef's daily soup selections 4

**SOUPE À L'OIGNON**
Classic onion soup, made with three types of onions and topped with melted gruyère 5

**EPINARDS ET CONCOMBRES À LA GRECQUE**
Spinach salad with feta and yogurt garlic dressing 6

**SALADE NIÇOISE**
Organic greens, flaked tuna, niçoise olives, anchovies, egg, tomatoes, and bell peppers 9

## Sandwiches

**FROMAGE AU JAMBON**
Roasted ham and gruyere with aioli on a baguette 8

**POULET**
Grilled chicken breast with lemon caper sauce, tomato, lettuce, and gruyere on focaccia 11

**TURKEY PESTO**
Thin sliced baked turkey with pickled red onions, lettuce, tomato, and fresh basil pesto on a baguette 9

**PORTOBELLO MUSHROOM**
Jumbo grilled portobello mushroom seasoned with Herbes de Provence, topped with roasted red peppers, swiss cheese, and aioli 11

**CRÊPE PARISIAN**
Thin sliced roasted ham and gruyere in a housemade buckwheat crepe 12

## Les Plats Principaux

**POULET À LA MOUTARDE ET AU MIEL**
Grilled chicken breast with honey mustard glaze 17

**CHAMPIGNON PARMENTIER AU GRATIN**
Braised portobello mushrooms, topped with mashed potatoes and Gruyere 16

**PORC À LA DIJONNAISE**
Sauteed pork tenderloin medallions with an orange compote sauce 18

**TRUITE SAUTÉ SAUCE AMÈRE**
Sautéed fresh boneless trout with a raspberry vinegar butter sauce, tarragon, parsley and shallots 21

**BROCHETTE D'AGNEAU À LA GRECQUE**
Lamb brochettes with sweet peppers, zucchini and echaote with a Greek citrus sauce of fresh rosemary, orange, lime and grapefruit juice 19

# CHAPTER 4

**C**assie and I are so close we are like sisters! I tell her absolutely everything detail by detail, and she does me the same way. We have been inseparable since the day we met! Cassie is cool she is a real tell it like it is type of chic, but she is a Diva for certain! Kind of ghetto sometime but still a Diva! I am the only child and I like it that way but if I ever had a sibling, I would say Cassie would've been the perfect one. I don't say this because she is perfect, or because she is so easy to get along with, because the truth is she can be quite bossy and stubborn most of the time. However, her heart is pure, and she truly understands me, and that is not always the easiest thing to do!

Coming up we did all the things best friends did! We slept over one another's house; we went shopping, bowling, and skating together and everything else! She is the only girl I ever really trusted. It's crazy how fast time flies! It seems like just a few days ago we were talking about what we were gonna do and who we were gonna be when we grew up, and here we are! We had big dreams and we had it all planned out! We were going to be successful! And we promised not to allow money or status change us. We vowed not to become the type of people who make it big and forget where they come from, and never give back. That was one of our biggest pet peeves. Being from Georgia we had seen many people make it to the top, some of them were even our classmates and peers. It just baffles me how a little money and a little fame has you catching amnesia or dementia right away! I remember one friend in particular became a famous singer! The girl could blow she stayed on the block with us and went to school with us and all! After she signed with her label, they relocated her to New York City. She was there about eighteen months before her single ever dropped. When we saw her video on television our entire town was excited! We hosted listening parties for her family and all! Her single went all the way to number one and that is when ole girl changed! The next thing we knew she had an interview with OPRAH! We love us some Oprah so once you made it there that is it! Anyway Mrs. Oprah was asking her to tell a little about herself and do you know that this heffa said she was from New York City? I wanted to reach through that television and slap her right in her mouth! Not only that, but she also hosted a "Derricka Gives Back" campaign, and the nut bucket claimed NYC as her hometown and didn't give a dime back to her real hometown! Our city was furious, her parents included! When she finally came back to do a concert, she could barely sell a ticket! Needless to say, her single was the only hit she had, and her "hometown" of New York City sent her dumb behind right back to Georgia, where she still is today working at a call center! Ha ha, I could sing better than she could anyway. So that is why Cassie, and I made that vow to never do that! After all these years we have upheld that promise.

Cassie is a highly decorated schoolteacher. She has received awards and recognition citywide, statewide and on the national level! She has even done some international teaching! It is her passion, and she is good at it. Her students love her and trust her with the inner most details of their lives. Even the parents would come to her about their personal issues. She is just that type of person. She runs a summer camp every year free of charge and she has a tutoring business, and she charges nothing for that either! She loved the attention, and she loved being able to give back!

She is the person to go to, period. One time one of her students' parents called her to come to their home because they could not calm their daughter down. The mom said she was crying hysterically and just would not listen. Cassie is as sweet as pie, but she has a no-nonsense air about herself that the kids didn't play with at all. Poor baby, this story in particular brings me laughing so hard I'm in tears, no matter how many times I hear it. Anyway, Cassie gets to the home and the little girl runs to her and falls apart in her arms. She was upset that her pet rabbit "Fluffy" whom she had got from Cassie was missing. Cassie gave everyone in her class a pet bunny after they learned about them in class. The kids loved it. Anyway, she was furious because she knew for certain that she locked the cage. The mom and dad were standing in the living room displaying a range of emotion. The mom was crying, and the dad kept turning his head to trying to hide the fact that he was laughing. The little girl continued in her story saying Fluffy had never gotten out of the cage before and she wondered what could've happened. She wondered why her mom cooked rabbit for dinner for the very first time, on the same day her pet bunny went missing. She believed her parents cooked Fluffy for dinner because at first, they lied to her and told her it was baked chicken! She was persistent and said it did not look nor taste like chicken to her and that is when they confessed it was rabbit. She was crying so uncontrollably they had to call Cassie to calm her down. It was at that time Cassie told her there were two types of rabbits. "Rabbits you can eat it's bunnies that you can't eat!" And just like that the little girl stopped crying. The funny part is the Dad still couldn't hold his composure and the Mom was still crying. When Cassie asked if indeed it was Fluffy the dad busted out the laughs he had held in for so long and the mom replied, "O girl!" Although they never confessed Cassie agreed with her student that they indeed served up Fluffy for dinner that night. When she left her heart was broken, and though it was already late in the evening she rushed to the store and purchased a basket full of groceries and took them back to their home. Cassie said they almost knocked her down trying to get those groceries into the house. She never asked them again if they killed poor Fluffy, but she said it was evident when they welcomed all the groceries in the home and the dad's eyes filled with tears. They were a very sweet family and very loving, but they had been going through some financial problems. If they killed Fluffy it was because they couldn't stand to see their daughter go hungry. A very heart wrenching story but I still crack up every time… poor little Fluffy!

Her heart is just that big. She loved deep and there was nothing you could do to change that part of her. Cassie and Donovan had been dating since our school days. They made a really cute couple! Donovan was into sports as well, but he and Devin were "pretty boys," and they had their share of girls chasing them. I think Donovan is more scared of what Cassie would do than anything else. When she wasn't busy teaching, tutoring, and running summer camp, she was helping him do things for the club. She loved promoting the different events and showing up making sure the women knew that he was spoken for. The club was doing well Donovan, Devin, and Ronnie were doing a great job. It was a classy upscale club. More like a lounge and restaurant! They stayed at capacity, and we stayed on the VIP list! They had the best DJ in town and their wings were the bomb! On top of all that they are always being innovative and had the newest ideas and music first. They had a theme for every day of the week. It wasn't that bumping and grinding type of atmosphere. And there were rarely any altercations there. They had live entertainment, open mic nights, poetry, bands, comedians, and celebrities passed through their like Norm passed through Cheers! You never knew who was going to just show up! The lines were always wrapped around the building. I have to give it to them; they are doing big things.

Donovan treated Cassie like a queen, and she deserved it! She has always been there for him and never left his side. His number one downfall is that he is a MAMA'S BOY! He has really come a long way, but it almost split them up a few times. It was always "My Mama said" this and "Mama said don't do that!" Oh, that burned her up. But on the flip side they say that you can always tell how a man will treat you based on how he treats his mother and sisters. If that myth is true, Cassie snagged her a good one. He was very romantic. She stays so busy as does he that they rarely have the time for an extended vacation. But he always finds the cutest most romantic ways to remind her that she is not only number one, but the only one in his life. That boy is super whipped! It is sweet though and precious to watch. He never waits until holidays to do it big for her. It is literally all the time. If it is her birthday, valentines, or Christmas it's a grand affair. Shoot even Ta'Ron picked up a few pointers from him. He affectionately calls her "Boo-Baby," he even has it tattooed on his neck. One of the sweetest things in my opinion that he ever did for her on no special occasion at all was the day he took her to a concert to see NEW EDTION, her favorite group of all time! They were in town on tour, and he had of course gotten her front row seats and backstage passes! He did the normal stuff like taking her to dinner and picking her up in a limo! But what we didn't know is that he had really put some thought into it. So here we all are intrigued by the stunning performance that these guys can still put on and they started to sing "Can You Stand the Rain!" As old as we were we ought to have been shamed for cutting up the way we did, but we didn't care. We were jumping up and down and screaming like giddy school age girls. And all the sudden Mr. Johnnie Gill himself said he needed a "Boo-Baby" in his life and asked if one was in the crowd. At first, we thought nothing of it, and we screamed and waved our hand right along with the rest of the women in the crowd until he repeated himself. Out of nowhere the entire crew, Johnnie, Ralph, Ricky, Michael, Ronnie, and yes even Bobby started to sing in harmony "Boo-Baby" and called her on stage, sat her in the chair and finished singing her favorite song! They proceeded on singing "Donovan loves you Boo-Baby," to the melody of "Can You Stand the Rain" and went right back into the actual song! We were both in tears! That was so sweet and thoughtful. When the concert was over, we all went backstage, and they were so nice. But I was impressed more with Donovan's creativity than anything else! They said they had never been asked to do something like that before but thought it was really sweet! After that night, the whole town knew her as "Boo-Baby!" Anyway, that was just a small example of how he treated her daily. It was no wonder girls were always in his face. He was fine, successful, a gentleman, a sweetheart, and a mama's boy!

One of her best qualities is that she is a great listener, and that is who I needed most today, Cassie the listener. When we have something to tell one another that just cannot wait, we call or text and say it's a "Diva Emergency!" This definitely qualified as one of those moments. I can't believe he is even on my mind. Cassie is a straightforward type of person, so she is going to spare me no mercy and that is what I need right now. It seemed like it took her forever to answer the phone. "Girl… I have a Diva Emergency… and I do mean emergency! Where are you at? This cannot wait, girl I need to see you now! Oh my God my heart is beating so fast! Where are you at?" I said in a panic as soon as she picked up the phone. "Um well hello to you too! What is wrong with you? Calm down girl. I am out gathering checks from the sponsors for my summer camp! I thought we were going to hook up tonight for ladies' night anyway?" I quickly interrupted her "Didn't I say this can't wait? Cass I am about to bust for real!" She tried to calm me down but to no avail. Sometime when you gotta tell somebody something it just cannot wait. She tried her best, but I really didn't know what to do and she was the only person I trusted. "Are you hurt? Is everybody alright?" she asked nervously. I calmed down because I could tell I was starting to scare her. "Nobody is hurt" I replied. "Ok let me finish up here and I can meet you in about an hour, ok?" I didn't respond "Tierra, are you there?" Hesitantly I finally replied "Yeah that's cool. Meet me at the park off 59th in an hour." She agreed and then we hung up. Damn an hour is a long time away. What was I going to do until then! I stopped by my favorite shoe store and bought 3 pair of shoes which shoe shopping usually always cheers me up, but I still had this anxious feeling that I could not get rid of. I put the bags in the car, dropped by Smoothie King and got us both our favorite smoothie and started driving toward 59th! The wait drove me crazy! She finally pulled up and I jumped out the car grabbing the two smoothies and my keys as I yelled across the park "GIRL!"

# CHAPTER 5

**W**hy are you acting so dog gone crazy girl? Cassie asked. "Cass you won't believe what happened to me today!" I then backed the story all the way up to me and Mommy's day out! And then I told her what happened! "And on my way out of the door I dropped all of my things and he helped me pick them up. Girl, he looked and smelled good, and all sorts of crazy thoughts went through my mind!" Who? She asked and I kept talking. "It doesn't make any since Cass I am in love with Ta'Ron and only Ta'Ron." Who Tierra who? She said angrily. "Why would seeing him make me feel this way? What is wrong with me? I haven't even thought of him since…." I am not going to ask who again Cassie yelled "Girl I am sorry; it was Juan Hernandez!" "From School?" she asked, "Yes from school!" As I retold the story, I really felt dumb. Why did I even think this was a Diva Emergency? I only bumped into the guy at work and he and his wife are looking for a home! All I have to do is my job and that's it!

"Hold up! I know good and damn well you didn't make me stop collecting money for my camp to come tell you you seen Juan?" Tierra come on now?" Truth be told I was starting to get pretty annoyed at her myself. If she would let me finish, I could tell her the whole story! "Spit it out girl" She said. Okay, okay, okay! I responded. "Well,

I guess it's more like "Diva Confessions instead of a Diva Emergency," You and Juan are old news, and I am quite sure he has moved on since you broke his heart in high school. Plus, you just ran into the man he told you he was in a relationship, and they were looking for a house, so it is not like he came looking for you, you just happen to work for the most prominent real estate company in town! Plus, what are the odds of yal seeing each other again? It ain't like yal exchanged phone numbers or anything?" She finally took a breath, and I did not respond. "Hello, I said you did not exchange phone numbers, right?" She asked again "Well not exactly, we just exchanged business cards and he asked me to maybe meet him for lunch so we could catch up and I could maybe help him find the perfect house, that's all!" I said defensively. "O hell no! Girl you cannot even play with fire and if you feel bad about saying hello to the man, then you already know that lunch is one hundred percent out of the question unless it is double date with your husband. Anyway, let me ask you this Tierra, are you going to tell Ta'Ron that you bumped into your good smelling fly suit wearing, smooth skinned ex-boyfriend, and that yal exchanged information and he then asked you for lunch and that you cannot get him off of your mind?" She chuckled. "Exactly! Girl, leave well enough alone. You are my girl but right is right and wrong is wrong. Give this lead up no matter how big the commission, because it will cost you more than you are willing to pay in the end!" Ugh I hate it when she is right!

"Go get out of that damn sun dress, take a bath, relax, and meet me at the club later honey, cuz you need a drink, and so do I! She said jokingly, but I didn't think it was a laughing matter at all! However, I knew I had to calm down, so I agreed! I stood up and hugged her and headed home to relax awhile. I knew she would give it to me straight up but dang! She got me feeling and an adulterer and I didn't even do anything.

I'm telling you my mind played tricks on me the entire ride home. As soon as I got into the car "Keep it on the Down Low" was playing on the radio, so I turned the station and "As We Lay" was going off and then "Secret Lovers" came on directly behind it, really? I turned off the radio but with all the silence in the car I began to daydream about spending time with him. So, I turned on the gospel station and blared it until I got home! I took me a nice long hot bubble bath and put on my pajamas. I then went and got an ice-cold bowl of green grapes from the fridge and flopped down on the sofa. I turned on the television and before you know it, I had fallen asleep. If it wasn't for the knock at the door, followed by a repeated ringing of the doorbell, I would've stayed sleep. I got up to check the door and I guess I moved too slow, by the time I got to the door no one was there, I opened up the door to find flowers! And not just any flowers my favorite flowers, Fuji Mums! They were so beautiful and full of color, there was no card in the flowers! I know that there is no way Juan knows where I live, I just bumped into him a few hours ago, so these have to be from my baby. I called Ta'Ron but he did not answer. I immediately went upstairs and started to get my clothes ready for tonight. Cassie was right I needed a drink, hell maybe even two. I pulled out a cute and simple little black dress, you know, the kind they say every woman should have. I pinned my hair up and popped a few curls in it and added my jewelry and a pair of my new blinged out pumps I just purchased today, grabbed my jacket, and headed for the door.

When it came to promoting you couldn't ask for a better person than Ronnie. Maybe because he talks too much and doesn't have a shy bone in his body. He is also great at marketing. By the time he is done talking to you he will have you ready to order a dozen of whatever he is selling. He has a swift and creative tongue too. He always has a rebuttal no matter what you say. He is extremely good at "creating a need" as it is said in the world of sales. I don't know if he will ever settle down though. He is just as smooth with the ladies. The funny thing is he always tells them up front he is not looking for a relationship or to settle down. Just friends who understands that she is not the only friend! And oddly enough these dodo birds go for it! I gotta say he does treat them rather well. He would make some lady a good husband if he could just be still for a little bit! Ronnie is the reason the lounge stayed packed to capacity. He knew how to get it done! I can say he is using the mess out of that marketing degree. Overall, he was a great friend and a great guy! When he was not promoting the club, he was also the community voice of the lounge. He volunteers at the Boys and Girls club every week and started and oversees the "Stop the Bulling" campaign, which he is very passionate about! He often uses the same artist that they pay to come to the club to show up at schools and community centers prior to them taking the stage. He is a very smart man. He could work anywhere he wants to. He graduated the top of class in both high school and college. People say he looks like Laz Alonso! I must admit they really do have a strong resemblance, but I never let him know that! Ronnie is my buddy; you can always count on him. He is very loyal and that is what I love most about him!

Devin takes "HEROES" very seriously. This is something that he and Donovan have been talking about doing from as far back as I can remember. When they put the upscale spin on it and required that all patrons must be thirty years old or older that really separated them from any other night clubs. It is the "Cheers" of the city. Devin keeps the A list clients in VIP and the Celebrities both in the crowd and on the stage. He gets a lot of help from Ta'Ron because of his connections, but I must admit, he is a go getter, and he holds his own. He also helps scout out new things to add to the menu so that they are more than beer and wings. They have chefs and an amazing wait staff, and he and Donovan train them personally. Although Devin is Donovan's identical twin, he has his own personality. Ladies swarm around Devin like bees around honey. He loves the attention. The bad thing for him is that he is so polite sometimes the ladies take his pleasantness as flirting, and he has had to run off his share of psychos. He almost tied the knot once, but she cheated on him and he dropped her like a bad habit unfortunately since then he hasn't trusted another woman, but he doesn't abuse them or dog them either. He is not into women who want to get physical right away because he said that is the number one sign that she is not what he is looking for. He is also a graphic designer, so he makes a lot of the flyers and business materials for the lounge, and for their community events. However, he is also into freelance photography and is always telling women they can be models and takes their photos. He is great at both.

He is just a women lover, all shapes, colors, and sizes, he really does look in the heart, I think that is so sweet!

Like usual when I arrived people were in line already and the doors were not even open yet! Devin and Ronnie were at the door scoping out the ladies in the crowd, bringing the ones that they like to the front of the line while the people who were there first started to get mad. This was a pretty nice size crowd of early comers. So, as I walked to the front of the VIP line, I hugged Devin and Ronnie and asked what was going on today, and that's when they told me that they were having poetry tonight but also India Arie! They said they told me a million times and they probably did; I just can't see me forgetting my girl was going to be in town! I was really glad Cassie talked me into getting out of the house now. They opened the door and let me in. Cassie and Donovan were already inside. I went to join her at the table and offered Donovan my help if he needed it. He said if they got too busy, he was going to take me up on that offer. T came out and hugged me and Cassie. He was working in the kitchen and doing great! He loved to plate the food the most! He could cook too but he really loved making it look like you are eating something straight off a magazine cover. He said he just wanted to come out and speak before they got too busy, because he knew he would not have any down time tonight. We didn't hold him long at all. The waitress came by with some drinks that had been prepared just for Cassie and I, and a bowl of popcorn. They actually had good customer service here. They turned the music up and opened the doors and the crowd piled in. Once the crowd settled in, they started the show. The poets were really good. Some were local and others traveled from surrounding areas to perform. I really enjoyed them. There was a real sexy neo soul type of feel in the lounge and the crowd loved it. They turned it over to the DJ for a short intermission before they brought out Ms. India. That was fine with me because it gave me a chance to talk to Cassie a bit. I told her how I went home and fell asleep and how someone had three dozen of my favorite flowers, in multiple colors delivered to my house with no card. She told me I was being paranoid! The DJ called the sexy ladies to the dance floor, so you know Cassie and I jumped right up! We danced a bit and then he slowed the music down. On my way to my seat, I felt a tug at the bottom of my dress. I stopped and turned around to see who it was and to my surprise it was Ta'Ron! "Baby what are you doing here? Oh My God it is so good to see you! I thought you guys were on the road for a few more days! I shouted over the loud music as I fell into his big muscular arms." "Yes, but we had a free day in between. I'm sorry I lied baby I wanted to surprise you! That's why I didn't answer your call earlier because I would have spoiled it! I figured you were calling because you received the flowers, I sent you! Which meant everything was going as planned! I do have to leave first thing in the morning, but I had to come see my baby! You aren't mad, are you?" He said. I wasn't mad at all more like relieved that it was him that sent the flowers and that it was him tugging on my dress. Cassie was right I was way too paranoid! "No baby I am so happy to see you! Thank you for my flowers you are so sweet! I am so happy to be your wife, thank you baby!" I said as I kissed him repeatedly. "Come out here and dance with your husband, can you do that?" I can do more than that daddy. We both started laughing as we took the dance floor and danced hand in hand. I didn't' want to let him go.

The DJ announced this was the last song until after the special guest. We took our seats. Devin came to the microphone and gave a great introduction to India Arie. She was phenomenal. She put on a great show! Ta'Ron asked to excuse himself because Donovan really did need a pair of extra hands. I told him that I understood and encouraged him to go help. India announced her last song and told everybody to grab somebody and hit the dance floor. Our men were busy working, so we sat there talking. Then I felt a hand on my thigh and a deep voice said, "can I have this dance?" I immediately said "of course baby, I thought you would never ask" I sat my drink down onto the table then I heard Cassie gasp. I looked up It was Juan, yes Juan damn Hernandez. I assumed it was my husband. I thought I was going to pass out! "I thought that was you over here. Wow you look good!" He said as my jaw probably touched the floor. "Juan I am so sorry I assumed you were my husband that is why I agreed to dance with you. I don't think that will be a good idea. Where is your..." he cut me off and said he was here alone. Then he apologized and walked away. I downed the rest of my drink so fast. Cassie didn't say anything. She just ordered us more drinks. Ta'Ron came back out about four minutes later. "Baby, are you ok? You look tense?" "I'm fine baby" I assured him I cannot believe this. Now who is paranoid?

I told Cassie I would call her tomorrow and she just shook her head in agreement. I tried not to think about it. Ta'Ron drove me home and said he would bring me back to pick up my car after we have breakfast in the morning. I had a great night with my husband. I felt like I should tell him, but every time I fixed my lips, no words would come out. I really am a blessed woman. He was always so good to me, and he always had me on his mind. Even though he traveled the world as a popular NBA star, my husband made sure everybody knew he had one wife and that he was a faithful husband. I was not about to allow the temptation of my past ruin my future.

My baby drew my bath and then joined me. I loved our one-on-one time together. He was everything I ever dreamed of and then some. I enjoyed being around our friends as well but there was nothing like our alone time. He always allowed me to be my goofy self. He was pretty silly too. He thinks he has what it takes to be a comedian, but I told him to leave that to T. We fully enjoyed our time together and the next morning, or should I say a few hours later, we headed out to breakfast as promised. We always supported the "hole in the wall" mom and pop style restaurants! We always enjoyed the home cooking and relaxed atmosphere. Plus, he loved when the owners came and asked for a picture that they can place on their walls. I was so proud of him. He took me to my car as promised and I cried as I had to say goodbye because he had to go back on the road again. He kissed me and promised that I would see him soon.

I decided to go ahead and go into the office since I had taken my half a day yesterday. When I got in, I checked my messages and I have eight from Juan. I asked my assistant Sheila to route his number to Tom on the 6th floor/ she agreed. I called Tom and gave him the heads up. I didn't go into detailed, but he promised to return his calls and find him the home he desired. What the hell is his problem and why is he calling me so much! This is starting to be crazy. I was trying to keep this as simple as possible but now this was turning into something more than a cute little reunion. I continued my day as normal, and I was starting to feel so much better. I even closed a deal! I pulled out my Asiago and cheese bagel with chive cream cheese and my cappuccino as I sat at my desk during my break, and I wrote a poem. Writing always helped me process things. I finished up all of my paperwork and then I called my dad. "Hey Daddy, do you miss me? You haven't called me in two days?" "Hey baby of course I do, why don't you come over for dinner tonight, we can eat, relax and then I will beat your butt in monopoly!" Dad and I were very competitive when it came to games. It was always a serious deal, and it drove Mommy nuts. "Ok Daddy I will be there but the only way you are going to beat my butt, is if you hit it with a belt, because you know I am going to win!" We laughed and I hung up the phone. "Good night, Sheila, forward all of my remaining calls to my voicemail, or encourage them to send me an email. I am gone for the day.

I went home to feed "Bella" my yorkie terrier. She was my baby! I loved dressing her and taking her around with me. I knew that because I was going to go see Mommy and Daddy that they would want to see her. Bella means "beautiful in Italian." She is truly spoiled, even by my friends and parents. She literally has her own room in our house. People can't get over that when they find that out. But I don't have any children yet and I wanted to do a themed room specifically for someone! It is so cute. Her room is pink, and orange and it has little dog paws all over the walls. She has a TV, a doggie bed, a play area, and all. It is so cute. I even iron and hang up all over her doggie diva gear and collars in her well-organized closet. I never heard of anybody doing such a thing. It seems I have inspired a lot of other puppy mommies, all over, thanks to Pinterest, Facebook, Twitter, and TikTok. She deserves it, she is a good dog. She is tough too. She is not intimated by the size of any other dog or any human. She will get you if you mess with us. I fed her, bathed her, and brushed her teeth. Then I dressed her and placed her in her matching carrying tote and we headed over my parents' house for dinner right after we took a picture and posted it to Instagram!

# CHAPTER 6

**"H**ey T what's up? I was wondering if Summer wanted to hang out with me and Bella today! We are going to go get our nails and hair done, go shopping and grab something to eat. I know it is Saturday, but I want to spoil my niece. Cassie is going to join us later because we are going to the spa to get facials and massages!" I said as soon as T answered the phone. You have to get out what you can in one breath when you were talking to him about Summer. He was still so overprotective with her, and I definitely understood. But we always had such a great time together. She is spoiled rotten, and I am part to blame. There is nothing she has asked me for that I have not given her including dirt bikes, four-wheelers, huge birthday parties and so much more. She has been through a lot, and although Cheyenne wasn't the greatest woman in the world, she didn't deserve to die that way, and Summer didn't deserve to grow up without a mother. I know that there is nothing that we can do to replace her, and I am not even trying. I just want to constantly remind her that she is loved and never alone. I don't want her falling into the stereotypes. She is a beautiful girl, and I don't want the first time she hears it to be when some knuckle head is trying to talk her out of her clothes and into his bed! So, I made it a point to spend as much time with her as I could! I pay for her vocal and piano lessons and basketball camp! If she is ever unable to do anything, it will never be because of money. Bella loved having her around; she is a very sweet, respectable, and obedient little girl! She is always so grateful, that's why I never get tired of giving her everything she wants and needs. Cassie and I take her school shopping every year and we always pull on her inner diva, while the guys keep her laced in the latest tennis shoes and of course "Jordan's." This girl has an awesome support system. I try to pull back now that T is out, but it is so hard.

"Hey Tierra, if she wants to go that's cool with me but she had one of her friends spend the night last night and I think they wanted to go to the movies. If I tell her everything you want to do, she is going to drop that girl like nobody's business. I don't want her to be that type of person, her word has to be her bond. Is there any way you can take her tomorrow after church?" he asked. Now he knows I cannot put off my hair appointments plus as long as the little girl's mother is ok with it, I would love for her to bring a friend so she can have someone to hang with when Cassie joined us. "The little girl is welcome to come along, my treat! Can you ask her mom for me? You can give her my number, and I will even take them to the movies if they still feel like going after our long day. I already promised her a girl's day and I thought she would enjoy this." I was too excited to cancel this date with my princess! He agreed that he would tell the girls and if they wanted to go, he would have them get dressed as he called girl's mother and that he would call me back. I was cool with that it was still early in the morning anyway. He called back and told me the girl's mom was ok with it and that he gave her my name and number and I told them I would be on my way. Her mother called, she started to cry and said she can't afford to do those things for Jasmine and that she was grateful that I would include her daughter. She said she works two jobs, and although Jasmine's dad is well off, he doesn't pay child support or spend any time with her now that he has moved on. That really broke my heart. I promised Diane that I would take great care of Jasmine and treat her just like I treat my Goddaughter. I told her to feel free to call and check on us throughout the day or whatever made her feel comfortable. I offered to come and meet her face to face prior to picking up the girls. She declined. She said that she trusts T's judgment. She said T had invited her to church tomorrow since she has to pick up Jasmine and I told her that she should come, that I would be there and love to meet her. She agreed that she would come.

I went and picked up the girls from T's new house! They ran out to the car with excitement. "Hi ma'am my name is Jasmine. Is Summer telling the truth when she says we are going to go get our nails and hair done, go shopping and go get something to eat and to the spa for massages? I have never done any of that! Are you sure it is ok that I tag along?" My eyes filled up with tears as I responded "Hey Jasmine I am Auntie Tierra and you are not a tag along, you are my guest! We are going to have so much fun! Your Mom has given me permission to get your hair and nails done and whatever else! Are you guys ready?" They screamed yes and ran toward the car. Summer stopped and gave me a big hug and told me I was the best! I couldn't help but to look down at Jasmine's run-down shoes. She was such a pretty little girl, and so well mannered. I couldn't hold back my tears.

I unlocked the doors from my keychain and told them to strap in their seatbelts. T hugged me and said just be you! My heart melted I was going to make sure this little girl had the time of her life!

As I drove down the road, I watched them laugh through the mirror. It reminded me of when I was their age. Diane said Jasmine has a set of identical twin brothers named Jeremy and Justin that are four and they have a different father than she does. She is just a hard-working single mom doing the best that she can. T said she is a good woman and a good mother. I used my Bluetooth in the car to tell the shop we had one more coming in to get the diva treatment! They said no problem. I loved just watching them look through the magazines trying to show me what hairstyle they wanted. I turned down so many! I am into girls looking like little girls not little grown women! They finally chose something nice, and the staffs started on their hair, nails, and feet!

When we left out of the beauty shop, we looked great! Jasmine and Summer's hair really looked amazing. Both of them had a good grade of hair and beautiful skin! Our nails and feet looked good as well! I did not allow them to get any tips, But cute designs is all girls their age needs. I asked them where they wanted to go. I named off a few neighborhood restaurants even a few expensive ones and they kept saying they wanted Pizza! I wanted to take them somewhere they have never been and may never be able to go! So, I talked them into doing both! I told them that we could have pizza today if I could choose the restaurant we ate at after church tomorrow. They agreed. We went to the local pizza pallor. They had great pizza and a small arcade on the inside. We ordered pizza and I went and purchased tokens and allowed them to run loose in the arcade. Cassie came and joined us, and I told her about the little girl. We decided that we would go all out and buy her some nice things when we went shopping today. I already asked Diane for permission. The last thing I wanted to do is offend someone. The girls were out of tokens again and I advised them to wash up so that we could eat. I Introduced Jasmine to Cassie and I asked Summer to say grace and then they dug right into the pizza. I told them not to get too full because we had to walk all the pizza off by shopping. They agreed and were so excited. We had the remaining pizza placed in a to-go box and headed to the shopping center. We allowed them to select a few things and then we choose some things for them. I started with buying Jasmine and Summer some new tennis shoes, mostly because of the shoes Jasmine was wearing. I found some things for Ta'Ron and myself as well and of course Bella! She had been with us all day and had been a really good girl. They had so much fun! I think Cassie and I had more fun shopping for them than they did! Once they had a few outfits, some shoes and jewelry they were ready to go! When we finished, we dropped Bella off for her grooming appointment and we headed to the spa. I did not allow the girls to get a full facial, just a basic cleanse and a massage! They didn't know the difference! Cassie and I went all the way! It felt great just to relax. The girls said that they felt like superstars! I told them that they were. Then Summer asked "God Mommy since we are all going to church tomorrow can we just sleep over your house tonight, and finish girls' night there. We can watch a movie in your theatre room and make popcorn! Can we please if Mrs. Diane and my Daddy say its, ok? And we got new everything today, so you don't even have to take us home to get anything!" She had it all thought out and Jasmine just agreed to it all! I didn't have a problem with it, so I called and got the ok and then we headed to my house.

I showed the girls to their rooms, and I gave them bath towels and wash cloths and told them that they needed to wash up and put on their night clothes before we made snacks and chose a movie to watch. Jasmine asked if Summer could take her on a tour of the house first. I said that was fine with me and off they went. We all relaxed had baths and put on our pajamas. I baked brownies and let them use the popcorn machine to make some fresh popcorn for the movie. The girls had a great time. I loved hearing them laugh and watching them smile. I know that one day I will have children of my own and I will be a great mother. After the movie, they talked and played games. It got late and I told the girls that they had to go to bed so that we could make it to church on time tomorrow. As they brushed their teeth and prepared for bed, I washed dishes and cleaned up the kitchen and then took some bacon out of the freezer so that I could cook breakfast for them in the morning.

I woke up early and begin to prepare a big breakfast. I made pancakes, bacon, sausage, eggs, and fresh fruit! I woke the girls up and we ate together as a family, I loved that feeling. We all got dressed for church and I had the girls round up all of their things as they were going home after dinner today. When we arrived at church T, Cassie, Donovan, Devin, Ronnie, and another woman was standing in the parking lot. Jasmine ran to her, and I assumed it was Diane. I greeted her and introduced myself. I then hugged everyone and told them brunch was on me today following service, and they all agreed to come, even Diane and Jasmine. Service was really good, and the choir sounded wonderful. The minister really brought a good word and I felt refreshed. As soon as church was over, we all stood in the sanctuary talking for a while and I told everyone I wanted to go eat at "Alejandro's." They were all very excited. Alejandro's was a five-star restaurant that was very popular. It was almost impossible to get a reservation there especially at the last minute or for a group as large as ours. I have an inside connection. One of HC&G clients manages the place, so I called in a favor.

We headed to Alejandro's, and we were seated very quickly. Diane and Jasmine were impressed at their surroundings. I told everyone to be sure to get whatever they wanted and not to worry about the cost. My friends knew that already, but I didn't want to look like I was singling Diane and Jasmine out, so I just made a general statement. Over brunch Diane opened up to me about her financial issues, Jeremy and Justin were there as well. They were so cute, with their little glasses on. She was asking where she should start if she wanted to file for child support for Jasmine. I told her that my father was an attorney, but he doesn't deal with child support but may be able to point her in the right direction. I asked her if she ever tried calling him and asking for help. She then said that he always tells her that unless she sleeps with him that he will not give her anything. She admitted that at first, she used to fall for it, because she was young and needed his help, but she stopped and he since got married and still wants her to sleep with him for child support that he owes. She said that he makes a lot of money as did his wife and that she was tiered of struggling. I told her how much a joy her daughter was, and I gave her my father's business card. On our way out of the restaurant she said that she was really scared on him, that even though they dated when she was really young, that he was physically, mentally, and sexually abusive to her. She then said that although they were dating, she was raped by him and became pregnant with Jasmine. She said she never reported it because since they were boyfriend and girlfriend, she felt that no one would believe her. I honestly didn't know what to say. I didn't want to show emotion in front of her for several reasons; one, because Daddy always told me to be careful because people will manipulate sensitive people. Two because I didn't want to look like a nut bucket in front of this lady and three because I don't know if anything she was saying is true. I just encouraged her to call my dad as soon as possible.

On the way home I couldn't help but to feel bad for Diane. I didn't want to get to involved. I just decided that if I could help I would, but I didn't want to make her think I was a bank. I have been used before and it is not a feeling that I want to feel again anytime soon. I called Ta'Ron on my way home and told him that I was taking a few days off and coming to spend some time with him. He was excited and told me to leave out as soon as possible. Cassie agreed to keep an eye on Bella for me while I was out. I called Sheila and advised her that I would be gone for a few days, and I knew she knew what to do. I booked my flight, packed my things, and packed up enough food and clothing for Bella and prepared myself for this trip I caught the first flight available to LAX! I was so excited to be headed to California. I knew the weather would be beautiful, and most importantly that I would have a few days with my husband. They were preparing for their playoff game against the Lakers, and he had several television, radio, and magazine interviews. But we would have a day to just enjoy one another's company.

When I took Bella to Cassie's she was still in school, so Donovan promised to take care of her until Cassie got home. I knew he would, everyone loved Bella. I called Ta'Ron as soon as I got through security check and let him know I was in route and then I called Daddy. I checked in my first-class seat and buckled in, with high anticipation of a wonderful next few days. I called Mommy when I landed as the plane taxied the runway and as soon as I got off, I called my baby to let him know I arrived. He was in practice which he had already instructed me, so I took a uber to the hotel, got checked in and put my things away.

# CHAPTER 7

The view in my room was beautiful. There were palm trees everywhere and the weather was perfect. You didn't' see many palm trees where I was from, and although we traveled a lot I was always amazed at beautiful scenery. I relaxed for a while and then left to do some shopping. No use spending time in a hotel room when you're in LA. I found something to bring back to everyone, including Summer and Jasmine. Ta'Ron will be free in a few hours and then we will spend time together. I had a ball shopping, there were so many shops there was no way I could go into them all, but I sure did try. There were so many people out and about. People were on the corners singing, playing instruments, juggling, telling jokes, and even doing magic tricks, all for any donation you were willing to toss in their buckets. I stopped by and watched several of them, after all the only time you saw this kind of entertainment on the streets of Georgia was when someone who was drunk or high stopped you while coming out of the store and just started singing Sam Cook's "A Change's Gone Come" often started and ended by the same line… "I was born by the river!" Then they would follow that up by saying "See… let me hold something" as they clutched their beer can wrapped in a brown paper bag tightly. So, I was really enjoying myself. There were even Muslims, Christians, and members of the Church of Scientology out there, all not too far apart from one another, telling you why you should follow them, while just a few steps away the physic was promising to tell you your future starting as low as $5.99! It didn't take too much to impress me. I remember thinking that they had true freedom in LA! Although everyone was standing there promoting their own thing, no one was harassing the next group which I thought was awesome. I was scared a few times when people who walked by me were dressed up in crazy scary costumes and it wasn't even Halloween! But everyone else seemed to keep it moving so I tried as much as I could to act like I was not a visitor.

I was walking back to the hotel, not because I was tired of shopping, but because my hands and arms were so full of stuff, there was no way I could carry another bag. Ta'Ron called and asked where I was, and he told me to stay put! I was glad because I was wearing high heels, and my bags were heavy and through all of the excitement I didn't realize how far away from the hotel I had actually walked. When he came, he was alone in a car, and helped me put all of my things in. I knew I was going to have to ship this stuff home or purchase another set of luggage, because my bags were already stuffed to capacity coming here.

As soon as my hands were free, I ran and jumped into his arms! I so needed a hug from him. He always knew how to make me feel better. Ever since we were young, he seemed to always know just what to say and exactly what to do. With all of this stuff going on with Juan I needed the security, protection, love, laughter, and affection from my husband. And just like always his touch made everything better! When I was in his arms it made me forget about all of the stress I was dealing with back home. He asked me how I was doing. I wanted to tell him so bad about all of the things I've been dealing with. But I didn't want to ruin our time together. "Oh, baby I am so happy to see you! I was so glad when you called and said you were coming. I miss you so much. What's new with you, how is work? How is everyone? What do you want to do? Talk to me baby." He said as he held my hands and stood and looked at me like he was dreaming. "I love you baby! I miss you so much! Look at you, Baby I am so proud of you, I don't care what we do. Today is your choice tomorrow you can take me sightseeing and then head to practice or rest or whatever! I need your head in this game! I know yal are taking it all the way this year!" I said. He then said that he wanted to take me to the beach where we could just relax and talk without being on video chat or the phone. I thought that was a great idea, so we jumped in the car and headed to Venice Beach.

We stopped by the store to grab a few things because he did not have any swimming shorts on him, and I didn't buy a bathing suit out of all that shopping I did! My hubby laid our towels out in the sand, and I laid down so that he could rub sunscreen on me. Everything seemed so perfect, the weather was amazing with just enough breeze, the water was beautiful, and the sunset was so gorgeous it was as if it was unreal! The water felt amazing and even the sand between my toes felt like marshmallows'. We had a great time enjoying one another. I can't even explain how it felt just to sit there and laugh and talk to my husband. Sometimes you just take the little things for granted. I know he is a superstar but to me he is just Ta'Ron, and I love him for that. What an amazing start to my trip, I was glad I packed up and came, I missed Bella though. We went back to the room and got cleaned up and met up with some of his teammates and headed out for a night on the town. We went to a party, and it was nice, there were a lot of actors and actresses there and other celebrities. I jokingly asked If Snoop Dog or Lion or whatever his new name is, was coming since we were in California. He was really the only person I hadn't met yet. He laughed and said, "You know he been and went back to Snoop Dogg, stop playing!" continued to enjoy the party. It was like we were on a date for the first time. He was the same ole gentleman as always, who swept me off of my feet so many years ago. We danced all night. I needed this trip! By the time we made it back to the hotel, we barely made it to the room, if you know what I mean! It was amazing. I remember just thanking God for this wonderful reminder of the awesome husband that I have.

The next morning, we got up and went sightseeing as promised. We went to Hollywood and took pictures of the new stars that I had been placed on the street since my last visit, we drove by celebrities' homes, and of course I did more shopping. I asked him to drive me to the "Price is Right" so I could play my all-time favorite game of "Plinko," and he chuckled and said maybe next time because he had to be locked in very early after practice because of the game tomorrow, plus it was not directly in LA. I was ok with just being with him. The only issue we had was that everywhere we went everybody wanted autographs. I understand why, but we rarely get alone time, and it was becoming too much. I guess I was wearing my frustration on my face, so we headed back in. We just sat and cuddled up watching reruns of "Martin" until he had to go to practice. I hated to see him go but I knew he had to do what he does best. I knew he would call before their lock in because he can't go anywhere or call anyone after the coach gives that set time. I just told him to come kiss me goodnight first and he promised to do so. I relaxed a little more and took a nice long hot bath and got comfortable, but still cute of course. I walked around the hotel and they happened to have karaoke going on in the hotel bar. I went in and ordered a drink and enjoyed the show. The Bartender brought me my drink and another one. I told him that I didn't order two drinks, and he pointed out the gentleman that sent it over. I politely asked him to send it back and tell him that I said thank you, but I am married. The last thing I needed was another Juan! He did as I asked, and the guy came over and sat beside me. He was nice I told him that I just wanted to have a good time. He said he understood and asked if I would sing a duo with him, because he could not do it alone. I told him if he promised to leave me alone I would, and we laughed. He selected "My Endless Love" out of all songs in the world but believe it or not the weirdo could actually sing, honestly, he could blow! Everyone gave us a standing ovation and after that we continued duets all night! He was a nice guy and was actually only being polite by sending me a drink. I told him that I just had to be more than careful. All in all, I had an awesome night! Ta'Ron came and kissed me goodnight in the bar and headed on in. At the end I did not know that there was a prize. We ended up winning two flat screen televisions! Since I was so far from home, I was going to have to either ship it or give it away. I decided to let hubby decide. I headed back to my room about one am and I had a great night sleep.

I was awakened by a knock at my room door. When I opened up the door, the doorman had fresh flowers and room service hubby had ordered for me! I smiled like a school aged girl! I love that man so much and he just does things to remind me of why he was the perfect choice! I had two dozen beautiful white roses and a blue bouquet of my favorite flower, the Fuji Mum! He ordered me an omelet and some fresh fruit and included a note that read "You are all I think of All I want, and All I need! And just like the flowers and fruit, you bring freshness to my life every day! I love you baby, see you at the game!" I could have melted! Now I wanted to do something special for him, but I didn't know what! After finishing my beautiful and delicious breakfast I decided to just relax at the resort. I went down and enjoyed some time at the pool and got a much-needed massage. Afterwards I rushed up to my room and just laid across the bed and chilled because the game started at six tonight. I knew I was going to go over to the arena early because Ta'Ron had already arranged my ride. I was dressed like a NBA wife and looking good! I had his Jersey Number added to the back of my red dress and I had on my black and red Jordan's! I looked like I could've been a cheerleader with as much gear I carried in! What can I say, I am a very proud wife and a great support system! I know I would do even worse when we had children and they began sports. But I didn't care, my baby loved it and so did the team. They have the other wives trying to outdo me, and they come up with good ideas, they just don't even come close to me. We always have fun though nothing serious, just friendly competition or at least, I think.

Today's game was no different! I was jumping up and down screaming and cheering for my baby like I had since high school, I wasn't ashamed or afraid! I always had fun anyway. I could always get the crowd to follow me, and I think I liked that part just as much. My baby was showing out tonight! I like to think that I am his inspiration! He was shooting three's all night and didn't miss! I was so excited! He always worked really hard. He is an intelligent businessman as well. He has a master's degree in business management but I'm telling you somebody has to give my baby a PHD for the way he is ballin' today! The half time show was good! I am not a Lakers fan at all, but those Laker girls danced their butts off during halftime! They had me waiting to join in! Well at least somebody from LA was doing something because they were getting whooped out there on the court! When they came back from half time they really put on a show! I felt so bad that they were being beat that bad especially on their home court! Baby was really on it! I was out of control! When I looked up, I was on the Jumbo Tron looking like a crazy fan! I couldn't help but to laugh! Needless to say, they won the game and of course they will advance in the series! I took tons of pictures and was posting on social media throughout the entire game! My favorite picture was of me a Ta'Ron putting on our "game faces!" What a perfect way to end my weekend!

The team went out to celebrate and I was right there! Cheering and getting the crowd all hyped up! We had a great night! Most of it the team spent recapping the game, arguing on who had the best move of the night and things like that. They had so much energy, they were so excited, and they deserved it. They are not often given the credit they deserve, but tonight they gave the people no choice because they played basketball and played it extremely well tonight! I miss being on the road with my baby and he reminded me I can stop working and come anytime I wanted to!

Championship time is almost here! Ta'Ron has been doing so well! I think my baby may be MVP this year! And he deserves it! He has been scoring like a school age boy and his number of assists is better than ever. His Turnovers have decreased, and he is the highest scorer in the league right now. Their team as a whole is doing exceptionally well and I know they are going all the way. This time of year, I usually take a lot of time off so that I can travel and support him! Cassie and the crew always meet up with us when they can during the playoffs. And when the team made it all the way, we always went to the NBA FINALS together. I have a good feeling that this is their year. I couldn't wait to tell Cass all about it! It felt good to smile again. I just hope I will be able to keep this smile for a while.

The next day was bittersweet as I knew I was scheduled to fly back home. I didn't really want to go but I knew there was something's I really needed to get straightened out back home. I was feeling happy again and I also knew hubby would be in our area soon and that they also had some home games coming up! That was definitely something to look forward too. But I packed my bags and had to buy that extra set of luggage because I sort of over shopped. Ta'Ron begged me to stay but I told him I would see him soon! He took me to the airport and made sure I got checked in and checked all of my bags. He held me in his arms which felt like heaven. I felt so blessed at that moment. I went ahead and went through the checkpoint and waited to board. I purchased a crossword puzzle to complete in case I didn't sleep the entire four-hour flight back home. I got comfortable in my seat and listened to the instructions from the flight attendant and began to daydream. I could see my life just the way I had planned it with my children and all. All I could do is smile.

They lady sitting beside me quickly interrupted my daydreaming session with her rambling. She seemed very nice, but she was very talkative, and her breath smelled like day old bread. She asked me about my trip and where I was headed to next. I tried my best to briefly answer all of her questions, but she just kept coming back with more. She then stuck out her right hand as if she wanted to shake hands and stated, "Oh I am so rude I am Megan by the way, and you are?" I went ahead and shook her hand because I didn't want to seem rude; my mind was really just in a different place at this time. "Hi Megan, I'm Tierra, nice to meet you!" After a while of hearing her life story about being raised on a farm in Texas and how she took care of horses like they were her siblings, the attendant announced we were now at the point where we could use our electronic devices. That was the best thing I had heard all flight long. As she stood up to get her laptop, I quickly pulled out my earphones and crossword puzzle, laid back and closed my eyes in hopes that Megan would get the picture. Luckily, she did, and I was able to enjoy the remainder of my flight. I do not know at which point I fell asleep; it must've been shortly after drink service. I remember drinking cranberry juice and that's about it! I didn't want to leave my eyes open for too long at once because I didn't want to hear the rest of her life story. The plane finally landed, and Cassie was there to greet me with Bella! It was good to see the both of them. Now off to baggage claim to pick up all the bags I have from shopping! Cassie is gonna flip!

# CHAPTER 8

I took the next day off from work just so I could rest. No matter how much I fly I still seem to get jet lagged and sometimes my ears even clog up which is really irritating and often painful. I was so tired. I guess I forgot how running around all day and night and changing my normal sleep pattern could really wear me out. I planned on just lounging around all day, and honestly, I tried. But I can never just sit around; I always have to be moving. I didn't do much as I normally would, just a little dusting, and checking on my plants and I did some rearranging of furniture in a few rooms in the house. After this trip, I feel as if I have been given a fresh new start, and I was ready to take it. I then sat down and thumbed through the stack of mail that came while I was gone. Nothing of importance was really there, except a Save-the-date postcard from HC&G, reminding me that their annual awards and celebration ceremony was coming up soon and the RSVP cut off dates. We were allowed up to three guests this year. I made it a point to go every year, it was always a great time, and I knew I would win something this year, as I did in the years past! I made a notation of it in my calendar. Maybe Cassie, Donovan, and T would go with me this year since my baby would still be gone. They always had great food and entertainment and we were always given really nice gifts too. After going through the mail and doing some minor housekeeping I took Bella out for a walk because I missed her, and she loved it. We went to the park and then to the lake and just enjoyed nature. On the way back home, I took her to the "Doggie Treat Drive Thru" and got her a snack! I liked the names of their combos. It was such a cute idea, anyway she loved that place, and she definitely deserved it! I felt bad for leaving her for the entire weekend, but I really did have a great time. Afterwards we just curled up on the sofa and just bummed around watching the Lifetime Movie Network and eating ice cream!

I started cooking dinner so that I could take the leftovers to work with me for lunch. I know that I will have too much work to do, to take an actual lunch break. With all this television watching today I caught a glimpse of some cooking shows and I decided to see what I could come up with! So, I took out some chicken breast and pounded them out just like I saw on the show. I seasoned the meat well and stuffed them with cheeses and spinach and then wrapped the chicken in bacon and popped it in the oven just as I saw on the show. I then prepared a nice, tossed salad to accompany it instead of pasta. I must say that it looked and smelled delicious. I have wanted to try new recipes for a long time. I will let Bella help me judge this one. When I took the chicken out of the oven it looked beautiful. I plated it up really nice, just to treat myself and poured myself a glass of Moscato. It was absolutely scrumptious! I will definitely have to make this for Ta'Ron, but he could eat about four of these by himself.

Cassie came by later that evening and asked if she could

host the twin's birthday party at the house. I told her I had to run it by Ta'Ron first, but I was almost one hundred percent sure that he would say yes. I knew for sure he would miss it due to his game, but he would do whatever he could for his friends. She said that she wanted it to be a surprise and because they are so involved with the daily affairs of the lounge, she knew she couldn't affectively plan it without them finding out before the party. I loved hosting so it was a great idea for me! She said she wanted to do an old school party theme and she was going to get a DJ and all. She asked if the pool would be accessible and if I would help with the food and if I would make the grills available for at least brats, dogs, and shish kabobs. I promised to do whatever I could to make it a memorable thirty-fifth birthday party for them. T's party was the only party we had since we moved in, except the housewarming that Mommy and Cassie gave me. I wasn't worried about him saying no, we really did love to have family and friends over.

We have an arcade in the house, but I told her Ta'Ron was going to make the party stay in a specified area, mostly because he would not be here, so it would probably be the back deck, pool, and pool house, but on the hard deck I would see if he would allow me to bring "Galaga" and "Packman" Arcade games out. He loved to show them off, but he doesn't like a lot of people roaming through the house and neither do I. Just the thought of planning the party got me excited. I ran to my office and grabbed us both fresh notebooks to write our brainstorm ideas in and flopped back down on the sofa. We came up with some awesome ideas! Everything from backdrops, food, games, party favors, entertainment, and so much more! She started writing out a proposed guest list! I needed to know how many people she planned on having in case I wanted to help her rent a building rather than coming to the house. But it was going to be a nice size crowd, bout sixty total guests if we included ourselves. I could handle that! Either way I knew I would contribute financially if for some reason we didn't use our house. I made myself a note to have the pool and hot tub serviced just in case. It could use it anyway. The pool house was equipped with showers and a nice lounging area that could hold about seventy-five people easily! This was going to be the party to remember. We got online and surfed the web for costumes, other party themed ideas, and whatever else came to mind. We found so much stuff. I was starting to get more excited than Cass!

We were on a roll; we occasionally got off subject as friends often do when spending time together! I had to fill her in on my trip! I went upstairs and grabbed the gifts from California that I had purchased for her and Donovan. I told her about me wining the television in a Karaoke bar in the hotel and she asked what Ta'Ron decided to do with it! I told her that it is being shipped here and that we are going to put together a package; with that TV, a signed Jersey from Ta'Ron, an autograph picture of him, and a basketball signed by all of the team members. Then we are going to do an online auction and split the money between his charity and her summer camp! She was so elated she started to cry. I thought it was a great idea she was always doing so much! With this package she should have enough funds to run the camp for a few years, especially since she already has grants and sponsors. I was happy for her. She tried on the new dress I bought for her, and she looked great.

Seeing her in that dress reminded me that I wanted to invite them to my awards ceremony in a few weeks. She said she was certain that they could come and that she would let me know for sure in a few days, after they have time to check their schedules.

Time went by so fast. We laughed and talked, and the ideas just kept flowing. Cassie looked at her cell phone and said that it was 2:36AM! I didn't' believe her so I looked at my phone, and sure enough she was right. It was just like old times, hanging out with my BFF and losing track of time. We used to have so many nights like this. Our personal and professional lives have become so busy that we don't get to do this as often as we would like. But I wasn't complaining! I needed these laughs. "Girl thanks so much for coming by! I enjoyed your company, this party is gonna be off the chain! Call me when you make it home safely!" I said as I walked her to the door, and she agreed. I need to get some sleep because I have to be at work at seven! So much for a day of rest!

When I arrived at work, I had a lot of voicemails and emails to return, so I didn't schedule any showings for the day. I came equipped for the day with the lunch I prepared and loads of water. I knew it was going to be a long day, and I was ready to tackle it. Amongst the many messages that needed to be returned, a handful of them were from Juan! He said he was having no luck with my colleague and just wanted a little advice. He asked if he could just meet me for lunch. I didn't think it was a good idea at first but after the amazing weekend I just had with the love of my life, I knew that I would never cross the line with him. Maybe going to lunch with him and setting the record straight once and for all would be a great idea. What could it hurt, just a simple lunch with an old friend, right? I could give him a few pointers that could hopefully assist him and his wife in their search for their new home. And I did have to be professional because of my job.

I returned the emails and calls from my clients, one by one, answering their questions and informing them that I was back in the office. I was only gone from work a few days, Friday, Monday and Tuesday; you would think I went on a weeklong cruise because of the number of messages I had. It was buying season and there are really some great deals out there. Because of the way the market is now, you can get a house valued over two hundred thousand dollars for about one hundred and forty thousand dollars. So, my client list was full, and they were anxious and serious about their dream homes. I didn't blame them; I loved my job, so I didn't mind the large number of calls and paperwork that was waiting for me. I had the pleasure of calling one couple and telling them that they had been approved for the loan we applied for prior to my trip! This was for a first-time homebuyer and there are so many programs out there right now that people can qualify for. I love hearing the reaction in their voices. It is a real treat to know that you are doing some good.

Sheila called and said I had a caller on the line, and I asked her to patch them through. It was Juan. I had intended on calling him, but I was so busy, and he technically is not my client. So, I wasn't going to put them on the back burner for him. I tried explaining that to him in the nicest way I could. He did not really seem to care, he just wanted to know if we were going to be able to go out to lunch and discuss things. I told him right off that it would be strictly professional if I did agree to meet with him. He said that he completely understood and that all he wanted was to find a house and catch up on old times, nothing more. I was fine with that as long as he understood it was going to be a onetime thing, about business and a short catch-up session. I wasn't trying to be rude; I have known the guy since my childhood. He asked if he could come pick me up for lunch. I told him that I was not taking a lunch break today that I could maybe do it on Friday which was only two days away. I told him I would be driving myself reminding him that this was in no way a date. He agreed to lunch on Friday, and I was just glad that this was going to be over with. I told him that I wanted to go somewhere very open and not quite quaint and secluded. He challenged me at first, but those were my terms, and I wasn't about to budge. It was the take it or leave it mentality I had learned from this job, and I was good at it. I told him I was busy, and I would see him Friday at Panera Bread at 12:30 downtown and I released the call.

I continued my work and then warmed up my lunch to eat in my office when Sheila reminded me that we had a meeting. I took my lunch into the conference room and sat there and listened to the new marketing plans they wanted us to adapt to. One of my colleague's suggested that I share my practices and that we adopt what I do and include it as the new Standard Operating Procedure. I looked up surprised at her suggestion, with my fork full of stuffed wrapped chicken and salad. I don't really think that I do something so special that it needs to become the standard. I just love seeing people's dreams come true and I said that in the meeting. I told them I take every case seriously and as if I have been entrusted with their family legacy. I just work hard to get them what they want at price that is affordable for them and I am always truthful. I agreed to share any best practices. I told them I sincerely get to know all of my clients, their likes, and dislikes because it helps you to understand them better. If their children are into sports, then I look for locations close to the ball fields. If they love to fish, you I look for property around a body of water. I just make sure that they know they are important to me and that I am working just as hard for my clients who I do not get the big commissions from, as I do for the ones whose commissions pay well. Word of mouth referrals keeps me employed and you never know who your clients know! I even take the time to send a follow up cards when they have been in their homes for a year. It is good to know that you were not just a transaction. Some of my clients have come into big money and come back and purchased new homes and commercial properties. I am not looking to tell anyone else how to do their jobs; I can only tell them what works for me. Our name HG&T alone is top of the line; I just feel their service should be top of the line as well. I told them again just to simply treat people like we would want to be treated! That's the secret the old "golden rule" and that is what has been working for me. Not to mention I know I am a blessed woman, and nothing comes to me by chance, but that God has graced me with it, but I didn't want to sound like a television evangelist, so I didn't add that part in.

When the meeting was over, I continued returning calls, finishing contracts, faxing over papers and returning emails. Before I knew it – it was time to call it quits for the day. It was a very long but productive day and although I had accomplished a lot, I knew that I would have to stay late if I wanted to make all of my deadlines. So, I told everyone goodnight and continued working in complete silence until I turned on my stereo. I continued to complete as much work as I could that involved me contacting other companies that were still open and leaving voicemails for those that were not. It was getting pretty late but I continued to return calls so that at least tomorrow we could move to the next step on majority of my caseloads because I had a stack of prospective clients who were ready to have consultations and some even ready to view homes, and I wanted to get to them as soon as possible.

As I sat there at my desk cramming paperwork and filing away reports I could not help but to get excited that my colleagues recognized my hard work! It felt really great to be appreciated. My company does a great job of recognizing their employees but still it's those informal recognitions like today that still make my day. I decided before I headed out from the office, I would send a site wide email of my best practices and basically recapping what I already shared with them in today's meeting. I feel so accomplished, and I love knowing that I helped someone else even in the little ways. Now off to get some much-needed rest, but I do have to take some work home if I really want to catch up on things. Once I was I the car I called Ta'Ron he said he was so proud of me and that I was his "Ambitious Mrs.!" He cracks me up. I think everything he says is cute when he says it to me.

# CHAPTER 9

**S**ometimes I wonder how it was possible for my mom to do such a great job being a wife and mother and balance an awesome career. It is really hard work and can become very overwhelming and I don't even have children yet. But if I learned anything from my parents it is to never makes excuses and do the hard work. Just being committed to my job has opened so many doors for me and I climbed the latter really fast. I am grateful for my life. It is almost perfect, well perfect in my book. Not everyone marries the man of their dreams, has awesome healthy friendships, a career they love, and no financial worries. But I must admit I have really been thinking a lot lately, and the one thing that my life is missing is a true family. Ta'Ron and I have been talking about having children for quite some time now but with his traveling and my schedule I don't see how we can effectively start our family. I really do want to have the "American Dream" family. You know at least one boy and one girl? I know that I would spoil them just like I do Summer and Bella. But I must admit I worry if I would be as good of a mother as my mother and grandmothers were. They were so attentive; they kept me involved in sports, cheerleading, and community activities, allowed me to hang out with friends but was strict on education and respect!

They did all of this while being awesome full-time wives and career women. Mommy says not to worry. She says that once I start having children it will all come naturally and I will automatically do what I have to do to ensure the safety, and wellbeing of my children. One thing is for sure I have some awesome role models to mimic. I am not rushing it; I know that in time it will come, it's just that I guess I have been having little baby fever lately. It seems like everyone at work or in the store is pregnant. They look so cute with their baby bumps, and I've found myself at more baby showers than housewarming parties lately. Even that I can get over but it's something about when I show a family a home and they have children it kind of gets to me. Then I am buried in a mountain of paperwork and that usually snaps me right back into my reality. I will be patient and I will wait my turn, but I won't be mad if it comes sooner than later.

I finally got all caught up at work and the work week seemed to fly right on by. I'm having second thoughts about having lunch with Juan. I just don't want to send any mixed signals, but he seemed to understand and reminded me every time we talked that he was married as well. I will go and hear him out, but I am not in the mood for stupidity.

With all of this work and travel Mommy and I have not met up for our lunch so today we will get back into our routine. I have to go out with her if I am going to make lunch plans with him. This time Dad suggested we tried this new "Soul Food" restaurant. He had tried it out with his colleagues and said it was very good and that the staff was very professional and that the ambiance was really nice. I love soul food, so it didn't take much convincing for me. Mommy was willing to try it as well because if Dad said it was good then it must be. So, we decided to trust him and made plans to meet today at "Auntie Mildred's Soul Café!" I was a little disappointed that we were not going to dress up or use crazy accents today but just to be in my mother's company was enough for me! Mom asked, "Tierra Michelle we are soul food, now how are we supposed to dress up like ourselves?" I just laughed I guess she is right!

The first part of the day went by really fast I was glad because I have been so tiered lately and I needed some good laughs and food and just time with those who love me. I left the office and told everyone I was going to be on a longer lunch and asked that my calls get forwarded to my cell after 2pm. Mom and I pulled up to *Auntie Mildred's Soul Café* at the same time. I greeted her with a big hug and kiss! Dad was right the ambiance of the place was very nice and this is just from the parking lot! As we walked in, we were greeted by friendly staff that yelled with excitement "welcome to Auntie Mildred's." The hostess asked how many and we answered "two" and she told us to follow her. She seated us at a beautifully decorated table close to the center of the restaurant and took our drink orders, gave us the menu, told us the specials, and said that our server would be right with us. As she walked away Mom, and I gave each other the "great service" look and giggled. The place was beautiful! It had lots of flowers around and mirrors but the way they put it all together it really worked. Each section had a theme to it which I thought was really cute. Each section was also named, some after food and some after people. The cutest section of all was the kid's section. It had a few arcade games in there and some tables and it was called the "Chitterling Pot!" I thought that was so cute and so creative. We were in the "Collards and Cornbread" section and ironically enough that is the free appetizer you get once you place your order, when seated in that section! Mom and I just kept saying that Auntie Mildred really thought this thing through! Our server came to the table with our drinks and our complementary bowls of Collard Greens and a plate of corn bread and took our order. Now my mom and both of my grandmothers were born and raised in the south and can cook just about anything and I go crazy over it! But I tell you what; Auntie Mildred put her feet and her neighbor's feet in those greens and in the cornbread! It was the best bowl of collards I had ever had, and mom agreed. When they brought out our food, I thought they were bringing the wrong order because there was so much food and only two of us! Our table was literally covered in plates and bowls. I hate that we had prematurely already put in our order for dessert! There was absolutely no way we could finish that food! I think I found a new favorite spot to come too! Oh My God everything was nice, and the staff was so attentive. And as if that wasn't enough, because it was our very first time coming, we got a mini dessert sampler tray where we were able to sample them all! I had already ordered the banana pudding and mom the peach cobbler, but we tasted everything from the best sweet potato pie to homemade cakes and everything in between. Then at the end before they bring you your ticket someone other than your server comes to the table to ask you about the service you received and the food. Then if there are no concerns, they give you your ticket and tell you that "your server will be back whenever you are ready!" Very classy place with phenomenal service and simply amazing food! Daddy was right… as usual! We had so much food left over we will not have to cook anything for dinner that's for sure! And on the way out we got to meet Auntie Mildred herself! She is a cute little old lady maybe about four feet four! She looks like she was about 65 but we were told that she was almost eighty and she is still in the back cooking! I told her how awesome our experience was and that we would most definitely be back and will spread the word. I asked if they catered, and they quickly gave me a brochure and told me that they did. Mom and I both completed a comment card and dropped it in the box on our way out and decided to go to the park and walk a bit because we were so stuffed!

The weather was so beautiful outside, so we walked around the trail located around the park, and just caught up on a few things! I really love spending time with my mom. As we walked around, I just imagined me doing the same thing with my daughter one day and I just hoped that I am as amazing of a mother as she is. Mommy said that she wanted to go by and see my grandma and take her shopping and I said I wanted to join her, so she called her to see what time works best for her. My grandmother is so cute! She is so funny and so full of wisdom. She has been working with troubled youth her whole life and is deeply rooted in church. Her schedule is always so full because she is involved in so much at the church and in the community. But like Auntie Mildred, my grandma looks amazing for her age, and she gets along very well and actually still drives, well speeds I should say. So, I am looking forward to hanging out with her as well.

The calls started to flow in from the office which was my reminder that it was after 2pm. I told mom that I would see her later and I walked her to her car and got my appointment book out of my car and walked back toward the park and sat on the park bench and took a few calls. It felt great just to relax. My hubby called and I told him all about the restaurant and the experience and he said he cannot wait to go. We continued to talk about how great his season was going and me traveling to the championship. I really miss him, and I know I need to travel to see him more often. Right in the middle of me telling him how cute Auntie Mildred was, I guess the phone died because I was still talking as the phone rang again in my ear. "Oh, Baby I was still talking, I didn't even realize that the phone hung up!" "Baby? Ooh I like that" he said "Excuse me? Who is this? I apologize I was talking to my husband, and we must've been disconnected. That baby was meant for him. How can I help you?" I quickly replied feeling a bit annoyed. "Ha ha no need to apologize it's me Juan and I was just making sure we were on for tomorrow or did you change your mind?" Ugh I rolled my eyes and hesitantly responded "Yes I will meet you at Panera bread like I told you there is no need for you to keep asking if we are still on, I have it written in my appointment book, and I will see you then…" my phone beeped, and it was Ta'Ron calling back thank God! "Well, this is my husband I have to go bye!" "Hello!" "Hey baby I lost signal, and it took a few seconds before it came back, sorry" Ta'Ron stated. "No problem baby I was really talking and didn't even know you were gone!" We both laughed and continued our conversation as if it had never been interrupted. I told him that I was going to work from home the rest of the day which was great because I had gotten so full and that I was going to eat my leftovers for dinner, so I didn't have to cook or make a salad at all today! The calls from work continued to flow in and I told him that I had to call him back and of course he understood. I set a few appointments, answered a few questions, and then called the office and told them I was going to work from home for the duration of the day. I grabbed my things and got into the car and headed home.

I stopped by the store to get a few things I needed for the house and a nice bottle of wine and headed home! I continued to receive calls until the end of business hours and quickly forwarded my calls back to the office voicemail system. I love the flexibility of my job! I took Bella for a walk and when we got back, I took my bath, warmed up my dinner and sat in front of the TV watching the Lifetime Movie Network with my bottle of wine! I watched the middle of one movie and caught the next one from the beginning. They always have great movies, but they are kind of lengthy and before I knew it time had escaped me. I turned off the TV and took Bella to her room. As I headed to my room, I received a text from my Hubby that said "Because of you my heart feels no pain, because of you I smile through rain. Because of you my life knows no sorrow, and because of you I look forward to tomorrow! Goodnight my beautiful Queen! I love you so much" I probably turned two shades lighter at the least! Ooh he knows how to make my heart melt! I smiled and texted him back that he made my day and that I loved him! I wish I could've said it the way he did but there was no need to try to outdo him as long as he knows he is loved and appreciated. I then laid down in bed thinking of him and just how awesome he is until I drifted off to sleep.

I slept later than usual, maybe because my dream was so good or maybe it was because of the three glasses of wine I had prior to falling asleep. Usually, Sheila would've called by now to see if I wanted my calls forwarded. I tried calling her to let her know that I would be in shortly, but I kept getting the voicemail. That is usually a sign that the day is going to be extremely busy. Either way I got dressed grabbed a banana, a granola bar and bottle of water and headed out the door to work. When I arrived, there was a group of people waiting in the main lobby. Everything seemed to be pretty chaotic. I didn't see them before but as I walked through, I saw Sheila and a lot of police officers all throughout the first floor. Sheila looked as if she had been crying and they escorted Sheila and I into a room. The officer stated that we would not be working at the building today due to the circumstances. But that Monday we would be able to be back to business as usual. Sheila started to cry harder. "Excuse me sir, what is going on?"" I'm sorry ma'am there has been a terrible accident and this building is officially a crime scene!" he said, "A crime scene what happened?" I shouted with frustration completely lost as my heart pounded super-fast in anticipation of his answer. "Well, that is what we are trying to find out. But I can tell you that two people are dead and another injured. I am sorry I cannot speak on the details at this time, but perhaps she can fill you in on what she knows." He said pointing at Shelia as he and the other officer left the room.

She was crying hysterically, and it took me a minute to calm her down. She finally started to speak. "Tierra this is crazy. Mrs. Estella came in and asked me to page Mr. Rudolph because he had forgotten his lunch and she wanted to bring it to him. I paged him but he didn't reply so I figured he had already begun cleaning the building and did not hear the page. She has been here several times, baked us cakes and all…. How could I be so dumb? I let her go back there anyway." She continued as she cried. "Apparently Mr. Rudolph was busy working and that's why he didn't answer, although he wasn't waxing our floors, but Melanie from accounting instead." I told her whatever happened was not her fault and she continued to fill me in. "The next thing I know Charley is calling the front demanding security and then that's when it happened. I heard gunshots!" she started to cry again and said if she would have followed protocol this wouldn't have ever happened. "Security rushed back there but when they got there it was too late! She had already shot Charley, Mr. Rudolph, and Melanie. And she had the gun to her head when they tackled her. She shot but they knocked her down in time, so she did not get a chance to commit suicide. Now Mr. Rudolph and Melanie are dead, and Charley got shot in his arm. But Tierra we just opened the doors, and she is always here, he has worked here for years. I didn't have a clue honestly. I feel so terrible." I couldn't believe what I just heard. Mrs. Estella was the sweetest little lady. She often brought him lunch and made desserts for the entire office. Mr. Rudolph and Charley worked in maintenance and had been working here for over a decade. We have met all of their family members and it was not out of the ordinary to hear that she dropped by. Many people have allowed her to head straight to the back without an escort. As for Melanie I feel terrible. She had a husband and three small children. I had no clue she was having an affair, especially with Mr. Rudolph, he was twice her age at least! Now someone has to call her family and not only tell him she is dead but that she was having sex with another man when it happened, and the man's wife killed them both. This was so unbelievable. They arrested Mrs. Estella Rudolph and took Charley to the hospital and then cleared us all out of the building and turned the entire building into a crime scene. After allowing us to gather a few things from our offices and allowing us to forward calls and to set up automatic out of the office replies on all voicemails and email accounts we were instructed to leave the premises. Sheila was still very broken up, so I called her husband to come and pick her up.

I called Ta'Ron but he did not answer, and Cassie was in training. My mom and dad were busy and at work, so I left them voicemails. Finally, I called T to tell him what type of morning I had. He said he had appointments with Summer but would meet up with me afterwards. So, I decided to go ahead and meet up with Juan for lunch. I didn't want to just go back home; this was a lot to soak in. When I pulled up at Panera he was already there and met me at my car. We walked in and ordered our lunch and he treated. When we sat down, I told him how terrible my day had been, and he was in total shock. I didn't go into detail with him because I had gotten all my facts from a third party, and he didn't know my co-workers like my friends and family did. Lunch was fine I really didn't have much of an appetite after what happen so I only had a bowl of soup, and I couldn't even eat that. Juan tried traveling down memory lane, but I really wasn't in the mood. He pissed me off he seemed so insensitive after a while. He only wanted to talk about himself and what he had accomplished and all of the material things he had acquired in life. I was polite but, in my mind, I was thinking this would be our last conversation. Somehow in his mind he thought that lunch was going well. When it was time to go, he walked me to my car and thanked me for lunch especially considering my morning. He opened my door and leaned in and kissed me right on my lips, I slapped the hell out of him and continued to hit him until he moved back. "Are you out of your mind? Don't you ever put your lips or hands on me again." He tried to apologize to me a million times saying that he couldn't help himself and because he knew what type of day, I had he didn't want me to feel alone. I got into the car and broke out unto tears. I started my car and when I looked up the idiot was still standing near my car looking in the window saying that I need to forgive him. By the time I made it to the first stop light he had texted and called me over ten times. I finally answered and told him that I never wanted to see him or hear from him again, but he continued to call so I blocked him.

I guess what had happened at HG&T finally made the news and everyone started to return my calls. I was already crying, and I just led Cassie to believe it was about work. She told me to meet her at her house and I agreed. When I got there, I was so distraught. When I finally pulled myself together, I told her what Shelia told me and I even told her that Juan kissed me! She was sad about what happened at work but pissed about Juan! She told me that I should tell the guys and let them kick his butt! I told her not to tell anyone and that I just wanted to lie down. Before I could get comfortable Mom, Dad, T, Donovan, Devin, and Ronnie were all there. I love my support system! They were all very loving and very helpful. Mom wanted to ask a million questions as did Dad. I just wanted to lay there and say nothing. So, after a while that's what they allowed me to do. The fellas changed the subject and made me laugh and Cassie poured me a much-needed glass of wine. My parents left me with my friends once they felt I was ok but only after I promised to stay with Cassie or come to their house for the evening. I promised that I would. Before I knew it, I felt so much better and when Ta'Ron called I didn't breakdown. My voicemail box was full of messages from Juan saying he was sorry and just wanted a chance to apologize in person, followed by text messages and emails. I didn't respond to any of them. I just wanted this nightmare to end.

The weekend was fine and Monday we all returned to work except for Charley and Shelia. We had a temporary secretary until she felt up to coming back to work, which was to be expected. The rest of the company seemed to continue on just with more rules. I had hundreds of cards, flowers, candy, and emails awaiting me when I arrived back. Stuffed animals, bracelets, rings, and necklaces followed behind them as the days passed all by Mr. Stupid himself. Because of what happened visitors were not patched through so thank God when he popped up, he never got a chance to see me. After a week or so it seemed to stop and just when I got excited it started all over again!

# CHAPTER 10

I am so exhausted, today was such a busy day, by the time lunch hit I lost count of the number of houses I showed. I had three clients close on their homes, which comes with a quick celebration followed by mounds of paperwork, and as if that was not enough to keep me going Juan will not stop calling me. He has called at least sixty times today alone. Why won't he just leave me alone? I hate that I ever went to lunch with him. I just thought if I finally did, and I was truthful and told him that I was happily married and not interested that he would finally leave me alone. But that plan backfired, and he has become an enraged stalker, sending singing telegrams, flowers, and notes to me at work, leaving voicemails and sending emails and texts. He has even resorted to teenage behavior such as disguising his voice so that Sheila will patch him through. I seriously need to file a restraining order before this gets completely out of hand. I know that sooner or later I am going to have to tell Ta'Ron because he is really starting to scare me with all his threatening voicemails and texted messages. I even had to block him on social media, and we were not even friends. I get that he is upset because I slapped him, but he had no right to put his fifthly lips on me. I am not sorry for protecting myself. He ought to be glad I didn't shoot his crazy butt. I told Cassie everything he ever did and said, and she suggested that I tell one of the guys! I didn't think that would be a great idea because they will shoot 'em. But I let her talk me into it and I finally told T what happened. I feel guilty because he is the one with the record so he is probably the last one I should have told; however, we are the closest out of all the guys. He told me that if he had to, he would come up to my job and escort me home every day! I told him that was ridiculous, and I promised to call him as I walked to my car. I felt like a prisoner. I just want him to leave me alone. The man is nuts! He seriously has full conversations with himself via voicemails and especially through texts. One text he loves me the next he is cussing me out. I have had to clear my memory countless times because he is taking up all the damn space on my phone. Now come on Juan! Really? But today was just so nerve racking. Before I deleted this set of messages this is what I saw...

- *"Good morning beautiful, my day just got a little brighter just knowing that you are mine. Have a blessed day and I will see you soon... real soon."*
- *Tee Tee Don't be ashamed baby I forgive you for slapping me, I know you didn't mean it I just caught you by surprise and you reacted I am not mad at you baby. I know I said that I was in my voicemail but that is because I just wanted you to call me back. I'm so in love with you and this time I am not letting you go. Call me back or text me if you cannot talk ok boo?"*
- *"Hey Bae it's me AGAIN!!!!!!! I know you are busy but I just want to hear your sexy voice that's why I keep*

*trying to call you. Guess you can't talk right now so I'll just settle for a text. I miss you!"*

- *"Damn just spit on me, I can't get a hello or Good morning? You know you miss daddy!"*

- *"WTF Tierra you pissin me off damn how hard is it to respond, ain't nobody that damn busy, don't make me come up there"*

- *Sorry Boo I just really miss you. Did you get my flowers and candy? Ooh I can't wait to taste you, you ready for that?*

- *"I'm trying to be cool with yo ass but since you wanna act then it is what it is. You will get what you want and I will get what I want. Too! YOU'VE BEEN WARNED"*

- *"What you doin for lunch sweetie? I want to see you & them sexy ass lips & hips. Damn you got a bruh on one. Can I have you forever?"*

- *"He can't please your body like I can. He hasn't even brought to his imagination the type of things I can do to you and do well. Are you ready?"*

- *"Damn don't sit here acting like somebody need yo sorry ass, you see me texting and calling and I know you have listened to my voicemails. How you gonna just ignore yo man and try to be on some bougie shit! I ain't gotta chase what's mine. You betta get yo head out the clouds and into the game sweetheart. Real life shit is here waiting on you, Do you want to snatch up this blessing or keep playing. I ain't gonna trip with you. You are my boo and you know it. Try to act otherwise and create a problem yo little ass can't solve!"*

- *"REALLY TIERRA????? WTF?????!!!!!"*

Unfortunately, the messages did NOT stop there. I didn't respond, not even one time. Leave me the hell alone dude! Jesus, please help this schizophrenic bipolar low life and remind him that he has a wife and that I am NOT her! Ugh! Why can't everything just go back to normal?

I have been taking all of my frustrations out on Ta'Ron, snapping at him for the littlest things, and yelling at him over nothing. It's like I am angry at him for not picking up on what's going on. I have tried to tell him so many times. I feel horrible; we have never kept secrets from one another, we never fight about anything. Juan is ruining my almost perfect life. I worked really hard to get to this point. And I have learned from the best on how to create and keep a successful marriage. My parents are still very much happy and in love and I know that we can do the same thing. I did not touch this man, nor did I lead him on. Why won't he go away? I cannot change my number. I am a real estate agent; this number is everywhere. This is so unfair. I wish I never would've bumped into him that day. I am a good person. I give big and love bigger! Why is this happening to me? His last voicemail today said that I would "get what is rightfully mine before long!" What the hell does that mean?

Anyway, I stayed at work way too long today and I need a nice hot bath and an ibuprofen. When I walked out of my office, I noticed that Sheila was still working too. I told her to stop whatever she was doing and to go home and get some rest. Everyone else had already left the building. She promised that she would, and I headed towards the car. I put my hands inside my purse to grab my cell phone, I called T as promised. "Hey, you, I am headed to my car and calling you as promised I had such a long day, you won't believe how many times he called me today. I don't know what to do T!" "Don't worry baby girl I got you!" he said, and I believed him I knew that I could always depend on T! As I unlocked my door, I heard someone behind me. I turned around and screamed to the top of my lungs. "Juan? Are you crazy you scared me? What are you doing here, are you following me?" He had a look of disgust in his eyes and started to ramble that he told me I was going to get what was mine. He grabbed my arm and started trying to rip off my clothes right there in the parking garage. I was screaming for T but in the hassle of me trying to punch him and kick him I dropped the phone. He started unzipping his jeans and pushing me inside of my car. I blew the horn like a crazy woman. All of this happened in just a few seconds, but it seemed like it was going on for hours. Next thing I know someone was pulling him off of me and beating him. I was trying to gather myself. My eyes filled with tears and my clothes destroyed. When I looked up, I noticed it was T! He had been parked a bit away so that I could not see him, but he could see me. "Tierra I am so sorry it took me so long; Baby are you ok? I begin to cry hysterically and screamed that he tried to rape me. Shelia came running and asked if she should call the police and T and I told her not too. Juan tried to get up and run and T chased him down and beat him again! I have never been so scared. "What the hell is wrong with you?" I yelled at him. Finally, T let him go and came back over to me. I couldn't get myself together. He begged me to calm down and stop crying. I told him and Shelia that they couldn't tell anyone! I didn't want my husband, my parents, or my friends to know what happened to me. They both promised not to say a word. T offered to drive me home, but I didn't want to leave my car there. I told Sheila that I would not be coming in tomorrow. T followed me home. It was the longest drive of my life. I couldn't stop shaking, crying, or cussing. I beat on my steering wheel so hard at one point I nearly lost control of the car. My throat was sore from all the screaming and yelling and damn near horse because of all the crying yet none of this was actually making me feel any better. In fact, I felt worse, powerless, like someone had just stolen my life. I tried to encourage myself to keep it together, but I was doing a horrible job. What is it that I did to make this guy attack me! I told him I wasn't interested, I slapped him, sent back all of his gifts, rejected all of his calls, and ignored all of his text messages. I cannot believe this happened.

When I got home, I pulled into the garage and entered the security code. T promised to come in until I calmed down. I hit the floor and burst into tears as soon as I opened the door. Bella came running from upstairs to the door, and she laid beside me, and T just wrapped his arms around me and let me cry for a minute. He then picked me up and laid me on the sofa and covered me up. He went upstairs to draw my bath water and came back with a couple of ibuprofens and a large class of water. Every time I thought about what happen I lost it! I kept begging T not to tell anyone ever. And he promised me over and over. He then helped me upstairs and I took a long hot bath and put on my comfortable pajamas and some socks, wrapped my hair, and came back downstairs. T didn't say anything as we sat on the sofa. He was just rocking back and forth like he was that night he found out Summer was missing. I didn't know what to say! I kept saying thank you and he kept telling me that I didn't have to say it! The tears continued to roll down my face. I couldn't help but to wonder what would've happened if T had not been spying on me. I would've never guessed this in a million years. My dad is a lawyer, and I could have that idiot underneath the jail by morning, but then I would have to explain everything and tell everyone how this has been going on for months and that I didn't want to tell anyone. This is all my fault! How could I have been so stupid! I knew that I never should have talked to him passed that day that we bumped into one another. How was I supposed to know that he was a psycho rapist? He looked like a normal guy; the guy that I had grew up with and once dated for a short period of time. How could he have become so infatuated with me? It is not like we spent a lot of time together or talked. I hadn't seen this guy in years. I have never done anything to deserve this. My chest hurt so bad it felt like it was going to explode. I guess I cried myself to sleep.

It was dark and my heart seemed to still feel like it was going to pop out of my chest. I am all sweaty and my hands are all clammy and I feel paralyzed. I cannot move. I hear breathing but it is not from me. I start to panic, and I lift my arm and try to use them to lift myself off of the bed. I don't even remember coming upstairs. I can't reach the nightstand to turn on the lights and then I feel it! He is on top of me, inside of me. The breathing is from him! Oh My God it is happening. How did he get inside of my house? I started to hit him and scream for T, hoping that maybe he fell asleep downstairs. I started to yell. "Stop get off of me, Stop, T help me T help!" Then he kissed me and whispered in my ears its ok baby I'm here, you are safe, it's not Juan baby it's me! I tried to push him up, but he put all of his weight down on my small frame. He got more excited once I woke up and realized it was him. He got deeper and deeper and I cried louder and louder. He started to yell at me and told me to shut up from the crying, that he has always loved me, and he knows that I love him, so why was I making such a big deal. He had such a tight grip on me and changed me into positions as if I was a willing participant. As he violated me, he told me that if he was going to keep my secret about what happened today with Juan that I was going to keep this secret for him. I begged and begged him to stop but he did not until he was finished. He carried me back into the bathroom and turned on the shower and watched me wash myself. When he felt like I was not doing it right he joined me in the shower and helped me wash. I couldn't stop crying. It made him so mad that he slapped me in my face, and then forced himself inside of me again. He said if anyone besides Ta'Ron was going to have me that it should be him not Juan. How could he say such a thing he was my best friend and he saw that Juan was trying to rape me, in all honesty he did but I keep saying attempted because I do not want to admit that he was ever inside of me and it was very quick, not that time constitutes rape but the shame of knowing I couldn't stop it was too much to admit at least today. When he finished this time, he washed me himself and dressed me back in my pajamas and laid next to me in bed with his arms wrapped around me tightly. I asked him how he could beat up a man for trying to rape me, and then come home and rape me himself, twice. He laughed and said "This ain't rape Tierra, you were always mine, and from now on you are gonna act like it!" I asked him what that was supposed to mean, and he said that every time he got a chance, he would do it again until I realized it is him, I was supposed to be with. He then told me to shut up and go to sleep! I couldn't. I cried so hard I lost my breath. That made him mad and to shut me up he entered me again! At that point I understood that I had to just keep quiet if I wanted him to stop. This time he humiliated me even more. He made me moan and say his name and tell him how much I loved him and how good it felt to finally have him. When I refused, he hit me in my face, or bit down on my nipple, or pulled my hair. I tried to keep quiet I really did but this just had to be a bad dream. It was finally morning and he still had me wrapped tightly in his arms. He asked me to cook him breakfast and the tears started to flow. I said sure he finally let me go. I went and took a shower and put on my house shoes and went downstairs. I went into the kitchen and turned on the water, I then grabbed my purse and keys and jetted toward the garage door he didn't suspect it at all because he heard the water running. I was halfway out of the driveway when he came running out of the house behind me. He called me and I did not answer at all. He sent me a message that said.

*"Do you know how dumb you are gonna sound when you tell everyone it was me who raped you, when even Cassie and Sheila know about Juan and Shelia even seen it was him. You tell MY secret and I tell yours! See you later Baby!"*

Damn what is wrong with everybody do I have a sign on my forehead that says, "take my cookies?" I don't dress or act like a slut! I keep it Diva and wear business attire and sophisticated clothes at all times. I have always been loyal and faithful to my husband and now in one day two men took that away from me. My phone rang again this time it was Ta'Ron, how was I going to answer his phone call and not breakdown? But if I didn't answer it, he would know something was wrong because he called every morning when he was away. "Good morning beautiful how are you doing this morning, I miss you!" he said. I burst into tears immediately and told him I missed him too. He said that he would be home soon and not to cry. There is no way I could tell him this over the phone and while he is focusing on the NBA Championship. I held my peace and told him I would call him later. I drove around town for hours. I had no clue where I could go. I was scared to go to work and scared to go home. This cannot be real, please pinch me.

# CHAPTER 11

**M**y life has been hell these last few months, now I have two stalkers, two secrets, and two reasons just to end it all. Mommy has been trying to use her expertise to analyze me. I tried my best to act normal, but I don't even know what normal is anymore. I have taken a break from work, which I often do around this time of year anyway to travel with Ta'Ron; the bad thing is when he comes home I don't even like having sex with him. And he is my husband. I made the normal excuses at first like I was on my period or had cramps and etc. But he is a good man and I really do love him. I can't process this. T has still been after me, and I am so outdone. I tried to be the same with my parents and Cassie because I don't want to raise any alarms.

I laid down in my bed, under my covers with all the doors locked including the door to my bedroom, and I just cried all day. I was so depressed, and I knew it, but I just didn't want to believe it. I thought about going to seek help from some anonymous group in the area but because everyone knows me, my husband, and my parents, I know that it will never truly be anonymous. I even used my company's EAP (employee assistance program) and called the help hotline. It seemed to help; however, they only cover three sessions, and after that it was back to being alone in my room with nothing but food to comfort me. At this point I wish Mrs. Cleo was still around, so at least she could tell me that this was almost over. I tried going to church but it just got worse, it took me awhile, but I did get there.

When I finally went back to church a few weeks ago, it took every piece of energy I had to get me out of the bed and get dressed. Cassie told me that no one from the crew had been there in a bit and I felt like I really needed to release it at least to God since I couldn't tell anyone else. I dressed in a very long and loose pant suit because I didn't want one single curve to show. I didn't need another man trying to force himself on me. When I walked in everyone was so glad to see me. I started out really well but then when the men kept trying to hug me it was like I had a breakdown moment. I knew they didn't know what happened to me, but I felt like everyone knew my dirty secret just from looking at me. But they were so nice and just escorted me to my seat next to Cassie and Donovan. The choir was very good, and I really enjoyed hearing them, it lifted my spirits. Every word spoken, every scripture read and what the preacher preached seemed to be just what I needed. When the pastor called for alter call, I went down for special prayer and after they were done praying with me, I felt so much better. As I walked back to my seat, I saw Cassie crying and she kept asking if I was ok. I didn't say anything I just hugged her and fell apart in her arms. Once church was over, we greeted everyone. Jasmine and Summer came and gave me a big hug, and my stomach hit the floor. I asked Summer where her dad was, and she stated that she came with Jasmine and Mrs. Diane because he didn't want to come today. I was so relieved. She said she was riding home with Cassie because Jasmine was going to spend time with her dad after service.

Diane came and said hello! She thanked me for all of my love and support and told me that the lawyer that my dad recommended has done wonders for her. She said she has started receiving child support, and that Jasmine's dad even started calling to speak to Jasmine and since they have had a few monitored visits that she was allowing him to take her out for the day and bring her home tonight. I was so excited for her. She even got a better job paying more than the two jobs combined and she said she had me to thank, and that she had been calling but I never called her back and that she thought she had done something wrong. I assured her it was not her fault at all and that I just had a lot of things of my own going on lately and that I was so excited for her. She then offered to take me out for dinner to return the favor I told her that was not necessary. Cassie and I walked with them outside so that the girls could get their things out of the car. Jasmine was so excited she said she was going to a movie. I told her to have fun. Then her dad pulled up in his silver Jaguar with dark tinted windows. He rolled down the window and said "Hey Princess" she screamed and ran toward the car. She swung open the door throwing her backpack in the back and reaching for her seatbelt. We all encouraged her to have a good time and then he leaned out of the car and said we will. I literally hit the floor. Jasmine's dad is Juan Hernandez? There is no way this is even possible. He looked at me and spoke as if nothing had ever happened. This time my heart was pounding so hard I knew I was dying for sure.

As he drove off Cassie and Diane helped me off of my

knees! I couldn't hold back the tears. Diane was confused and asked Cassie was I ok, and she asked if I knew him and what was the problem. Cassie told her I was fine and that I was going through a really tough time. She said ok and hugged me and said that she was praying for me.

Cassie came and got into the car with me! And we started to talk until I realized that Summer was in the car too. Donovan came to the car and reminded Cassie that they were going to be late and then he asked me if I would drop Summer off at home. I just started screaming and crying. I didn't want to say no to her because I love her. But I am afraid to be anywhere around him, but nobody' knows so here I am looking like the psycho. When he witnessed my temper tantrum, he said that he would go ahead a take her home now and by the time he returned Cassie should have me calmed down. Summer kissed me and told me that she loved me and that no matter what it was I would be alright! As much as I wanted to believe that I just couldn't make myself. Summer asked him if I was ok, and he told her that I just had the "Holy Ghost!" I wish that was all I had. Cassie started talking to me! I wanted to tell her everything, but I didn't know how. But before I could start talking, she just assumed it was because I had just seen Juan, and I didn't correct her. She said not to worry that she would tell T! I begged her not too. She looked at me very strangely and asked me if everything was ok. I then told her that I wasn't alright, but I was going to be. By this time, I had calmed down and told her I was going to go to bed. Donovan came back and they promised to check on me later. I drove myself home and ran into the house locking all the doors, setting all alarms including the one on the gate. I had changed all the key codes already. Although I had everything set and secure, I didn't feel safe at all! Church is supposed to be the safest place of all I should've just kept my ass at home. I'm starting to go insane; I could feel my mind slipping away. I just want my peace back.

Oh my God I had just gone down and had prayer and started to feel so much better and just like that the feeling had returned. Both of the little girls that I love and had spent so much time with are the daughters of the two men I hated most. This is so surreal! I have to be dreaming. This is unbelievable, and he had the nerve to say hello to me, as if he is just being polite to a stranger. I am more confused now than ever. If I turn him in, he will go to jail, Diane will lose her child support which she had just thanked me for, and Jasmine would lose her dad again. And it would all be my fault. There was no fix to this solution. Do I stop caring for these girls who need me, because of this? I do not have any children of my own and I love the times that we have. They are precious and I love them. My heart is hurting so bad! I feel so insecure. Everything in my life was falling apart and fast. I felt like I was losing my mind. I can't even go to church. I vowed I would not go back again unless my husband was home, and that is exactly what I did.

It has been weeks and all I do is sit here in this room. When my parents or my husband call, I act like I am busy doing this and that! I have been working out! I have no choice all I do is eat and sleep! As I was sitting down watching talk shows on TV that made my issues feel nonexistent the phone rang. I looked at the caller Id and saw that it was Cassie and I allowed it to go to voicemail. She called back-to-back to back. She then sent me a text saying this was an emergency and then called back again. This time I answered the phone. Cassie was in a panic, breathing heavily and crying. I couldn't make out what she was saying at first and so I asked her to calm down. She then asked me to meet her at T's because Mama Shirley had passed away and he and Summer were not taking it very well. I was sorry to hear the news, but I didn't know how to tell her that I could not come over there. I told her it would probably be later because I was in the middle of a project, which was a huge lie but hell I had been through enough. She begged me and said she needed me to be there. How could I tell her no after all the times she has been there for me? I was so nervous. As I got dressed, I hid weapons in all the layers of my clothing & my pocketbook. And I put on a sweat suit and some tennis shoes just in case I had to take off running. I practiced my "normal" face in the mirror for several minutes before I headed out. It sounds crazy but when you have to fake something like this you damn sure better be good at it. All I need is for T to snap on me and attack me in front of everyone or worse get so mad and tell everyone what happened that day in the parking garage. Although I knew he ran the risk of me telling what he did at the time I was nervous as hell.

I felt bad, Mrs. Shirley was an amazing woman, and she was always there for everyone. When I pulled up, there were cars everywhere. Then it hit me. I called my daddy and told him, and he said that they would be on the way which made me feel so much better. I knew I would be safe with Daddy there. When I walked in T was crying and had his left hand over his eyes, and his right-hand patting summer who was crying with her head on his lap. I honestly didn't know what to say. Had he never raped me, I would have ran up to him and hugged him and tried to comfort him, but instead I was layered with fingernail files, and pocketknives, afraid as can be. I had tried calling Ta'Ron, but he didn't answer. When T finally looked up, he was shocked. He yelled my name and ran toward me. Before I knew it, I was running backwards, almost right out the door. He finally remembered, and stopped moving towards me and said that he was so glad to see me. I finally froze in place because everyone was looking at me. He came and hugged me, and I had no choice but to hug him back because I didn't want to look coldhearted. And to everyone else he was still my best friend. He broke down crying so hard. I cried as well as he slid down to the floor on his knees with his hands around my waist. I was crying because I thought it was about to happen again, right here in front of everyone. I just started screaming "NO, NO, NO!" Summer and Devin came and said she is in a better place. I had forgotten about poor Mama Shirley I thought he was trying to rape me again. He came and sat next to me on the sofa, and I tried to rub his back! Then he turned to me and said he loved me and that he was sorry he was such a horrible friend. Before I could respond Mommy and Daddy walked in and I ran to them like I was a seven-year-old girl! I had already made up in my mind I was leaving as soon as they did, because I knew they wouldn't stay long. They sat down to talk to T and I went and found Cassie. She was still crying. She said that she assured T that I would sing at the service. I reluctantly said of course but inside I was saying hell no! I loved Mrs. Shirley but this was becoming too much for me to handle. Everyone finally stopped crying and they pulled out the cards and dominoes the men that were there started to play, while the ladies tried to organize all the food that was in the kitchen that people were still bringing in. We then made plates and before I realized Mommy and Daddy had slipped out and I was still there.

I made him a plate and took it into him after we finished feeding all of the kids first. He grabbed me by my waist and brought me close to him and said thanks. I tried my best to keep a straight face. I kissed the top of his head and said no problem. I thought I was going to doo doo right then and there. I told Cassie I had to go to my parents' house, and I told everyone bye. T said he would walk me to my car. I told him I was fine, and he didn't have to, but he said it was late and he wanted to make sure I was safe, and Ronnie agreed. I wanted to slap him in his face, so I before I knew it, I did! No one saw me thank God. "Damn girl that hurted!" he said as he grabbed my hands and walked me to the car. He said he was sorry about everything and asked me to forgive him. He started crying and said he didn't know what came over him. I cried too and told him that I am scared of him and that out of all the people in the world I could not believe he hurt me. He promised that if I forgave him, he would never do it again and would allow me my space. I said ok, and he released my hands. As he walked back into the house he turned back around and said "I am really sorry boo, and I do love you, I really do! Sorry, ok?" I just nodded my head yes as the tears flowed.

I got in my car and went straight home. I thought that I would feel different when he apologized but I didn't I was more confused than ever. Was I just supposed to now act like nothing ever happened and go back to being his best friend? Was he really sorry or was he just emotional because of his loss. Or is he trying to get me to let my guards down so he can do it again? It had been weeks since he had seen me or heard my voice, was he sincere? Had he ever done something like this before? I was glad I didn't have to use my knives, but I had too many unanswered questions to just start forgiving him now. Until I felt comfortable, I wasn't going to forgive him, and even if I did, I was going to stay far away from him forever. I must admit I slept so much better that night!

# CHAPTER 12

Life itself has been so exhausting but Bella has been such a blessing. She is such a loving companion. I know she is a dog, but she is everything a girl wants, security, protection, and love! Lord knows I need true love after all I've been through lately. Just having her around has kept me alive on days when I really just wanted to end it all. It's amazing how a little four-legged creature can bring you so much joy. I finally made a doctor's appointment because I can't seem to keep anything down lately. I just want to make sure everything is ok because we are all headed to see Ta'Ron, and the championship game and I really want to see my husband, but I have to be in good health. The stress is really getting to me, and I want to look and feel my best so I can be the best cheerleader as always! My bags are already packed because I knew the team would make it all the way! This road trip should be great, all of us together again. I hadn't even considered the fact that T was coming. I felt like I would be fine since everyone was riding together and because I would be with my husband the majority of the time. I just hope that this appointment goes well!

Cassie called and asked me if it would be ok if we changed the location of the twin's birthday party! She said she didn't want to offend me but because of everything with

Juan and work she didn't want to add too much pressure on me. I'm glad it was her idea because I didn't want to let her down at all, but just like most situations we were on the same page, I love my Bestie! I still promised to help her with the planning stages of the party when we returned. She said that she already put the deposit down on "Premiere," a very beautiful all occasion building in the heart of downtown with a fabulous VIP rooftop and the best view in the city!" Hell, that is a better idea anyway! Premiere? Oh, he better propose to her soon! She is always doing "wifey" type things for him, but hell she ain't wifey yet. It's not that he doesn't love her; I think he really just wants the club to go to the next level before they move forward. She is just a caring person, and she deserves the best. Damn she loves this man for sure. I didn't tell her, but I plan on asking Ta'Ron if we could pay the remaining balance as a gift to his best friends and ask him if we could help with food and drinks as well. I know he will be fine with it, but I still want to discuss it with him. I am so excited that I will have a chance to have my husband back. I can barely wait to spend quality time with him and put all of this drama behind me. Maybe I will book us a nice cruise to Costa Rica for just the two of us. We absolutely love it there. We have been there a million times it seems, yet we keep going back and each visit feels like our first time. The weather is amazing, and the food and people are perfect. The water is crystal clear blue, so blue it seems unreal, and the lifestyle is truly set up for someone who wants to escape their troubles. It is heaven on earth, and we need to go somewhere where we can just blend in with the crowd! Whatever we decide I really don't mind as long as we get away and have some alone time! I know that will make a worlds difference and put everything into perspective for me.

I got to the doctor's office and as usual it was super packed in there. Why do they always seem to book seven or eight people for the exact appointment time? Oh well, as irritating as it may be there is nothing, I can do but wait. I filled out all the necessary paperwork and went to the waiting room with everyone else until they called me. An hour had passed, and they still haven't called my name yet. My head was hurting, and I was hungry and ready to go. I went back to the front desk to make sure they hadn't mistakenly overlooked me. The clerk assured me that I was still going to be seen and I hadn't been overlooked but they were really just really busy. Shortly after I sat back down, they called me to the back. The nurse asked me to give a urine sample, which was easy because I had been sitting out there so long, I had to go anyway. They weighed me, took my blood pressure, and took some blood samples. She asked if this was just a routine checkup. And I told her yes it was but that I had been feeling sick lately and I wasn't sure if I had the flu or if it was all stress related. She said that a lot of people had been sick lately and asked if I had been eating a lot of sea food, I told her I had not. She stated that there was some food poisoning going on as well mostly they found related to fish and shrimp from a local market. I couldn't honestly remember what I ate because I have been eating so much. She walked me back to a room and said that the doctor would be with me shortly. When he came back there, he made short talk in reference to my husband and the games. I told him that I was heading out within a few days to go and join him. He asked me to wish him well and offer his congratulations to him. I told him that I would and reminded him that they had not won yet but that I was with him in believing in advance that this was their year. He laughed and said "Yes that too sweetie but I was talking about congratulating him on being a father! Tierra you are not sick honey you are very much pregnant!" I couldn't believe what I was hearing I had waited to hear those words for so long, but this is some seriously bad timing. I started to cry, and the nurse and doctor comforted me and assured me I would be a great mother. They asked me to disrobe so that they could do a full body checkup and of course I did. "Yes, ma'am you are going to have a little star, make sure you come up with a great way to break the news to your honey. But you may want to wait until after the championship or he will not be able to focus. When was the first day of your last period?" I hadn't even realized I missed my cycle there was so much going on I had no clue when it was. All I could do is shrug my shoulders and cry. When they asked if I was happy or sad, I told them I was happy, but honestly, I was excited but scared. "Well, we estimate that you are about eight to ten weeks pregnant. That would put your due date approximately late October!" he said. "Pregnant? Pregnant? Now, after all I have been through. God is this your idea of a joke because this is not funny at all!" Any other time I would be walking on clouds. We have been trying for so long and it finally happened. A slight grin came across my face until I remembered I had been raped. "God please don't let this be Juan's or T's baby," is all I remember repeating on my way home. My eyes were bloodshot red and swollen from all of the crying. I was so furious! All I ever wanted was a family and now I am more stressed than ever. How can I tell anyone! I don't know what to do or what to say. I will take the doctor's advice and keep my mouth closed until after the play offs. Damn I would've rather had the flu!

Do I tell Ta'Ron what happened now, or do I wait and just keep it a secret and never say a word? It's not my fault at all so why do I feel so guilty? Why do I feel like I must hide this from my husband, when I am the victim? He would understand but be upset that I didn't tell him when it actually happened. What would T think? After all he knows exactly what's going on and I'm sure he will have a fear that it is his and that the truth will have to surface because of it. I knew I was keeping the baby, but it wasn't until this happened to me that I began to understand why some women have an abortion. This is a lot to handle. I'm strong, but I am not sure if I am built to handle this type of pressure. "Try not to stress this baby could belong to Ta'Ron" I kept telling myself. God this cannot be real! I literally cried all day and all night I didn't answer any calls whatsoever. I want to be a mother but not like this. Why is all of this happening to me? I am a good person! I just want to kill them for doing this to me! Right now, that doesn't sound like a bad idea... UGH!

I didn't sleep well at all I tossed and turned all night long. Trying to find a comfortable position but I couldn't. Even when I tried to think about something else, my mind still would revert back to the possibility of this baby belonging to my used to be best friend and now my rapist T and even worse Crazy Juan! This kind of thing is what you see on TV in one of those lifetime movies I always enjoyed watching. I can tell you there is nothing enjoyable about it, when you are the one going through it! I thought about the baby and that cheered me up a bit. Would it be a boy, or a girl? Would I have twins? How would the baby look, would they be athletic or artistic like we are? I tried so hard to see the positive in it. Telling myself over and over that God wouldn't put more on me than I can bear and that he must think I'm pretty tough because this is a lot! I wondered what theme I would use to decorate the nursery in. How will I tell my parents, and why did I have to get knocked up under these circumstances? Maybe I should just tell my family with excitement and never even act as if there is a possibility of this baby not belonging to my husband. But I don't want to hurt anyone especially when this is not my fault! I have to believe that this would all work out because if not I am going to go crazy and get depressed and this is not how I planned on living at this age in my life.

I eventually was able to get a few hours of sleep and I called Cassie to see if everyone was awake and packed up so we could leave as scheduled. She said that they were and would be headed to get me in a few and would pick up T last because he stayed by the highway! I told her that was fine. I went ahead and took a Tylenol as the doctor said I cannot have aspirin and pulled my bags to the door and relaxed on the sofa. Shortly after I sat down, my Dad pulled up to pick up Bella. They are taking care of her and watching the house while I am gone. Daddy was being Daddy still trying to give me money as if I was a little girl going on a school trip. And reminding me of all the things I need and need not to do! I just smiled and said yes sir and walked him to his truck. I swear Bella knows what's going on. She normally loves going to my parent's house, but she didn't want to leave me. I almost broke down crying as I assured her, I was ok. They finally left and I did one final walk through in my house and removed all the garbage. Devin knocked on the door and came and assisted me with my bags. I was starting to feel so much better. This trip is going to be so much fun! Once I got into the truck everyone was in such a great mood. Cassie reminded the fellas that we still needed to get ice and a few things from the store and so that is where we headed next! I decided to get some ginger ale and crackers just in case I started feeling sick on the road. The last thing I wanted to do was alarm my friends of this pregnancy.

We were leaving in plenty of time to make it an official road trip. We decided to stop a few places to see some sites and relax and take pictures and then we would continue. Ronnie was in charge of that, and he had everything all together, so we were nervous and excited. There was no telling what he has planned. After leaving the store we headed towards the highway to pick up T. My stomach began to feel a bit queasy, and I knew to sit in the front row of the SUV next to the twins and to allow T and Ronnie to have the back. We were all going to take turns driving but the men insisted on doing all the driving and so that leaves me and Cassie to relax. When Donovan was driving, she would sit upfront with him and other than that she sat with me. This made me feel so much better because I didn't want to make a scene if T gets close to me. When we pulled up to get him, I could feel myself start to shake a bit so I just took deep breaths and tried to act as normal as possible. He said hello and went to the back and immediately started clowning. After thirty minutes or so I loosened up and started to feel comfortable. He didn't overdue speaking to me. He occasionally asked me to pass him something from the cooler, as did the others, but other than that he kept his distance and I appreciated that. When we pulled over, he helped me out of the truck like he had always done and continued to talk to the guys. Maybe things really are going back to normal; maybe I don't have anything to worry about after all! Ronnie and Devin were excited they knew there would be thousands of ladies there and that we have VIP access all tournament long, which includes after parties as well as Day Parties. They spent the majority of the time talking about who would pull the most women. Our road trip is already creating new memories. Ronnie picked some interesting places to stop and see to say the least. Some places were interesting, and others were places like the largest strip club, which Cassie and I could've done without! Nonetheless we had an awesome trip to Miami for the finals.

When we arrived in Miami the streets were packed full of people. Some wearing swimsuits, some in team gear, others in day-to-day clothes, some who looked as if they were headed to a costume party and absolutely everything in between. We had been to Miami several times before, for getaways and such but this was something entirely different. We wanted to get checked into our rooms immediately so that we could shower and change and hit the town. We already knew that it would be late tomorrow afternoon before we had a chance to see Ta'Ron. The best thing about Miami is no matter how late it is the city is always up and ready to welcome you with open arms. We got checked into our hotel, and as usual we were staying at the top-of-the-line hotel, it was beautiful. The hotel was the host hotel and there were celebrities all around. We actually reserved our rooms under the group rate for the team and team families. Cassie and Donovan shared a room, Devin, Ronnie, and T happily shared a three-bedroom penthouse suite in hopes of being able to entertain and impress a group of young women throughout the trip. I had a room of my own of course because I knew that when he was available my hubby would be in there with me. My room was laid! It had everything you could possibly think of in it. It was better than the room I had in LA just a couple of months ago. There was a huge hot tub in one area of my apartment style room, surrounded by mirrors and blinged out wine glasses and accessories. It was gorgeous, sexy even. It had a huge blinged out chandelier that hung over the hot tub and that could be dimmed for mood setting purposes. There were complimentary robes and house slippers that felt like royalty, super white, super soft, just perfect. There was a sitting area and an entertainment area. The bedroom actually had a door to it with another bathroom in it, as if the huge bathroom as you first entered the room wasn't enough. As soon as I swung the huge double doors open, I was excited. The bed was enormous, it looked like it was two king size beds put together. The patio could be accessed from the sitting area or from the bedroom area. The view was beautiful, and in the entertainment area there was already a couple of bottles of wine that I Knew I was going to crack open. Oh, Damn I can't drink!

We all took some time to relax and shower and then got dressed and met up to go eat and hit the town for the remainder of the evening. We all looked great! We knew that the possibilities of the night were endless as there were so many parties, concerts, boxing matches, after parties and etc. going on all day every day, so our clothes had to match what we might get into, and since we were VIP, and I was the wife of a high profiled NBA star I had a reputation to uphold, and I loved it! We hit the city hard that night. We had a great dinner, went out for dancing, did a little site seeing, went to a late-night armature boxing match that was very entertaining, and hit up a celebrity hosted after party that lasted longer that my body would allow me to hang. They had live entertainment at the party, and they gave a show as if there were performing in front of a packed stadium. Ronnie and the fellas were having the time of their lives. They were getting and exchanging number as we knew they would, and they were really in what Cassie, and I jokingly called "Mac Heaven!" I was tiered but I didn't want to be the one who ended it all. It was after five in the morning and well past my bedtime. But just as my eyes started to close, they brought out another special guest and I got excited all over again. Ronnie came by and asked me to dance with him and of course I did, or at least I think I did. I think my body was moving but I'm sure I wasn't video girl material at this hour. He said that he was tiered but wanted to go have breakfast before we headed back to the room because he said he didn't plan on getting up until evening! As the song was winding down Ronnie and I started our exit from the dance floor and Cassie and Donovan met us and stated they were tiered. I told them what Ronnie had just said and Donovan was all over the breakfast idea. Ronnie went and rounded up T and Devin who were still living it up but said they were tiered as well. As we walked out of the party we could see a long line of people in line outside, who were stilling trying to get into the after party. I was amused but I must admit the party was great. As soon as

I sat down in the truck I must've dosed off because I don't even remember putting on my seatbelt, let alone pulling up at the twenty-four-hour diner spot nestled deep in the hood of Dade County. It too had a long line of people waiting to be seated and a bunch of people walking out of the opposite side of the building with the classic Styrofoam to-go boxes. Devin said this is where everyone goes, that the food was amazing and that is why people wait. So, we all agreed we wanted to see what all the hype was about, and we would wait and experience it as well.

The morning air had a little chill to it, so I went back to the truck to get my jacket. T was leaning against the truck on his cell phone and told whomever he was talking too that he would call them back. I shut the door and began to walk away when he grabbed my arm. I quickly snatched away in fear. He apologized and said he didn't mean to scare me or make me feel uncomfortable but instead just wanted to know "Are we good, you know back to normal, my friend? I miss you girl, damn! I just want to know if you can forgive me, and we try to move forward. Is that cool?" I didn't know how to respond to that, and I was pissed that he put me on the spot like that. We had such a great time, and all was well, why did he have to verbally remind me? "Uh yeah we straight." I said hesitantly "Straight?" he replied with a slight attitude "What the hell does that mean, straight?" "That means let's try our best to move forward, but I cannot make promises at this time. I am trying the best that I can, but I trusted and loved you and you hurt me. That's what I mean by straight dumb ass!" I yelled as I walked away. He ran to catch up with me. "I'm sorry Boo that wasn't fair. I know it will take time and may never be like it used to be, but I swear I'm sorry and I love you and I just want to make sure you are ok is what I guess I'm asking!" He then grabbed me by both of my shoulders and turned me towards him "Tierra Michelle I am so sorry; it is true that I love you beyond friendship and always have but I had no right to." I cut him off pushing his hands off me. "Respect me enough to give me time and space! Love me enough to never hurt me again and please don't bring this up again. Part of my healing is at least trying to forget. This is crazy and hard to deal with especially alone T I can't tell anyone, so let me deal with it in my own way, and I promise to try not to hate you forever. Right now, I hate you and what you did and my peace that you stole, I hate that you are trying to force me into a friendship just like you forced yourself inside of me. It's like being raped all over again. Please T I am trying can I get a little help?" I felt my eyes welling up with tears. I can't believe I finally got a chance to confront him, and I did it with boldness that alone made me feel so much better. "I hate it when you call it rape, but I know why you do. Honestly, I was hoping when you found out it was me and not Juan that you would open yourself up to me and make love to me the way I always dreamed you would. But when you didn't, I guess I was embarrassed and pissed. Tierra I am not making excuses I hurt you and I hate my damn self for it. But I am sorry. I know you love that nig... I mean Ta'Ron but you don't know everything babe and it just pisses me off sometime. But I take responsibility for the choices I made the good and the bad and yes, I will be more understanding. Can I start with helping you put your jacket on and walking you back to the line? Baby I'm sorry I wish I had better words, but I love you and I'm sorry. I have never done that before and will never do that again to you or anyone else. Ok?" "Thank you that's all I ask T but what do you mean I don't know everything?" I asked with a look of total confusion on my face. "Psst I'm just talking trash baby girl, don't trip. Let's go get some food. Ya boy is hungry. Can I buy your meal?" "You better buy it sucka!" I said jokingly trying to lighten the mood and change the subject. We walked back and joined our group and there were just a few more people in front of us. We were asking what the specialties were. We were told everything was awesome, but they are famous for their huge thin homemade pancakes and overstuffed omelets and potatoes. We finally got in and got seated. Cassie and I decided to go with the crowd and order the house special. The guys ordered so much food I felt sick to my stomach just hearing them order out loud. They brought out so much food it was no wonder we saw all of the to-go trays leaving the building. It looked as if they used a dozen eggs on my omelet! It was huge and overstuffed with all of my handpicked toppings just like the lady in the line said it would be. It seemed as if I took a million bites and didn't get even a quarter of the way through it. The pancakes were so good. Huge, thin so they had the crispy edges on it just like Nana makes. And the potatoes were very good, a little spicy but delicious. I tried to drink some of my orange juice, but I was stuffed and started to feel sick to my stomach. I prayed silently that God would at least allow me to hold it all down until I got alone in my hotel room. I quickly asked for a few boxes to put my leftovers in, and Cassie joined me saying that she needed some as well. The guys had the special and pork chops, steak, and everything else and swapped food so that they could try it all. They ate a lot more than Cassie and I combined but at the end even the fellas had to get to-go boxes too. We sat there and really enjoyed ourselves, it was nice. Before long, it was after seven am. We left and drove back to the hotel which was a little ways away from the diner. When we finally arrived at the hotel, we all hugged each other goodnight and laughed at the fact that it was after eight in the morning. I was so tiered, but I figured I would sleep much better if I had a bath, especially since we had been around a lot of cigarette smoke. But I honestly couldn't wait to use my robe and house slippers. I got good and comfortable and slipped into my oversized and comfy bed. It didn't take long for me to drift off to sleep, but not before T's comment kept running through my head. What did he mean that I didn't know everything about Ta'Ron? I tried not to over think it, but I couldn't let it go. O well at least I'm not throwing up! I drifted off to sleep before I could think too deep.

# CHAPTER 13

This bed is absolutely amazing! I have to see what type of mattress this is because I will be buying one as soon as I get back home. I slept like a baby and woke up feeling extremely refreshed. I woke up about 1'oclock which means I didn't have a full eight hours of sleep, however, I felt like I had slept for days. Maybe it was because of T's apology or the fact that I was given the chance to let off some steam. Whatever the case I feel so rejuvenated. I was hesitant about calling everyone to see if they were awake, but when I did Cassie said that the guys woke up a little bit ago and had been in the gym for hours. She said she wanted to come up to my room but didn't want to disturb me. I told her to come on up.

"Girl we are way too old to be trying to stay up all night!" she said as soon as I opened the door. "Exactly girl, but I didn't want to be the one who cancelled everyone's fun, so I just tried to hang!" we both laughed. I told her that we will get to see Ta'Ron from about 3:30-5pm and then the first game was tonight at 7 and after that the two teams were having a combined meet and greet tonight. So, we were in for another long night. I showed her what I was wearing to the game and to the meet and greet and we decided to take it easy until time for us to head out, so we decided to go to the pool and chill out. On our way we stopped by and told the guys and they decided to join us. The guys were splashing and acting crazy as Cassie, and I relaxed pool side and took in a little sun. We occasionally had to remind them not to get our hair wet because we had limited time to get dressed after we meet up with Ta'Ron. They laughed and talked trash and said they wouldn't get it wet but they started splashing again moments after each promise. I was glad to see everyone having such a great time. We all went back upstairs and got dressed and I told them to meet me in the hotel restaurant for appetizers with my hubby. I knew he wasn't going to eat because he had a game, but I knew it would be awhile before they got another chance unless they ate a hot dog or something at the game. They all agreed to meet me, and I reminded them to pack their change of clothes for the meet and greet as well.

We all headed up to get dressed and Ta'Ron called and said he was going to be a few minutes late. I was disappointed but I know he is here to work so I acted as if I wasn't bothered at all. "Ok baby I understand, I'm about to shower and get dressed. I can't wait to see you. Hold on baby somebody at the door!" "Somebody like who?" he asked "I don't know crazy that's why I said hold on" I said sarcastically as I walked toward the door. "Who is it?" I asked there was no response and they knocked again "Who is it? Okay stay out there!" I said as I walked away from the door. Ta'Ron made fun of me saying I thought I was tough. They knocked again and I ignored it and kept talking to him. Finally, a voice of a woman said Housekeeping and I walked over and snatched open the door ready to give her a piece of my mind and asked her why she didn't answer me when I asked her several times before, who it was. I was ready too, but when I opened the door, I saw the back of a man giving the housekeeper money as she walked away. He turned around and said, "Hey Tough Stuff!" and started laughing hysterically. It was my baby he wasn't late at all it was him all along at my door! I jumped in his arms and started kissing him while asking him why he did that. I said "You ain't late boy, you early!" "I'm early for you, but we will be late meeting up with them if you know what I mean!" Ooh Lord he was still so smooth "Yes I do baby let me call and tell them you will be running a little late" I said as we giggled, and I reached for the phone. "No need to do all that baby we will just have a quickie ha aha hah, and if not I'm sure they will figure it out!" We both laughed and the rest as they say is history.

We were only a few minutes late meeting everyone downstairs. And I was so energized and ready for the evening as you could imagine. The guys went crazy when they saw Ta'Ron! "What up Sniper? What up Big Baby? Oh, my dawg is here!" And many other slurs came from all over as they hugged and greeted one another. They clowned all the way to the table. I smiled so hard; it was so good to see the crew all together again. We had too much fun. I had to warn them to calm down because he had a game to play, and they all finally settled down. I allowed the fellas to catch up because I knew I would have his attention again late tonight. Cassie and I chatted and watched as they reunited, and we occasionally commented on their topics. Ta'Ron left to head to the center, and we assured him we would be the best cheering squad there and he laughed and said that was what he was afraid of. We continued to sit and relax and reminisce and also talk about tonight. "We are NOT staying out to 8am this time!" Cassie boldly stated with her hand on her hip and her eyebrows slightly raised. "Hell, we are too damn old for this! Now I'm all for having a good time but we gonna pass out trying to hang with these kids!" We all laughed and told her to sit back down, but we all agreed. "Girl sit yo crazy butt down, we ain't going to plan on it but we are going to have a good time and go with the flow. When you are ready to go you have to say something!" Devin said while making faces and hand gestures at Donovan insinuating that Cassie was nuts.

We headed to the game and while in the car Cassie and I practiced our cheers and chants while the guys mocked us and made fun of us, but it didn't matter to me or Cassie we just kept coming up with more. I was starting to feel so at ease, things were finally starting to feel normal again. I was dressed to kill, fresh from head to toe as usual, to remind all the women who drool over him that he had a fine wife and no need to look elsewhere. Plus, the paparazzi was always trying to get pictures of me as well and they weren't gonna catch me off guard looking all crazy if I could help it! The guys continued to plead with us not to do our cheers and embarrass them, but we didn't care we always had so much fun at the games. I quickly reminded them that they didn't have to sit courtside next to me and be subject to such humiliation, that they could always go and purchase a regular admission ticket, and no one would ever know we were together. They jokingly started chanting one of our cheers. I took that as a sign that all of the sudden they were cool with the embarrassment after all. They finally left us alone and made their own conversation until we arrived.

When we pulled up to the valet there were camera crews and paparazzi all around. As soon as I exited the car, I was approached by ESPN asking me for my prediction of tonight's outcome of the game and who I thought would win this year's NBA Playoff. Of course, I responded with the typical friendly and respectful response; "Both teams are great teams, so I expect it to be a very interesting game. But I know that we will take it all the way! We are hungry and it is our year! And it would just be an added bonus if my husband brought home that MVP trophy as well" Then I giggled and walked on, occasionally stopping for a photo opportunity or a limited interview. I never really mind responding to ESPN because I have never had a bad experience with them. However, I learned the hard way a few years back, that you cannot be so generous with some of the other networks. I guess it's all a part of journalism and ratings, but I learned that they will turn your words around just to create a buzz. I wanted to slap the hell out one network in particular, when they changed my simple statement about the team's former coach and his oh so highly profiled infidelity & drug scandal all around and upside down! But it's all good I sold more houses and got so many referrals as did my company as a whole. So, what was meant for bad worked out for my good and lined my pockets.

We found our way to our seats and really enjoyed ourselves. The game was intense, and the fans were even more intense. My baby was out there showing out despite of the bad calls the referees were making. Cassie and I limited our cheers because we were so engaged in the game, but we threw one or two in here and there and the fellas dropped their heads in disbelief. I'm not here to impress anyone.

I love being my crazy goofy self, and I am my husband's number one fan, not some Heffa with her face painted and hair colored waving around pom-poms. Plus, it's been a minute since I felt like this, I miss this feeling. Just as I had predicted we won the game! I went nuts in the stands like a crazed parent at their child's game. "That's my baby! That's my baby" I hollered as I jumped up and down and tears fell from my face. I joined the mob and rushed the court to celebrate with my man. I didn't get to love on him long because of all the people who wanted interviews. Oh well it was time to turn up and we were so ready!

We made it out to the night scene again and the crowd was "turned up." Everyone was hyped all up from the game and others were just glad to be a part of the after party. The fellas talked us into stopping by a local hole in the wall before meeting up with the team for the official after party. It was packed wall to wall with people. The room was filled with the stench of sweat, marijuana and bad breath. Not exactly what I was looking for, but I couldn't deny that they were having a great time, so I joined in and held my complaints. Eventually we made our way the after party and I didn't let my husband out of my sight. We had such a good time. I was overwhelmed with gladness, and I could feel his excitement. The party was nice very nice, but I could only concentrate on being by my man's side and celebrating his success. This trip was much needed, but this win was needed even more. I hate the fact that I have to head back without him. But I know it will only be a short while until we are together again. I can't wait until my baby is home, I truly miss him.

assie has been battling with the thought of going to visit her mother in Illinois next month. She, along with Donovan usually takes the trip to "Chi-Town" once a year for the last few years and they stay a couple of weeks. Her mother moved away a few years ago when she got divorced from Cassie's Father, and she now has a new man in her life; "FRANK!" Now Frank has got to be the weirdest person I have ever met, and personally I don't like him at all. He thinks he is God's gift to women. He walks around talking like an old, retired pimp, wearing tight white linen pants and different color floral Hawaiian shirts with the first two buttons always unbuttoned to show his nasty taco meat on his chest. As if that isn't awkward enough, he talks in third person constantly as if it's normal. I swear he must have thirty pair of those pants all tight and all white! "Frank is in the Hizz-ouse, so grab ya ladies unless you want new babies cuz Frank neva says no to stank!" That is his favorite thing to say whenever he enters a room, as if anybody cares that he is there at all. He is otherwise a decent looking man besides his clothes and Beetlejuice looking teeth. He always smells like evergreen trees and cigars and tries to convince everybody that its designer cologne. "Naw Baby Frank don't stank. Frank don't stank!" He would say as

Cassie, and I wiped his wet kisses off our cheeks with frowns on our faces. He is one of those people you must see with your own eyes otherwise he sounds like some fictional character from a comedy movie. Have you ever met someone who believes they sincerely know EVERYTHING about EVERYTHING? Well, that is Mr. Frank. You cannot have a conversation or debate about anything because he has already done it at least twice and already thought about three times as much. Unfortunately, he is wrong more times than not, yet he will never admit he is wrong he will just say something like "They must've just changed it because that's not what it used to be." How miserable must a person be to be ashamed to admit that they learned something new? All pride to the side if you don't know you just don't' know and it is ok to admit it. Heck, I have heard the saying all of my life that you should learn something new every day, but Mr. Frank sure doesn't feel that way. Yep, he is definitely annoying, yet I learned how to deal with him and trust me that is from a distance!

Apparently, there was a little blow up between Cassie and Frank the last time she visited, and she vowed she would never go back to visit her mother as long as he was there. He is one of those petty old men. You know the type of person who has never really had much and now that he does, he feels as if he has something to prove. When Cassie called me after their fight, she was pissed "GIRRRRRRRL! All I know is you betta bail me out of jail, this fool don't know me! He got me messed up!" I tried to interrupt but she rarely took a breath long enough for me to jump in. She was mad for real. She continued on saying how he was just doing stupid teenager stuff like following her around, repeating everything she said as if he was a parrot, and immature things like that. But this time he went a little too far with his "I'm the man" tactics and shenanigans. This time he got in her face while Donovan and Mrs. Reynolds weren't around. And he gave her some drunken speech about if he didn't want her around all he would have to do is say the word and her mom would stop talking to her and one of his family members would beat her up. Now although Cassie knew it was all a dream in his crazy head, she just got pissed and went off on him and that is when he stepped in her face and things got a little heated. All the talk is fine because everyone knows the only thing he can do is run his mouth, and people allow it because it makes him feel better about himself. Well Cassie grabbed his little stubby finger and twisted it when he put it in her face and touched her nose and she said she kind of twisted his arm a bit. He acted like he wanted to actually hit her after that, and she dared him to. They were still arguing and fussing when Donovan and Mrs. Reynolds returned. She told her mom that he was doing all the little kid stuff to her, and they all ripped into him immediately. The thing that has her the angriest is that she cannot tell her Mama everything because she knows her mother and not to mention Donovan would completely snap and lose it and poor old Frank would be a distant memory. She doesn't want to do that because he treats her mother right, and she seems to really love him, and Cassie is torn with whoopin his ass and making him understand that she ain't the one or breaking her mother's heart. So, her frustration is coming from not being able to tell everything that happened.

If he would just settle down, he would be an ok dude.

Seriously he is alright when he is not drinking, which seems to be all the time unfortunately. I think personally he just tries way too hard. Maybe he has always had to be that way to get people to like him. What he is not understanding is that it is doing the complete opposite and it is weird and annoying. He obviously has issues all around. He has children and grandchildren of his own, but they do not communicate with him at all, not even on major holidays. Even when they attempt to patch up the relationship, he finds some crazy way to mess it up and then blames everyone but himself for the fall out. He is a drunk and I mean an authentic drunk. He drinks waking up and amps it up throughout the day and goes to bed drunk. By 7 am he is literally drunk, like tore up. He is the type of guy who cannot hold his liquor and starts trouble but is actually very weak and too scared to even try to back it up so he runs to Mrs. Reynolds in hopes that she can smooth things over. The crazy thing is he is only this way with family. If they are out in public or at one of the many events she hosts, he is on his best behavior and never embarrasses her and treats her really well. It is like watching the modern-day version of Dr. Jekyll and Mr. Hyde play out right before our eyes.

My only thought was what an idiot! "Girl I'm only mad because I want to knock him out, but out of respect for my mother I'm just keeping to myself. I'm not playing if I snap you better come get me Bestie ha ha ha you know Chicago got real jails!" Cassie said jokingly and I assured her that I would not only have her bail money, but I would catch a flight and slap his stupid ass myself! Whew I tell you people never cease to amaze me. Selfishness and pride are the ugliest things you can ever adorn yourself with. They will surely keep you miserable and alone, let's pray neither happens to him.

Cassie was really hurt and rightfully so, but she is being a bit stubborn about the whole thing. She is stuck on saying no to the visit; however, her mother has really been reaching out to her to return to Chicago while assuring her that things are different now! Cass and her mom have a great solid relationship and have always been close. I told her never allow anyone to separate her and her mother and she said she would never do that, but she never wants to put her mother in a place where she feels the needs to pick sides because she knows she will choose her. However, reality is she has her own life in Georgia, and she didn't want her mom to be alone all because her drunkard idiot of a boyfriend doesn't know how a real family works.

Mrs. Reynolds seems to be happy, and I guess that is all that really matters. Like Cassie use to say, "As long as he puts a smile on my Mama's face, he is alright with me, but the moment that changes that's his ass!" He thinks it's a cute little quote, but I know my girl, she is not playing at all. When it comes to her family she will go there with no apologies! And trust me you don't want her to go there... ever. I decided not to continue to pressure her. After all it is her decision and I know she will eventually do the right thing. She was always there for me, so it was my turn to be there for her and nagging her about the same thing over and over was not going to do the trick anyway. However, I did lay it on pretty thick because apparently her mom is being recognized by the city for her help in the community and of course she wants Cass to be there as she accepts her award and a key to the city. Mrs. Reynolds has started a few community groups and hosted several major events since her relocation. She focuses on women and children, and she does a fantastic job. She used to do a lot of the same things when she lived here. She is obviously creating quite the buzz especially to be in a city as large as Chicago and make a huge enough impact in such a short amount of time to be recognized and to receive a key to the city. They are also doing a big story on her in the newspaper and local news channel because the work she is doing has touched so many. Someone heard about it and contacted Ebony magazine and they are coming to the event to get pictures and to interview her. Naturally she wants Cassie in the pictures and wants her to be interviewed, but Cassie doesn't want to be in any pictures with you know who, but I know she is seriously considering going now that she knows that. I cannot imagine her allowing what happened between her and Frank to miss this huge moment in her mother's life. If I hadn't been traveling so much and if I wasn't pregnant, I would go with her. Anyway, I allowed her to vent and then I changed the subject to something I knew would make her smile, the party.

We continued the final planning stages of the party for the twins and that took her mind off of the subject which was my intent. Everything was coming together, and we were days away from the actual event. Cass was so nervous she wanted everything to go off without a hitch and although I was constantly reassuring her that it was going to turn out great, she was still scared. I was excited too, but I had to be careful not to take over as I often did. It was never intentional, but I seem to always be the planner, the organized one, you know the one that holds it all together.

So, a lot of times without thinking I tend to take charge of things without anyone even asking me to. They joke about it a lot, but they like my ideas and the fact that they can guarantee that I will get it done. But when Ta'Ron said that we could help out financially he said, "Baby let Cass throw her man a party!" Then he laughed and continued. "I mean, I know you mean well Baby but don't take over. You can offer ideas but don't bully her into accepting them, 'cuz you know how you can get." He continued to carry on in detail and I cut him off. "Whatever!" I said as I chuckled knowing it was true, but I was kind of mad that he felt the need to bring it up. Like I said I knew it was true so I promised him that I would only assist her and that I wouldn't turn it into one of my spectacular events unless she asked of course. Anyway, we are two peas in a pod she is just as talented and has just as many great ideas. I am sure it will be a sexy-sophisticated sensational event.

Invitations had already been sent out and everyone was already confirming their spot, so the little details were important because there is going to be a lot of people there. Once we finalized all of the party details it was time for us to go shopping and find something to wear. I can no longer fit my clothes the way I like them to fit. I have a mini baby bump already and I want to look cute and comfortable. Cassie wants to coordinate with the twins and so we headed out to see what we could find. "Girl I'm just so nervous. I hope it all works out. I know the location is flawless, DJ Novelty is just ridiculous, and the food and entertainment will be talked about weeks after, but I just have butterflies in my stomach, like something crazy is going to happen and it scares me!" I chuckled while shaking my head. "Don't laugh Tierra I'm serious. I don't know how I will react if this party isn't absolutely perfect!" "Aww Boo!" I replied jokingly "Don't trip it will be amazing just focus on how he will feel when he sees all the thought and love you put into it. I just can't believe it is finally here. Two more days and it will be party time. Everything is paid for, and you know they provide immaculate security at your venue so there is no need to worry. What you need to focus on is what you are going to wear to really make his head spin!" She laughed uncontrollably for a few moments. "Whew… You are a nut! I know that's right girl I need everything sitting tight and sitting right… in its proper place, okay?" We continued to joke and laugh as we continued shopping, and both found an outfit that we absolutely loved. She dropped me off at home and I continued to work on a few decorative touches on the party favors and then showered and went to bed.

I slept so well I woke up in a great mood. I felt like Aaliyah! I was all in my bathroom mirror using my brush as my microphone as I performed "Back and Forth," as if I was on stage in front of a packed house at Radio City; singing at the top of my lungs "It's Friday and I'm ready to swang pick up my girls and hit the party scene tonight oooh oh it's alright um. So, get up and let this funky melody get you in the mood 'cuz you know it's alright yea…" I continued jamming throughout the house as I ate breakfast and took Bella out to handle her business. I even had a great stress-free day at work today, which I hadn't had in a while. I got a lot of paperwork completed, I wasn't feeling sick and Juan though he was still as crazy as ever must've been busy because I got mostly emails from him and one of them included a creepy poem, he wrote which I don't really know how to take. I wasn't sure what the next step should be, but he seemed to otherwise be backing off, so I really didn't give it much thought at the time.

*From: juanito79@memail.com*
*To: tmhunter@hcgreality.com*
*Date: Fri, August 28, 2022*
*Subject: Just open it*

*Hey Tierra, I know you have received my other emails and honestly, I am pissed that you feel that ignoring me is ok. I heard what you said loud and clear about seeing you at church when I picked up my baby girl. The only reason I didn't put it out there that we knew one another is because I do not want my ex all up in my business. All of that put aside I wrote you this poem and I just wanted to share it with you. Maybe this will better explain my feelings to you without scaring you away. I love you always baby girl and I understand we both have a lot to lose. Enjoy your day my queen.*

*Never Let Go*
*People come and people go - some of their true purposes you may never know*
*Yet there are those that upon your first meeting you just know - that you love them so*
*        Never Let Go*
*Everything doesn't come easy - life is complex it is a puzzle a game of chance*
*It's up to you to keep perusing - don't give up just because of your current circumstance*

*Never Let Go*
*They may push they may run – But if you keep on chasing their confusion you'll soon overcome*
*They may hide they may even fight - but if you keep trying, they'll see you just love them with all of your might*
*Never Let Go*
*Your mouth says no but I've looked into your eyes- I know what you want is me by your side*
*You can continue to ignore me telling yourself lies. But I know you want me near and soon you will realize*
*Never Let Go*
*I know what I want - I'll never leave you alone so please stop asking me to do so*
*I love you Tierra Michelle Jackson-Hunter and I will NEVER LET GO!*

Like I said creepy, but it was nice not to get a thousand calls, packages and all for a change.

I knew it would be awhile before I was able to see my husband face to face and I had to tell him about this pregnancy. I had sent him a package that should be arriving today, and I am about to faint in anticipation. So many times, I just wanted to blurt it out on a phone call, but I thought that if I did that it was robbing him of a great memory. I didn't want to mail a pregnancy test that just seemed way to disgusting. So, I had a onesie shipped to him that on the front side said, "Sniper never misses a shot," and on the back it said, "That's my Daddy!" I was so nervous. I was hoping he got it and I didn't have to explain it, but I knew he would. He finally called me and at first, he acted like he was just making his normal call which drove me insane. He was talking normal and not a hint of excitement was in his voice. I knew he had received the package because I had been tracking it all day, and I see he signed for it about thirty minutes ago. The suspense was driving me insane, but I held it together and he finally screamed "I never miss a shot huh?!" I am gonna be a Daddy is what you are telling me? Girl!" He was so full of joy and thanked me for the sweet gesture and told me we needed to hurry and tell our parents because he was not going to be able to hold this news in and will be telling everyone he sees. So, we definitely called them, and they were so excited. They asked who else knew and we assured them that they were the first to find out and that we will just tell everyone else later today. Mr. Hunter loved the idea of the onesie and kept saying "Yeah my son never misses!" It was cute and sweet. We agreed to just hurry and tell the others so we can tell everyone. He did not want this to be a secret at all and I agreed. Once everyone knew they watched me like a hawk, literally reporting everything back to my husband like I was child. They did not care how mad it made me they left out no details at all. I was excited, the extra love you get when you are pregnant is nice. Especially at work. If you even coughed next to me someone was letting you have it.

Things seemed to be going along pretty good. I was in good spirits, and I was feeling good physically as well. The guys kept an extra watch over me, and my uncles were even popping up out of nowhere to make sure I didn't climb anything or change any light bulbs or almost anything at all. I cannot lie, it was nice, but it did get a bit overwhelming from time to time. I kept it all to myself because it was all done from a place of love, the entire family was excited, and this was great news for us all. I think that our mothers were more excited than anyone. They promised not to take over, but it was the first grandchild for them both, so we knew they were going to be extra. I just prepared myself for the ride.

Back at work the office was busy as normal and the day went by pretty fast, and we had a farewell party for Tina Marelli; a great coworker of mine who is relocating to Virginia Beach because her big shot husband, who is super sweet, is taking over as President of a large accounting firm there. I'm excited for them they are a wonderful couple. Unfortunately, because of the terrible event we had awhile back we still cannot have visitors in the building so he could not come to the party. We all hated to see her go, and it showed in all of the amazing gifts and awesome words of encouragement that was shared with her at the farewell luncheon. When she hugged me, I just broke down. I was so embarrassed these hormones are really something else. She said, "we better get an invitation to your shower, Craig and I want to be the Godparents!" I just wiped my face and shook my head yes, but honestly, I hadn't thought that far. I hope she doesn't consider my head nod as a firm yes. I was scarfing down the snacks and I didn't even feel ashamed. No one cares how much you eat when you are pregnant. They had the cutest little Knick knacks and party favors; it was very well planned. My favorite thing was the homemade sugar cookies shaped like a hand that read "Bye for now" I just thought that was so cute, plus they were delicious. The rest of the day at the office was perfect, and I didn't stick around working when 5:30 hit I was out of there. I was ready for this weekend, real ready. I am so happy that my boss gave me my own parking spot once I announced my pregnancy. Now I don't have to park in the parking garage and therefore I don't need T to watch me because neither he nor Juan was going to try anything in the front of the building. God truly works in mysterious ways. I am happy I didn't have to "expose my truth" as pastor always calls it, to get this favor!

After work I headed to Cassie's house. She offered to cook dinner if I came over to help with her last-minute jitters with tomorrow's affairs. The evening was nice, but I should've known it was too good to be true. After dinner Donovan offered dessert and wanted to play cards. In walks T! I hadn't seen him since our last altercation. I knew he would be at the party but not tonight's dinner. He actually kept his cool aside from giving me a crazy look every once and awhile. I tried my best to act as normal as possible, but I quickly excused myself after the first game and asked Devin if he would walk me outside to prevent him from trying to follow me out. On my way out the door he grabbed me and pulled me very close to him and I couldn't act too suspicious, so I immediately pushed away and said, "Stop Punk you play too much you hurt my arm." Devin defended me "Damn Bro be careful our little one is in there." Then T sarcastically replied, "Don't I know- Good night babies!" and then he laughed and went back to the card table. My heart was beating so fast but once I made it outside, I felt better. When I got home, I double, and triple checked every door and every window and then I called my parents to check in with them. I stayed on the phone with my daddy until I drifted off to sleep. I slept through the night without interruption and woke up ready for my day.

Another successful night of sleep and God knows it was much needed today is a busy day. I have a hair appointment and then an appointment to get a manicure and pedicure done and I could use the pampering. If I have time after completing all of that and after picking up the cake and taking it to the venue. I want to squeeze in a facial since they really do not like to massage pregnant women without going through a lot of steps that I won't have time for today. Either way I'm excited about the party and I'm feeling like a lady again. I mean I know I'm still a lady, but I lost my ability to feel beautiful and free and now it is slowly coming back. My only fear is that T will try to pressure me to talk to him tonight. I prayed about it the best way I knew how.

*"Dear God,*

*Thank you for all of the many blessings you have given me. Thank you for my beautiful family, awesome friends, and amazing job. I know that I am guilty of not talking to you as much as I should have and I know I don't know all of the fancy words and clichés to say an impressive prayer, but I am asking that you not allow me to make tonight about me. You know what I am dealing with and going through and you know how torn I am but please react for me and do not allow my enemies the opportunity to see my weakness. Please keep me safe in Jesus name Amen!"*

I still had my same problems when I finished praying but I felt so much better. I went out and enjoyed my "me time" and ran my errands; including dropping the cake and party favors off at the building. Then I came home took a long hot bubble bath and a nap so I would be ready for the party. I felt so rejuvenated. I didn't get my facial because I ran out of time, but I still felt gorgeous. My dress fit me like a glove and for the first time I wasn't ashamed of showing off the fact that I was pregnant despite the uncertainties. I felt like a million dollars although I had a million problems. I valet parked my car and walked into the party looking absolutely flawless from head to toe. And for the first time in a long time, I smiled, and it wasn't for show, it was real. I was ready to take on tonight. Cassie was at the front entrance she looked gorgeous, red carpet ready. She greeted me with a hug and continued to walk through the building. Everything looked amazing and people were already showing up. The VIP area was laid out for a king. We started taking selfies and posted them encouraging everyone to come out tonight.

The party went over so well, way better than we ever imagined. The twins flipped out when they saw what an awesome job we did on the party. We already booked the most exclusive venue in the city and had the best food the top DJ and an A1 guest list. Everybody who was anybody was there along with hundreds of other people that we have never seen before. Everyone was having a great time Ronnie was dancing like a maniac and the ladies were falling for it as usual. He looked like he was on an old episode of soul train. I laughed until I cried, joining in with him occasionally but I frequently lost my breath and had to step back.

The DJ had everybody on the dance floor from start to finish. And I tell you pregnancy adds a whole new meaning to the song "Wobble" I felt dizzy as hell after a few turns and had to sit down and catch my breath. There wasn't a thing to complain about outside of my feet feeling like elephant hoofs because they were so swollen. Dang I'm not even that far along and I am going through the change fast. It seems like as soon as Babe announced it everything just came out of hiding. I was in some pain but tonight wasn't about me, so

I choked it up and pushed through it. Request after request hit and I simply couldn't dance another step. "Alright we are about to slow things down for all of you lovers out there!" The DJ said. That was my cue to get off the dance floor, so I headed off the dance floor to check on the caterers. Everything was already going well I wanted to make sure there was still plenty of food. I just wanted everything to be perfect for Cassie I know she wanted this party to be epic. I almost made it off the dance floor and I felt someone come behind me and wrap their arms around me tightly like a snake does its prey, while "There's A Meeting In My Bedroom" played loudly. He then whispered in my ear. "You look so sexy and smell so delicious I will never let go!" Everything in me said turn around and slap the piss out of him because I knew it was him quoting lines from his serial killer ass poem. My heart skipped several beats, and I remembered the prayer I prayed today, when I asked God to react for me. So, I tried to pry his wet clammy hands off of my body, but his grip was too tight, and he kept pulling me closer. I didn't want him to squeeze my stomach after all to my knowledge didn't even know that I was pregnant. And if he found out he would surely flip but I guess he can see now. I stood firm with my feet planted as much as I could plant them praying for relief. I continued to try and peel his hands away when T walked by heading to the bar and saw me and the look on my face. He walked up and said, "Babe, we need you," and then told me to walk off as he stood on the dance floor talking to Juan. The next thing I knew security was escorting him out. "Are you ok?" he said when he came back. "Yeah, yeah, I'm alright. Thank you" I said, and he said, "No problem" and actually walked away.

I was beyond grateful. Grateful for him getting rid of Juan and not acting up.

DJ Novelty called the twins to the stage so that we could sing happy birthday to them, and Cassie was about to explode with excitement because of the surprise she prepared for him. She and I carried out the two cakes with the candles lit as Donovan's celebrity crush Jasmine Sullivan came out and took the happy birthday song to a whole new level. Hell, I knew she was coming, I booked her but once she started singing, I damn near dropped the cake I was holding for Devin. She has such a beautiful voice. I seriously think Donovan was about to pass out. He was going crazy kissing Cassie over and over saying thank you a million times. When she finished her song, he could barely blow out the candles he was so hype, and Devin just stood there smiling and giving us the thumbs up. She continued with her performance and the crowd was fully engaged.

At the end of the party the twins took the Mic to say thank you and they called Cassie and I to the stage. We all stood there with our arms wrapped around each other while Devin occasionally rubbed my belly. Devin's speech was short, sweet and to the point. Just as cool and smooth as he always was, the ladies were hollering! "Dude this party was legit! We appreciate the love, Man I'm just like …man speechless!" He said. Donovan was all over the stage acting like some hip-hop hype man. It was clear to see he was happy and very well pleased with the overall turnout. "Tonight, just confirmed everything for me and bro. It's a great feeling to know you are loved but an even better feeling to be shown love. This is all love, and we thank you all for coming out tonight and a huge thank you to these two ladies for planning a birthday we will never forget. I love yal! Cass babe, you showed out… Jasmine Sullivan… Boo! That's some real... man I love you so much. I asked Devin if he would be ok if I did this tonight and he was more than supportive. I just didn't want to take away from his day. I mean we shared it our entire life, but I just knew tonight was going to be special. Cassie you are everything a man dreams of in a woman. You are loving; supportive, understanding, and you will go to battle for me. Today I wanted to surprise you, but you surprised me instead, you are always a step ahead and I need that balance in my life. I know you feel like you have waited forever but tonight I want to put an end to your wait." He dropped down to one knee and I started ballin because I know how much she loves him and has been waiting for this moment. I can't believe that they didn't let me in on the surprise, but o well. Cassie immediately started shaking and crying as he grabbed her hand and continued. "Baby I am not the most perfect boyfriend; I don't know how to do this the right way, the romantic way you probably dreamed of the way you deserve. All I know is, I love me some you and I want to be me, just Donovan. Baby will you please marry me?" she quickly responded with "Yes!' and they engaged in a kiss and the crowd went wild. I couldn't control my emotions. My best friend has been waiting on this day forever plus I'm super hormonal. It was pretty embarrassing; I mean I was too through. Either way I didn't care. I was thinking man every time we have a party someone gets engaged just another way she and I are connected. I am so excited! Of course, they went off on their own and we finished settling up the party. Thank God we don't have to clean up I am tiered as hell. I feel like I just ran a marathon. It all worked out just as we had hoped.

I promised my parents I would spend the night with them instead of driving home because they stayed a lot closer to the venue than I did. Plus, they were treating me like a baby ever since they found out that I am expecting, and after what happened tonight, I was glad that I was not going home alone. When I used my key to open up the door to my parents' house, they were up waiting for me on the sofa, and I just laid down across their laps and let them love on me until I drifted off to sleep. My mom woke me in the morning for breakfast and asked if I was going to church and I told her yes, I would go. When we left church, I noticed I had a few missed calls mostly from hubby and Cassie. Before I could call her back my phone rang again. "Heffa, you don't see me calling you? Perhaps it's because my rock is blinding you!" She then let off a loud screech and a crazy laugh. "Oh my God girl I'm getting married" "I know I am so happy for you girl I cannot wait to get started. What did your Mama say? "I asked "I haven't told her yet. Donovan and I decided we will tell her in person when we go see her receive her award in Chicago. Then we can celebrate all of our good news together!"

Cass has finally decided to visit her mom now that she has some awesome news of her own to share, and she wants to be able to share it with her in person which I completely understand. She is so excited, and I know her mom is going to flip out when she tells her. I am so glad things turned out this way. I knew she would come around eventually, and this is just perfect. It is now a win-win situation for the both of them. I am so excited, my girl, my sis, my BFF is getting married to a good man and she deserves it! They just got engaged and my mind is racing with ideas for an engagement party. I get so pumped I have to calm myself down. I know she may want to plan that one herself, but I am going to blow her mind when it comes to her wedding shower and bachelorette party. They are both going to be epic, straight over the top and ridiculous just like we like it! I'd like to meet the person who can top what I'm about to do, yep, they do not exist. Oh, and if she lets me get my hands on any part of this wedding, it is a wrap. I can hear my baby now telling me not to take over ha-ha, and I also see myself straight ignoring him and everybody else who won't let me be great. I am totally kidding I remember how stressful it was for me that we ran off to Hawaii, so I will make sure not to make her feel the same way. Finally, another reason to celebrate, Lord knows we need it.

"Hey Girl, I'm leaving church about to go eat with my parents, but I promise I will call you back." She smacked her lips and gave out a heavy sigh and reluctantly let me off the phone and I returned my husband's calls. He was concerned when he didn't hear from me. I reminded him that I was at church with my parents, and he laughed and said that he had forgot and was about to come find me himself if I had not finally called him. I was finally able to go into details with him about how awesome the party turned out and how smooth his boy Donovan was with the proposal. Of course, he already had talked to the fellas, so he was all caught up. "I miss you Baby" I said "I miss you too Baby and I will see you and my little one soon. Say hi to mom and dad for me, ok? And answer your phone when I call!" I laughed and I promised to do both.

# CHAPTER 15

**M**y husband is on his way home and Cassie is on her way to Chicago. Time is moving fast, and the baby is growing beautifully. I am so glad that the season is over, and I am looking forward to having Ta'Ron home. Hopefully this will bring balance back to my life and this should surely deter the crazies from coming after me… at least, I hope. I woke up this morning and made sure everything was in order. I just want everything to be perfect when he gets home. His flight is scheduled to land at seven-thirty tonight and I swear it cannot come soon enough. Even Bella is acting as if she knows he is coming back. Life on the road is a sure sacrifice. I am grateful for all that he does, and I know he is happy, but even after all of these years I am not use to him being away. It will be hard sharing him with his friends and family. I must admit that selfishly I want him all to myself, but I know that's unhealthy and unrealistic. In the back of my mind, I wrestle with the thought that this baby could not be his and if I should tell him and even what his reaction will be. But I will lay all of that aside for now and just focus on enjoying time alone with the love of my life.

I ran a lot of errands making sure I had all of his favorite things in the house and that we had all the necessities so there would not be a need to go out. My heart was beating fast as if I was meeting him for the very first time. Everything about my body has expanded and exploded into almost double its normal size so I haven't felt sexy lately. I thought it would be a good idea to take a trip to the "Goodie" store and pick up some new lingerie and other things to make this reunion even more enjoyable. I just hope he is not disgusted when he sees that everything that use to be snatched is now moving around with a mind of its own. Despite of my concerns I went ahead and made that trip, and I did find a few pieces I talked myself into. The saleswoman was sweet and very helpful and assured me that my husband would not have any complaints. After making my purchase I headed to get some more candles and scented oils from my favorite shop downtown. The shop is called Mesmerize and is locally owned and operated by a cute couple from Ethiopia. Everything is natural and they custom make all of their candles and scents. I was a bit apprehensive the very first time I went there. On your first visit they have you fill out a questioner which I thought was different. I don't know how asking me a few basic questions lead them to create a perfect scent for me, but they did it and I have been a faithful customer ever since. I was so impressed I bought everything they suggested without question. I am a walking advertisement and I even got Cass and Mommy addicted. Today I am going to load up. They even sell scented rose pedals which I need because I plan on making today feel like Valentine's Day, it is definitely going down. "Hey Nadia, I need some stuff today my husband is coming home! I want my regular scents in candles, oils and bath bombs." She chuckled and started preparing my order. She noticed I was pregnant and suggested I try a new scent that would surely knock my husband off of his feet. I trusted her because everything was always unbelievably amazing. I told her to go ahead and give me that too. We exchanged small talk as she prepared my order and then she came with a big bag full of my things. She took out a large soy candle and asked me to smell it. "Nadia! You did it again. What in the world is this one called? It is the best one yet." The smell was indescribable, almost heavenly yet sexy all at once. She said she threw in a massage cream in that same scent that will also prevent stretch marks. When I left there, I knew tonight was going to be perfect.

I sat in the truck outside of Mesmerize and I called and ordered our dinner from his favorite restaurant Bengie's and asked them to have our takeout order ready about eight-thirty. Bengie's alone is going to win me points. My husband loves their food. They have a lot of things you cannot get everywhere like fried cauliflower. Everything there is delicious however he gets the same thing every time. Fried cauliflower, garlic butter grilled shrimp and pork chops with spicy steak and veggie skewers. He will always try what I order as my order is rarely the same and even if he loves what he tries he will not change his order. Everything is going as planned now all I have to do is relax and enjoy this time with my husband.

I arrived at the airport right on time, his plane was just landing, and he had to get his suitcase. When I saw him coming around the corner, I smiled so big and so hard I was sure I looked like a crazy person. He spotted me and came right over to greet me with a hug and kiss. "Baby you look so beautiful. Now I know what people mean when they say that you are glowing!" He always knows what to say. We got his bags headed to the car and I just could not stop staring at him as we held hands in the car. "Oh, Baby I almost forgot, stop by Bengie's before we go home, I got us a "to go" order!" His face lit up like a Christmas tree in Time Square. "Girl you are a keeper you hear me, a keeper!" He said as he laughed and swiftly switched lanes preparing to exit. Finally, we made it home and Bella greeted him and completely ignored me all night. The night was absolutely perfect; He turned his phone off and gave me his full undivided attention, which wasn't a shock as he always was so attentive and respectful. We sat and watched several episodes of "Blue Bloods," one of our favorite shows, and I brought him up to speed, occasionally going too far ahead at times. He plopped his big feet across my lap, and I had to remind him that my belly now sticks out much further than it ever had and that he needs to be careful. We continued to enjoy television as I massaged his feet. "Oooh wee! Don't start nothin' you can't finish babe!" I continued to massage his feet as I laughed and shook my head. "Ok I'm warning you. You know I been gone a minute, right? Watch yourself!" I responded sarcastically and told him that I had to go to the bathroom and pushed his huge feet off my lap. "Wait, you just can't stop like that!" he screamed as I walked upstairs. "My bladder says otherwise!" I yelled back.

I really did have to go to the bathroom, but I also wanted to slip on one of the outfits I had purchased earlier. Being pregnant I fall asleep at the drop of a dime, and I was afraid if we sat and watched another episode that I would fall asleep before we got a chance to do anything. "Babe, are you ok up there? Do you want me to pause the show 'til you come back down?" He hollered. "No go ahead I will be back down in a few, I'm ok, just gonna go ahead and shower since I am up here." I responded. I went ahead and showered and set up the room as quick as possible before he came upstairs wondering why it was taking me so long. I got dressed and walked over to the stair railing and leaned over trying to look sexy with my big belly hanging over my newly purchased sexy gear and yelled down to him. "You can keep watching tv, I'm just gonna go to bed." He looked up at me and yelled as he grabbed for the remote, I am coming up to join you, WOW!" That three-letter word helped me regain my confidence, Nadia was right he loved it and those candles had the ambiance set in our bedroom. I needed to remind him that everything he needed I could provide, so I did just that. He acted as if my weight gain and baby belly didn't even exist. I love my husband! As I laid my head across his chest, I felt so safe, so happy, so restored. Just like that, in a blink of an eye, I felt normal again. I wanted to tell him about T and Juan, but everything was just so beautiful I didn't want to ruin it, plus it was his first day back home. I will tell him when the time is right, I think.

I woke up and prepared a big breakfast and decided to serve it to him in bed, he was snoring so loud I hated to wake him up, after all I knew he was extremely tired from all the traveling. I set the tray on the nightstand and began to pull the door closed as I walked out of the bedroom when he rolled over. "Where are you going? Come chill with me." "I made you breakfast but you were sleeping so good that I didn't want to wake you." I said as I came back into the room and crawled back into bed. We laid there laughing and talking and sharing the food I had prepared for him until we drifted back off to sleep again. He woke me with a kiss, and I teased him that he had morning breath, and he ran and brushed his teeth and showered. The small things like this are what I miss about him most. Today I know he is going to receive phone calls and I am just going to play "good wifey" and act unbothered by the numerous requests for his attention. I don't mind because I know that I am never lacking in that department. When it comes to me, he spoils me with love, attention, affection and, anything I ever dreamed of. As a matter of fact, I need to go through my closets and make some space in what is to be the new nursery and move my things out of there. I am telling myself that things will get better from here, that everything will smooth itself out. Now if I could just make myself believe what I say all will be well.

Once I got dressed, I joined him downstairs on the sofa. He was on the phone, and I didn't disturb him, I just laid my feet across his lap just as he had done me the night before, and he knew I wanted him to return the favor. I could tell by his conversation that he was on the phone with one of the fellas, and they were planning on getting together and I just enjoyed the moment, although Bella was jealous and kept jumping on the sofa squeezing between us. Once I heard him say congratulations, I knew he was talking to Donovan about his recent engagement to Cassie. He was giving him advice and encouragement in his own way, which was full of laughter and sarcasm, yet it seemed to be well received. When he got off the phone, he told me that he wanted to take me out and to not make any plans for the day. He also said the fellas were going to come over tonight to shoot some pool and I said ok, that I was sure Cassie was coming as well. I was so wrapped up in the thought of spending quality time with him that I honestly forgot that T was amongst those he considered his boys. I went to the bathroom, pulled up my hair, put on some makeup, grabbed my shoes and my shades and I was ready to spend some time with my Boo. I had no clue what he had planned, and I tried not to ask, although I was anxious. I was enjoying the simple things like not having to drive all the time and taking selfies like crazy. First, we parked and went for a walk, which I loved. We walked into a high rise building and took the elevator to the 5th floor I finally asked where we were headed, and he said Oh just to chill. When we got off the elevator it opened up to a beautiful sitting area with a receptionist and he went up to the counter to confirm his appointment. They called us to the back and walked us to a private room with mats on the floor. I was clueless. In walked a tall well fit lady with long blonde hair and she asked us to take the mat on the floor. My first thought was, "I am not dressed for this, I look too good to be on this floor." I didn't say a word and Ta'Ron helped me down on the mat and sat behind me. She started giving us a speech about how excited she was and how happy she is to be a part of this. I'm sitting down on the floor in my husband's arms looking like I just stepped out of a magazine, and I am puzzled. I guess she could tell by my expression that I had no idea what was going on. She introduced herself and said she was going to allow my husband to tell me what was going on. He said "Baby ever since you told me you were pregnant; it is all I can think of. I know I was away at work, but I feel like I missed out on everything. All the parenting classes, your doctor appointments, everything. I reached out to Mrs. Nixon, and she is going to do our private Lamaze classes starting today as well as yoga. So that is why we are here." I was so moved I wanted to burst into tears, but he was always making fun of how emotional I was, so I held it in. Then I looked at him and he looked teary-eyed and so I lost it. I enjoyed our session with Mrs. Nixon, it was awesome. That is one flexible woman, she was so sweet, and patient and I couldn't thank her enough. As we walked back toward the car we stopped at a stand and got ice cream. I was still emotional crying as I ate my ice cream, like a weirdo. To our right, there was a group of men singing acapella and they had a bucket sitting on the ground in front of them. Just a few feet away was an empty bench. It immediately reminded me of Los Angeles. We must have sat and listened to them sing for about an hour. They sounded amazing and I felt like they were there just for us. I gave a very generous donation; I was sincerely overwhelmed with gratefulness for today. By the time we got home I was whooped. I went upstairs and took a nap. I didn't even realize that I had been sleep that long. Cassie came upstairs to let me know she was here. She said she waited an hour after getting there before waking me. When I looked at the clock, I realized my nap had lasted over 4 hours!

I got myself together and went to greet everyone before Cassie and I sat out by the pool. I didn't want to be rude after all they were equally my friends. The guys were rowdy. I mean just loud as usual blasting music and hollering over the music having a great time. We didn't stay in there long at all; I just made sure my husband didn't need anything from me. They had ordered wings because I was sleep, which was fine with me. I wasn't hungry so we left them to play catch up. The sight of T being there did not even bother me. We sat with our feet in the water and chit chatted about the wedding and her thoughts and ideas. She was so excited, we decided to get an early start on the planning, I promised not to take over but not to allow her to procrastinate. After a while we decided to get in the pool so we went inside so that I could get some shorts and a shirt for Cass and myself since I couldn't really fit my bathing suits anymore. When we came back to the pool, the temperature was so perfect. It can get very hot in Georgia and stay that way even in the evening time, so this was a great way to cool off and just relax. We reminisced about our childhood and what we always dreamed our lives would be. Just as we got into the good part, the loud fellas came out with drinks in their hands singing Jagged Edge's "Where the party at." We are 90's R&B fans to the max. Soon they went and got shorts from Ta'Ron and came splashing into the pool- O well there goes the girl talk. Thank God I am pregnant, so no one picked me up and threw me as they always did. Sadly, Cassie took enough for the both of us. When they finally calmed down, we sat around tossing around memories about the good ole days. We talked about high school, college, and just the days on the block as we affectionately called it. We laughed so hard we cried real tears. It seemed like every other story one of us was put on the spot with a memory that we would rather not hear about, but we continued to share them anyway. Overall, the night was great no incidents, and no uncomfortable encounters with T. It was a late night as to be expected. It was really good company; It didn't seem like it was that late. 2am had come without warning it seemed. I remember watching everyone walk to their cars and thinking that despite what I have been through and the secret that I was literally carrying I was still pretty blessed.

# CHAPTER 16

I was really enjoying being loved on and pampered by my husband. Now that he was home, being pregnant didn't seem so bad and the days seemed to fly right on by. It was time to find out what we were having so that we could plan a baby shower, and theme for the nursery and to do some fun shopping. I kind of wanted a gender reveal party but I didn't want to overload Ta'Ron, nor did I really feel up to doing it myself. My feet and ankles are so swollen that they have grown together, and you can't even see the point in which they are supposed to separate. I still was ready to do some major baby shopping, after all this is our first child so I have a right to go overboard. I had been stocking up like a crazed coupon lady-buying pampers and wipes, wash cloths and bath supplies and now I have a room full of that sort of stuff, but no clothes just yet outside of white t-shirts and onesies but that's no fun! I have been putting off finding out the gender for as long as I could because I really wanted him to be here with me. Well today is the day, and I am so nervous. All we want is a beautiful healthy baby of course but he wants a son and I want a princess I can doll up. All I have now is Bella and she only lets me go so far. I think it would be great and so much fun to make her all girly and beautiful with little dresses and hair bows etc. But bae is set on a boy. He said he always wanted a boy first so that no matter what we have later they will always have a big brother to protect them. When you look at it from that perspective I can understand where he is coming from. All I know is that I am in love with the little goober already, although it has invaded my body and jumps on my bladder like it is a trampoline. I cannot wait to see the babies face, but I must admit if it doesn't look like my husband I will probably faint. I will tell him before delivery though. I do not know why I am so terrified; I know I did nothing wrong, however it is like the secret comes in and consumes you and before you know it you are deep in and lying and covering up for people you have no need to protect. Honestly, I try my best not to think about it hoping it will all fade away like a bad dream and my life will go back to what it was before only with a family of my own. If I am honest with myself, I am scared of Ta'Rons reaction to T to Juan and towards me for not telling him upfront, but I do not want to be like one of those women on Maury who years later is bringing the baby and three potential men on the show for a DNA test because she is 100% certain about all of them. So, when the time is right, I am just going to have to let it all out and I pray we can get through this. The thought of it all has my stomach feeling as if I turned it inside out. But today I am just going to focus on us spending time together and finding out what we are having.

"Don't be taking all day Baby! Go ahead and get ready I do not want to be late and have to reschedule the appointment!" he started in trying to urge me to hurry up! "I am just about ready it's you who moves super slow babe," I responded back jokingly, and it was true I can be a bit of a diva but when it is time to hustle I do just that. Meanwhile his favorite argument when I tell him to hurry and start getting ready is "all I gotta do is..." which is followed by an entire laundry list of things that he acts like only takes seconds. I will be ready, and he will finally jump up and start moving around talking about he is almost ready, boy how? But today was a different story I believe that we were both just so excited that we damn near woke up ready! "I will be done in less than five minutes baby how about you?" and all I heard was scrambling through the house which let me know he had sat down and started watching ESPN and lost track of time as usual. On the ride to the doctor's office, I was so nervous I felt like a child excited about the first day of school or excited about Christmas day. Maybe a better way to describe whatever my body was feeling was that feeling you had as a teenager when you knew you were going to run into your crush, and you played the conversation and events out in your mind in advance like a movie. The ride over seemed to take forever as did the waiting room which is the worst part of any appointment. I never did understand why doctors and hairstylist all make several appointments so close together just to have you sitting in the waiting room reading magazines for an hour or draining your cellphone's battery down, playing games or catching up on social media. It is like they know when you finally get deep into a movie or phone conversation and like clockwork, they come calling your name. I'm like man now I have to wait to see what happens on the show.

They finally called us, and my nerves immediately kicked into high gear. They escorted us to the room and stated that I needed to get changed and that the doctor would be in shortly. While I was getting changed Ta'Ron decided to make comments that almost cost him his entire life. "Ooh baby I think I see where those six pounds they said you gained went!" he said as he was cracking up looking at my booty as I changed into the infamous hospital gown. The look on my face must have been one of hell and fury because he suddenly stopped his giggling and tried to say he was just kidding and that I looked amazing. "Keep on and we are gonna know just how your eye got swollen as well." I said as I was rolling my eyes trying not to laugh but lost it anyway. As we laughed hysterically, the sonographer came in and begin to crack jokes like "I'll have what you're having" everyone was always so nice and always made you feel comfortable. "Ok Mom and Dad are we ready? Do you want to give any final predictions before we see what is baking in there?" Before I could answer he jumped right in "Oh I know it is a boy I am just here to prove it to her." I just smiled and shook my head as she placed a huge heap of freezing gel on my belly and begin to move her magic wand around. The heartbeat was nice and strong, and I remember baby telling me that I better not cry as we listened to the best sound ever. "Ok here we go guys, I am going to turn the screen to me just for a second and then back to you guys you just let me know when you are ready." We said ok but, in my mind, I wasn't ready I was so nervous. I knew we would be happy no matter what, but we are both also competitive and so we both wanted to be right. We gave each other the look and nodded our heads as we replied in unison "we're ready!" she turned the screen around, and I swear it moved in slow motion. "Congratulations you are definitely and without any doubt having a baby boy!" We were both so excited, but he started jumping around and running in the room like he had just won another championship ring. "What I tell you- yeah- that's what I'm talking about!" I knew then I would never hear the end of it. "That's ok baby we will go to Cold Stone after this to celebrate. That should make you feel better, but just don't blame me if another pound gets added to you know where!" All I could do was laugh I was overjoyed, but I was happier to see how excited he was. The whole ride to get ice cream all he was talking about was what he was going to do and how he and the boys were going to plan the shower and it was a basketball theme and so on and so forth. I agreed to some things, but I am not letting those nuts plan my shower that is a hell no. Just to see how the news made him feel warmed my heart and made me even more terrified at the same time. All I could think of is what if after finally having the boy he always dreamed of we find out it is not even his. I know that would be devastating to him and a tear dropped from my eye, and he just reached over and grabbed my hand and held it and rubbed it. When we pulled into Cold Stone he reached over and kissed me and said, "Thank you baby" and I promise I wanted to break down like an enraged lunatic, but I just kissed him and said thanks to him as well. We decided to take a walk at the nearby park, and it felt so good we were only stopped a few times for autographs as he put on shades and a hat. I didn't mind and neither did he, we were in such high spirits that nothing else mattered at all. As we walked, we were trying to decide how to reveal the baby's gender to our family and friends and we tossed out some name ideas. We then started to talk about what we would name him. Anything that started with the letter T was a no for me unless we named him Junior. I did not want people nicknaming him "T" considering the circumstances. I played it off well and we agreed that if we did that T would swear, we named the baby after him. He laughed and said that was out of the question. Little did he know I could not agree more. Our phones were ringing off the hook from everyone wanting to know but we just couldn't decide if we should tell them now or not, so we just let it ring. I know my Mom and Cassie were going insane, but I just wanted to enjoy the moment with my husband and catch the earful from them later.

We could not hold it in at all, as soon as we got home, we decided to call our parents first. We knew that if they found out that someone else knew the sex of their first grandchild before them, that there would be hell to pay. So, we called them both at the same time and told them that they would be having a grandson and they all screamed and cheerly loudly. It was a great feeling. I told them we had decided on a baby shower and theme. I had to keep my promise since I lost the bet he gets to decide which we knew already it would be basketball. Little did he know I was already brainstorming on how to jazz it up a bit and I knew it was going to be an event to remember. We got off the phone with our parents and decided to text the crew and tell them to meet us tonight at one of my favorite little hole in the wall spots. It was a cute quaint little bar and grill, but the food and drinks were amazing. I can't drink of course but I knew they would be celebrating hard. Hey if I can't drink at least I can indulge in some amazing chicken wings and pizza. They all agreed to meet up with us about eight o'clock which was perfect because it gave us time to relax a bit before heading out to grab a few things and reveal the gender in a more intimate setting just with our close friends. "Babe I was thinking we would all sit down and order food and talk right and then ask everyone again for their last predictions. After that we will have the waitress bring over a round of shots for everyone. Now here me out because it's a boy so we will just order a round of Hpnotiq because its blue and instantly everyone will know it's a boy, and then we will order bottles of the good stuff and just celebrate. Yeah, I like that, what do you think baby?" He kept rambling talking so fast jumping up and down and clapping like he was leaving the huddle on the court. "I like that baby, cute and simple!" I replied and so we sat down and talked about how we thought the night would play out and quickly made come calls to get some last-minute personalized items made to give them.

After relaxing we got up and did some last-minute running around. Watching my husband move with so much excitement about starting our family is so sexy to me. I just kept staring at him and smiling all day. Occasionally he would catch me staring and say "What?" I would reply with "Nothing Baby just looking at you!" After a few times I had to gather myself before he thinks I'm crazy. After we finished doing all of our last-minute running around and headed home to get dressed. I could not decide what to wear I must have changed ten times at least. When all else fails you can never go wrong with a little black dress even if it is maternity style. As I walked past the mirror in the master bedroom closet, I must admit I was really feeling myself and then my Ta'Ron stepped behind me looking super fine and smelling amazing. "Ok Sir where you think you going, lookin' like you lookin' and smellin' like you smellin? Let me find out!" We laughed and headed out the door to Wiz's. As we pulled up the crew was already hanging out outside waiting in anticipation. "I'm nervous all the sudden Baby." Ta'Ron said as he chuckled. I asked him why and he said he had no clue. I told him they were going to be excited either way plus they are just happy he is home. We got out and they greeted us with hugs and the normal "Hey Baby Mama, Hey Baby Daddy jokes!" It was a very nice crowd in there and the music there is always good. They escorted us to our reserved table, and we tried to just keep up the small talk, but they were not having it. "Aye Man, we ain't trying to hear all that. Are we having a niece or nephew or what? I can't take all this suspense Bro!" Devin said as he rubbed his hands together. Everyone joined and agreed, and T had the nerve to chime his ass in "For real though I gots to know." I could've slapped that serial killer smirk right off his face. "Chill- we got yal. Let me call Sophie over here to get this party started." Ta'Ron said nervously. Sophie was our favorite waitress at The Wiz, she was always cool and made sure we were well taken care of. Her cousin Amber is one of the best bartenders in the city if you ask me, and when they both are working together you can guarantee the night was going to be magical. The Wiz gives you all the feel of a big club, they even have VIP treatment, but they are small so if you do not get there early you are not getting in unless you have some pull. We had already called ahead to reserve our spot however even when we do not, they always walk us right on in no questions asked. Just as he finished telling them he was going to get the waitress she walked up with her arms out to hug me screaming hey family. We have been coming here for years so at this point she seems like a cousin. I told her they can't wait, and she said she had us set up and ready and would bring out the pizza and wings and then the shots so we could kill all the curiosity. It only took a few minutes for her to do just as she had said but for some reason it seemed like an eternity. When they came to the section the staff really made a big deal of it and it was very sweet. They marched around like they did if it was your birthday chanting and clapping and once Cassie saw the blue shots on the tray she screamed "A nephew," so loud and literally started crying which mad my emotional behind start bawling. I could feel someone rubbing my back and I gathered myself and said hey we are celebrating, but this time I was not alone there was not a dry eye in there. We turned up and fast, it was such a beautiful moment I wish we had captured it on video, but we were all so caught up in the moment we didn't get their reaction. I did not want the night to end. We talked ate and cried for hours. Cassie and I talked about their upcoming trip, they were packed and ready to hit up Chi-Town! It feels good to be surrounded by so much good news and positivity because these last few months have been insane. When we got home, we were both out with the quickness. I do not even remember getting undressed. Tonight, was definitely a night to remember.

# CHAPTER 17

The next few days were pretty smooth. We spent most of it planning the baby shower and getting the nursery together. I was really missing Cassie. I was so glad she was enjoying her trip and that things were running smoothly. She said that even Frank was on his best behavior and that they were so excited about the news of their engagement. Cassie said her mother was so happy that she was literally telling everyone even during her interviews. I am so proud of Mrs. Reynolds, she is really an exemplary woman, and this award and recognition is really well deserved. Cass made sure to call me nightly and fill me in and ask to see our progress on the room. Our parents are going overboard, literally dropping off carloads of stuff every day or we were signing for packages that they had shipped directly to us. To say that our son was going to be spoiled and well-loved is definitely an understatement.

I don't even know why we are having a shower we are not going to have room for anything else in this house. Ta'Ron got the nursery painted and trimmed already and has really been showing off on his "dad duties." There are boxes all over the house except in the actual nursery. Hubby said that room has to be clean and clear in order for his creative juices to flow. The theme for the shower and room are his as we bet, and I lost. Both are basketball related themes, but he still wants them to be a bit different. I clearly do not get as much input as I want in the room However, I get to have lots of input on the shower ideas, but the room is all him. I am not worried he has amazing taste. I am just excited to see Hubby get so involved; he has some amazing ideas and this morning he surprised me with a huge surprise that literally dropped me to my knees. He sent me out on some errand to get a few things that he acted as if he could not live without. I was fine with that because any excuse to go shopping is a great excuse in my book. He said that since the area of town I had to pick the stuff up from was near my favorite nail shop that he set me an appointment for a manicure and pedicure. I'm always down with some good pampering. When I made it back to the house he came and got the things from the car and set them down in the garage next to the other boxes. Then dragged me in the house and upstairs. "Ok baby check this out -I wanted to surprise you. I got a lot done while you were out today. Be honest though let me know what you think of our son's room so far. I had some help of course, well I paid for the help but either way this looks good." He kept rambling until I cut him off. "Baby!" he opened the door, and I can promise you I never expected to see this at all. The crib was up and in place. Hanging on the wall above it was a basketball goal and oversized net. It was way too cute. On the walls he had framed autograph Jerseys from himself and a few of his teammates that they donated and all kind of team memorabilia. The lighting and overall ambiance of the room was incredible. As you can guess there were basketballs everywhere, but my favorite part so far was the LED sign with his name mounted to the wall. "Oh my God this is so perfect!" I said as I stood there in complete shock. Now we can start bringing all the other stuff in and set the room up so I can start my part which is the organizing and finishing touches. The chair and reading nook area was so creative. I could not wait to have it all come together. "Baby you did an amazing job I love you so much!" I told him as I kissed him and as he directed me out of the room so he could finish working.

As I sat in the sunroom and continued on my part of the guest list for the shower, I remembered to add Sophie, Amber, and the others from the Wiz as we had promised. And of course, I added Tina as I had promised them before they moved away to Virginia. I tried to concentrate but mind kept drifting away about the paternity of my son. I knew it was time to finally tell Ta'Ron. I am scared which is crazy because I know that the only thing, I am guilty of is not telling him when it happened. But in good conscious I cannot allow him to be at the baby shower let alone the birth and not know what is going on. The tears started to flow down my cheeks, and I sat the list down and picked up my phone and texted T. "I am about to tell Ta'Ron!" I must have typed and deleted the message a dozen times before finally pressing send. I threw the phone down wondering what the hell did I just do. There is no turning back now, and it needs to come out I am tired of carrying this secret around, this shame that does not even belong to me. I picked up the phone and called my doctor's office to inquire about prenatal paternity test and the receptionist explained that this prenatal test is still 99.99% accurate and that it was not invasive. I explained that I had been a victim of assault and that I haven't shared that information with my husband yet, but I wanted to tell him and come get all the answers so that our child comes home to a healthy environment. I explained that I knew both of my abusers and that the secret was killing me, and I needed it to be done as soon as possible. I had a ton of questions, and I tried my best not to overwhelm her with questions, while still whispering because my husband is upstairs. I think I would rather him walk in an hear me than me have to spark up the conversation myself. She continued with a lot of medical mumbo jumbo and in a nutshell told me it was a simple sample of blood and safe for me and baby. I told her that I had a baby shower coming up soon and that I had to know this information before then. I scheduled the test which she explained the doctor would do another full checkup and sonogram while I was there as is his standard requirement although just a few weeks ago we just had one. She said she had one in the next 6 days, and I took the appointment which means I had no time to play around I had to tell him tonight. I hung up and noticed I had eight or more texts and missed calls from T. "You better be ready to find out yourself, find out about your husband and his own skeletons, cuz I ain't holding shit back no more." So, let's see how this plays out- I promise you it will be nothing like you imagined. What you think we gone fight, nah baby girl its way deeper than that and he know I can change everything in a millisecond. But honestly, I want to know as well and like I said I really am sorry, but it Is what it is so let's go, I'm ready" What in the world is he talking about and why does he keep making references to my husband. I wrote back "My husband and I did nothing wrong; this is on you bruh and Juan. So, let's go indeed." I replied back. Then he said that he didn't do anything "this" time but to hold on tight cuz my world was about to be rocked. I started screaming and cussing so loud Ta'Ron rushed downstairs to see what was wrong. This is obviously not the way I wanted to tell him, but I was so damn mad and confused I just started talking and couldn't stop. I just let it all out. "I set a paternity test up for us next week because when you were on the road Juan raped me and when T came to make sure I was ok he also assaulted me, and now I don't know if Legend is yours or one of theirs. I am terrified and I know I should've told you right when it happened but I am scared and I did nothing wrong and T said that if I tell you what he did, that he can blow up your whole life and that you know what he means and I am confused I don't know what the hell is going on but I will not bring my son into this chaos and I will not hurt you because I did not cheat, this happened to be by crazy ex a dated for a small minute in high school, and by a close friend and I am losing it baby I can't do this. Please forgive me but you were on the road in the middle of a championship, and I just wanted to tell you face to face and no time ever seemed appropriate. After you showed me this nursery today there is no way I can move forward without telling you everything. I hope you will be able to forgive me for holding this!" I blurted out all in one breath. He was pacing the floor with tears in his eyes punching his right fist into his left hand. "Forgive you? Baby you did nothing wrong, yes, I wish you would've told me the moment it happened, don't you ever hold info from me to hell with basketball I would have dropped everything and come right home, and you know it. I am gonna kill both of the asses you can bet that. And T has been all up in my face this whole time? Yes, we are going to the appointment, and I don't care what it says this is my son and I will be the only one on the birth certificate and the only one in his life and I don't' give a damn about what nobody has to say about it. As for T yeah ok, he wanna play like he got something to hang over my head we can let it all be known cuz when it comes to you, I do not give a damn!" He was going off I was trying to calm him down, but he was running through the house putting on tennis shoes and grabbing keys. "What is T talking about Baby I don't get it- what is going on?" I asked. He yelled as he was running out the door "Just know I love you and I literally don't give a damn what T is on- its his ass today!" You could hear tires screeching and all I could do is call Cassie- "Oh my God girl I told Ta'Ron, and he is flipping out and took off out of the house. I don't want him to get into any trouble. I do not know what is about to go down." I was crying and out of breath. She just said she would call Devin and have him go over to T's as we were sure that is where he was headed, and he stayed closer. I didn't know if I should go over there or not and although Cassie told me to stay home, I got in my car and headed over to T's house. When I got there you could hear them fighting in the house from outside. Ta'Ron was on top of him punching him and I started yelling at him to stop tried telling him lets go home. And that's when T started saying weird stuff like Ta'Ron has lived his life all of these years and asking Ta'Ron how it felt now that he stepped into his life. I was so confused. What the hell is going on. He said that he wasn't worried about the police being called because they would both go to jail and that's for sure. I asked a million times what was going on and Devin came barging in the house and pulled Ta'Ron off T and separated them. They both cried like babies and my husband charged at him again. T apologized over and over but kept asking for an apology from my husband in return. Ta'Ron hit the floor and started crying uncontrollably and said he was sorry and that he has always taken care of him "But my wife Bro? My wife? You know I can't let that shit slide!" T replied "I know I know and that's why I didn't even really fight you back I deserve all of this, but all my life people have been looking at me like I am a monster. I have been holding on to shit that ain't mine and you tried to play me. When this happened with Tierra, I swear I don't know why or how it happened though and I am dead ass wrong and yes now this may be my baby. I may be guilty of rape Bro, but you are guilty of murder!" T yelled back and Ta'Ron charged at him again. All the while I am crying like crazy and yelling "murder what the hell is going on? All three of them were yelling at me to go home and I told them I would not leave until someone explained to me what was going on. That is when they all started trying to explain at once what happened.

"Baby I am going to tell you everything but not until after I go whoop Juans' ass this part isn't finished yet and I swear I will let it all out cuz it's been weighing heavy on me for a long time. T said he was going as well and now I'm like what in the world is going on- I mean I want Juan to be addressed but not like this and the fact that they are back be being on the same side after he found out what really happened was disturbing. All I could do is replay those words back in my head that T would throw out here and there and in his text messages. I screamed to the top of my lungs "Stop it! Just stop it- I need you here to help me raise our son and I can't have you in jail for Juan. Now sit down and start talking now!" They could tell I was fed up with all of the foolishness and he came a kneeled down in front of me and started off telling me that he never meant to hurt me, and that he never thought in a million years this day would come but that he was glad it did and that is when he dropped it on me. "I am going to tell you some things that are going to be hard to believe but please do not interrupt me or ask any questions, just let me get it all out first and then I swear to answer any questions you have, ok?" I shook my head yes while wiping the tears off of his face and kissing his lips. As he grabbed my hands he said "Baby do you remember back in the days when Cheyenne was murdered? The whole community was out trying to find Summer and find out what was going on? Well T and I… we made it to the house and Spice and Summer was there and... well remember when you made it to the hospital I was covered in blood and T had got shot well... I am the one who killed Spice!" He started crying and both T and Devin stood behind him comforting him. "WHAT? What the hell are you talking about T killed him and understandably so and that is why he went to jail!" I hollered in complete disbelief "Baby listen, please hear me, it's time. T did not kill Spice I did! T decided on his own at the house before the police came to take the wrap because he knew I was up for draft and that I had a chance to go to the NBA and because I did it to get his daughter back and avenge the death of Cheyenne that it was his family and that he would do the time if it came down to that. So, when he says that I am living his life that is what it means. You remember how I never missed a payment or a visit the entire time he was locked up? It was me Tierra, it was me and I am sorry, it all happened so fast.

I was so mad I don't even remember the full details of how it unfolded but it happened. We were both trying to be good friends to one another. So yes, he spent all that time in jail for a crime that I committed while I went on to the NBA got rich and got the perfect family. I was going to tell you but once the case closed and T went to jail, we decided that I would live for us all and I promised we would look after Summer which we have. Now that this happened, I am just messed up, I committed a crime protecting his family and he committed a crime against mine! I'm hurt upset, confused, embarrassed and ashamed and you don't deserve any of it," he explained. My heart pretty much hit the floor I never expected to hear this at all. I wish I didn't know, I thought that by telling him what T did to me would make me feel relieved, but I feel more torn now than before. In mind all I could think is no matter what the DNA test says the father of my son is either a rapist or a murderer. I could not be consoled. T was right this pain was way too much to bear. Now that I released one secret, I picked up one much bigger and I did not know what to do about it. T jumped in "I am sorry I had to get this weight off of me, it was destroying me. What I did is unforgivable and if for some reason I end up being this baby's father I will secretly sign off on anything and everything and never open my mouth. I am dead wrong for what happened Tierra! You know I love you and it was the heat of a crazy moment and I did it and you didn't deserve it and I think in some weird way I was really getting back at Ta'Ron. Either way I won't show up at anything and I will pull all the way back but believe me when I tell you- I already did the time for this crime. Yes, it sounds Hella messed up to say but its real. We don't have to be friends anymore, but I promise you I am not doing another day in jail, and you know that would mean everyone would find out the truth. Which means all that you have, and all that he built would crumble. I am not trying to blackmail yal for a single dime, he will tell you I never asked for anything financially, ever, but what I am asking for is what's left of my dignity. And if yal gone have the big family the fortune and the fame that is the least yal can do, and again it doesn't excuse anything I did to you and I take full responsibility for that- I just at least wanted you to know what was weighing heavy on me. And Bro I swear I'm legit sorry and I am leaving this all in this room, it's up to yal what you do next." T said as he started cleaning up the mess from the fight they had made. I honestly did not know how to feel I was in the greatest shock of my life. Yes, I was mad as hell that he had violated me and finding this out doesn't change the fact that he raped me, but I should I feel compassion for him because of what happened between he and my husband years ago? Devin stood there just as shocked as me and said he was driving me home and told Ta'Ron to follow him so that he could bring him back to his car later, I could barely stand let alone drive. When I got home, I crawled up on the chase lounge and bawled for hours. I had the worse headache and heartache you could ever imagine. I was in total shock; I had a range of emotions flowing through my body I just wanted to scream and fight and break things and every time Ta'Ron checked on me my anger only grew. How could he keep something so big from me? Why didn't anybody tell me after all of these years? Did the fellas know? Did Cassie already know? Was I the only idiot walking about here with my blinders on? Are these people even really my friends to stand by and allow me to marry a man that they knew committed murder, and no one felt that I needed to know? I was a wreck. The more I tried not to think about it the more my suspicions grew. At this point I hated everyone, all I knew, all I was so proud and happy about was a complete lie, and now I am about to bring a baby into this reality show lifestyle. This is not how I imagined my life at any level. I am a genuinely good person, I know I am not close to perfect, but I honestly don't believe this could be really happening to me. As I sobbed on the sofa with my head buried under the covers, he came and tried to check on me as he had been doing the last several hours and I finally just snapped. "Don't you dare touch me! As a matter of a fact don't you ever touch me in life again. I can't believe you thought it was ok not to tell me about this! How am I supposed to move forward? Am I supposed to just remain married to you and raise this baby with you like I do not know? Oh my God this is insane!" He just looked at me with tears in his eyes reaching to grab me and the next thing you know I slapped him. "I said don't touch me damn it! Do you think I am playing with you? I need some time Ta'Ron I just cannot handle anything else. This is supposed to be one the happiest time of my life and I feel like I was just assaulted for the third time, and this time by husband!" I was in so much pain I started gasping for air. My chest was hurting, and I could barely form any more words out. This situation had literally drained me physically and emotionally. I could feel my body shutting down on me. He must've seen it on my face and ran to the bathroom and came with the garbage can and just on time. I just started throwing up and crying and I could not stop. He held my hair back and cried a cry I had never heard a man cry. He apologized constantly, and just kept saying he did not want anything to happened to me or the baby and how he needed me to calm down even if I hated him at the moment. He tried convincing me to go get in the bed, but the thought of getting in the bed next to him only infuriated me. I fell asleep but only for moments at a time. I would wake up crying and my body ached all over. This was by far the worst day of my life.

The next several days were silent in our home. I tried to avoid seeing or speaking to him. I couldn't eat, I was giving very short answers to all of his questions. He tried to spark up conversations and at least get me to eat, but this was a pain I could not bear. My eyes were the size of Garfield, swollen from all of the uncontrollable crying. I had nothing left to throw up and therefore my throat and stomach was in turmoil. Eventually he came in the living room with a plate of fruit and slammed it on the table. "You can be mad at me all you want, you can even hate me and continue to threaten to divorce me, but what you will not do is harm my baby. So, you will eat damn it and I will not ask you again. I do not expect you to get over this in a few days but damn. You act like I had time to process your secret as well, you dumped your shit on me too Tierra! We both assumed we were protecting the other by not telling them and obviously we were both wrong. If we get through this, I promise to never withhold anything from you again, and I hope you would do the same. Baby this isn't fair to either of us. What do you think I should've done, went to jail and left you out here alone? I have held this secret for years and threw myself into work, never cheated on you and never did drugs to make sure I never did anything else that could cause me to lose you. It may sound selfish and self-centered as you called it, but the way you are crying now is what I have wanted to avoid you doing all these years. I was wrong and I am sorry, but I am also not just some cold-blooded murderer. Yeah, you think I can't hear the things you have been mumbling under your breath. You say that you are so concerned, but you have not once asked me what actually happened and anytime, I try to explain you shut me down. So yeah, you sit here like your life is the only life that was turned upside down and you pout all you need to, but you gonna eat, I'm done with it- do what you feel like doing!" He said as he continued to go off about how I was assaulted not once but twice and how I kept it from him not allowing him to protect me and both secrets caused this pain. I was mad but I wasn't dumb. I knew the things he was saying was the truth, but I really didn't even know how to start moving forward. He wasn't talking to any of the guys, and I wasn't really talking to Cassie. We both felt betrayed by them all- that they all knew things they should've shared with us. I sat up and grabbed a piece of banana off the plate and cried so hard as I bit into it. As he walked away, I yelled "I don't know what to do? I don't know how to move forward!" He said he didn't either, but he knew me and was willing to listen and try and not just point fingers.

He came and sat back down next to me, and I just fell over on his lap and cried. He rubbed my head and we cried ourselves to sleep. When we woke up, we attempted talking to each other. He ran me some bath water and as he walked me upstairs, I apologized for not telling him about Juan and T. He stopped me and reminded me that I was a victim, and he is sorry for not understanding how hard it must've been to tell anyone even him. I apologized for not at least allowing him to sit down in private as his wife and at least listen before going crazy. But I confessed that above all I was terrified that this was going to destroy our family. We both promised to try. "Please just be patient I'm upset and hormonal and I am doing the best I know how." I asked him as he washed my back. He agreed and asked that I give us a fighting chance and if at the end I felt I could not move forward he would understand. He asked that I not judge him on that one incident from the past. I promised not to do that and apologized for all the hurtful things I had been saying. I then asked him to tell me what actually happened that night. Once he was done explaining I realized he had really been carrying a lot. I told Ta'Ron because of all of this, that if we were even going to attempt to move forward that I just wanted to take the test and put it all behind us and under no circumstance wanted him approaching Juan unless he contacted me again. I couldn't imagine adding even more on top of this. He agreed and said as long as I was ok because he didn't want me anymore stressed than I already was. I went ahead and let him know about all of the emails and how T stepped in at the twin's birthday party when he came. I just had to get it all off my chest. I felt bad cuz the thought of my husband holding me just angered me. How could he have kept something this major from me? Our entire marriage was built on a lie. I then quickly remembered how I felt when I held my secret in and now, I am wondering if telling was the right thing to do. The fact of the matter is that it is all out now, and we have to move on or move forward. It was selfish thinking at its finest. Thinking he should just forgive me, but I get to wallow in his secret and complain. I cried and asked God for forgiveness. I didn't know if I wanted to be friends with these people, I have spent almost every day of my life with. Try explaining to family and friends I want to leave this "perfect" marriage for something I can't even bring up. At the same time, it wasn't cold blooded murder, when he explained the story and the more, we talked he explained that Spice started shooting and that's how the shoot-out started, he literally was protecting Summer and T and ultimately saved T's life, so why do I feel so miserable? He is clearly the great guy I thought I was getting.

I didn't tell my family about this new information. I could not even fathom hearing all of their responses or just adding this burden to anyone else. The thought that I would add grief to our parents was enough for me to know that I could not do that. Devin filled Donovan and Cassie in on everything that happened. When they got back into town, Cassie and Donovan came over to have a couple's dinner with us and offered to come with us to the doctor as support during the paternity test. I told them I just wanted it to be me and my husband. We apologized for pulling back from them, but the truth is I was pissed I didn't know if I wanted a divorce or what. They said that they understood and just sat with us in awkward silence watching tv until it got really late. I was dreading the test results as it is, the thought of anyone other than us being there just gave me anxiety. I appreciated the gesture, but It was going to take a little time for me to process the thought that they may all have already known. My thought was I would see how I felt after getting the results. T had went ahead of us and submitted a sample it made no sense to have them in the same room any time soon.

When we checked in the appointment it was the normal routine get weighed, give urine, and blood and a sonogram and wait on the doctor, they explained that it would be a two day turn around for the test results and it seemed more like two years. Meanwhile we had to act like all was well and keep working on the nursery and shower and at this point it was all just becoming overwhelming. But as the days passed, we were getting back to being close and it was after a real long deep conversation we were both put in situations where we kept something from one another, thank God it wasn't infidelity so we agreed that this is something we would overcome and just try to proceed. We approved the print of the invitations, and our parents were still spending money left and right. I had ordered decorations the coordinator needed for the shower, and it was driving me insane not to be more hands on but hey I am the mother this time. I still have not completed the baby registry yet with all that was going on I just hadn't been in a shopping mood, now that is something that I thought I would never say. If I am really being honest, I just don't want to celebrate anything until I know if this is my husband's baby. I don't think I have ever prayed so hard since the assault. As we were getting the labels together for the invitations printed, I got a call asking if we could come in that the results were in. We left the print shop and headed straight to the doctor. For the first time ever, we did not have a long wait in the waiting room. They called us back immediately. The first person to enter the room was a therapist and I immediately burst into tears. She started in saying we may get some news that we are not expecting and that we need to keep an open mind and be there for one another. I knew then that we were about to have our world shaken yet again. The doctor joined and asked the therapist to stay in the room as he went over the results. "Just rip off the band aid please I can't take it!" I screamed. They explained how its standard and blah blah blah. The doctor started talking and I just wanted to throw up- "we tested two of the three potential fathers and the results from both are back. I must admit there is some shocking news and so I will get that out of the way. The good news is the father is not the person we did not test so there is no need to notify him at all! The great news is that Ta'Ron you are the father! I asked the therapist to stay however, because the other day when we ran more test, you are most definitely the father of twins and not just one little boy, but of a boy and a little girl!" the look of confusion that must've rested on our faces must've been priceless the doctor continued "She is here because you have been preparing for one baby and you are most certainly are having two healthy babies and by your husband!" I think we sat in awe for a few minutes until I broke the silence by jumping up and saying, "I told you we were having a girl!" as I started crying. Ta'Ron was so excited we were so happy that the paternity was behind us but now we are having 2 babies. "Good thing we didn't print those invitations yet, we have some changes to make, and another nursery to do!" he said as he grabbed me, and we embraced for what felt like hours. This was news worth sharing. We left and at that moment it was like our marriage was restored. All the fear and anxiety I had been feeling the last week was instantly lifted. I held on tight to the paperwork and we called T and let him know the news but that by law they would send him his own paperwork, or he could go pick it up to see for himself that he is not the father. We did not tell him about their being another baby, for once this news belonged to only the two of us.

# CHAPTER 18

It has always been said that time flies when you are having fun and I am witnessing first hand that this could not be any more true. We looked up and after making the changes to the announcements that we are having twins and finally mailing the invitations few weeks ago the days have gotten shorter. We have now two nurseries just about completed but Legend has way more stuff than our baby girl. I felt like this surprise was God's gift to me after all that has transpired. I get a princess and her room is crazy amazing. Girly doesn't even begin to describe it. Her room does not have a basketball anywhere near it, but she does have some very special pieces as well. And yes, daddy reached out to come celebrity friends and she has the hookup on some autographed memorabilia as well. The baby shower had already been planned so we stayed with the Slam Dunk themed shower which actually worked into our favor since he is being all but celebrated for a two-in one deal, as if he made these babies alone. I just give him a hard time I actually think it's cute.

We had not heard from or seen much of T at all since we found out about the paternity results, but as the shower was quickly approaching. We wondered if he would he show up or not. We absolutely did not want any drama happening, but we wanted Summer to be there, and we also didn't want family and friends asking why he wasn't there. So, I brought it up in general conversation. "Babe, do you think T is gonna show up at the shower? I asked and immediately he said he was thinking the same thing but did not want to be the one to bring it up. We both laughed, something I did not believe would be possible especially so soon. He asked how I felt about it and truthfully for the first time it did not matter to me and with that being said we decided not to reach out either way and just let it all happen naturally. If he comes, we will play it cool if he doesn't, we will remember that this day is about us. We had a lot of guests coming and I had booked a maternity shoot in between all of this chaos so we were also preparing for that, and I was excited. My girl had arranged for me to get my face beat by the best makeup artist in the ATL. I had been planning so much this time I let the photographer have full creative control over the shoot. I just wanted us to show up and smile. The plan is to have a few of the finished shots displayed at the shower. We were able to do just that, and the proofs were insane. He really outdid himself. I immediately booked him for family photos right away, for after the twins come. We got glammed up for this shoot which was fun since the shower was more jersey and sneakers so there goes the best of best worlds again.

They day is finally here, and my phone was ringing off the hook with questions from everyone. I had to literally just power it off and let it charge. I'm trying to get done and be on time and every time someone calls it slows me down, as if these two babies don't slow me down enough. When we arrived, it was more beautiful than I could've ever imagined and there were gifts everywhere. I never did the registry, like I said he had so much already, and we decided to allow people just to know the theme of both rooms and the sex of both babies and just take whatever they decided to bless us with. Our people never disappoint so there was no need to steer them. And between Ta'Ron and I and our parents everything else was bonus anyway. We really just wanted to enjoy family friends and food of course. The games were fun and the energy in the room was so beautiful. I smiled for so many pictures my face was tired for real. We danced, ate, laughed, and mingled and everything was flowing great. As we were opening gifts, we spotted T. I am not sure how long he had been there, but he was chilling and commanded no personal attention. These babies have way too much stuff I have no clue how we will get this stuff home it is unbelievable how much stuff they got. Tina put me on the spot about being the God Parents again and I actually told her we had not had time to think about it yet and she did not give any push back which was helpful. At this point I am just trying to get through all of this, and we will worry about all of that at another time. For the first time in a very long time, I was starting to feel happy again.

Cassie and Donovan were finally ready to set a date for some time next year and we were all excited to be able to be there for them, they have held us all down and it was their turn. Anything they could think of we were willing to be on board in whatever way possible. As the weeks passed by, they grew more eager as they should, and we accompanied them to the local bridal shows in the Atlanta area. Cassie wanted to get more out of the box ideas and between social media and these bridal shows she should have a lot to think about. The wedding was not anytime soon but we definitely know how fast time flies. Our favorite part was walking around the expo hall tasting all the samples of wedding cake. I was having too much fun with that alone. The guys enjoyed that part as well, along with the fashion show of bridal party. They gave them so many samples and free gifts that we had several large tote bags of goodies when we left. After we left the Bridal Show the fellas were going to meet up with Devin to hang out and for him to show them this major project. Whatever it was it must've been a big deal because he had been working on it in secrecy for a while. They needed some time to reconnect with one another and just chill. So, Cassie and I decided to go back to her house and go over the stuff we just collected and just chill out a bit. We finally had time to catch up on her trip to see her mom and just other girl talk that didn't include any of my drama. She wants a very intimate wedding just close family and friends, but she wants to find a way to incorporate some of her students as they are her babies. I have been so busy I haven't been able to volunteer and help out in her classroom like I love to do. I love helping chaperone field trips but those has slowed down since covid. Although things are opened back up and so called back to "normal" a lot of things have changed. She said that she had about four students she really wanted to participate a couple from this year and couple from the previous year. She is a great teacher and has great relationships with the students and their families. She has continued to be a mentor or aunt in many ways to these kids and it is much needed. I thought that it was so selfless that on their big day she was still finding a way to include her students. That is Cassie for you, well Miss Reynolds, soon to be known to all the kids as Mrs. Wright, literally. I love my best friend nothing like having a true friend you can depend on. We laughed and talked the night away and before you knew it Donovan was walking in saying "Yal still up talking? That don't make no sense its after two o'clock in the morning." I jumped up laughing and said I better head on home, I called my husband on my way home and he talked to me while I drove home telling me how much fun they had and how crazy everyone was acting. I made it home safe, and sound and I am really feeling great about the new direction we are heading in It is feeling natural again, I am beginning to believe we can get through this.

**CHAPTER 19**

Seriously I am getting so uncomfortable. These babies are in there having a soul train dance party on every single organ I have. I cannot get comfortable in the bed to sleep, to sit up and watch tv, or anything else. I get a lot of walking in showing houses and I have still sold quite a few without taking as many clients as I normally do. I was just relaxing but sitting around got boring, so I begged my husband to allow me to go back to work if I promised to take it easy. Plus, I wasn't about to lose out on winning the trip to Bora Bora all because I was pregnant. If I was going to lose it wasn't going to be because of this pregnancy. If someone else wins I would not be mad at all, but I am very competitive within myself so even at part time I needed to show them why I am number one year after year. This year there are so many in the running and I love it. At a time, we thought the market was going to be slow due the Coronavirus it did the exact opposite, and we cannot keep a listing passed a day really. It is a great time to be a Realtor and our office is doing what we always do, stamping our name all over the city and closing these deals. We had a Q & A session at the office for high school seniors, and really anyone interested in learning more about the business. Just encouraging people to get licensed and telling our stories. No matter how many times I am introduced I am always humbled at the intro, just hearing all of the things that I have accomplished in such a short amount of time is heartwarming. I love telling the raw truth about the days when the money was not flowing in. I am very transparent. The main thing people ask is why I work if we are rich. That is probably my favorite question, I always tell people no matter what your partner does you want to have your own identity and more importantly achieve the dreams you have so you will be fulfilled. The fact that I get paid well is just a bonus. The blessing in our partnership is we can both stop working today with our new family and retire well. We have been very good with money, saving and investing from his very first contract and really being able to live a debt free life. That may not be the goal for many, but we want to live carefree, this is the way to do it. Plus, I love to shop and travel, and this helps with that as well. In sports there is a new younger more skilled player drafted every year. You never know what can happen and that includes injuries and all. Plus, he wants to retire young so we can enjoy or family. That has been our plan since high school, and we are now in a position to make that happen. Being surrounded by other entrepreneurs like the twins and other professionals in our circle just keeps us going, we all have a career and a hustle as we like to call it. You should always have more than one stream of income is what I always tell the kids when they ask me questions like this. And I won't lie I have a great advantage to the rich because of my husband and it makes being part time easy because the homes I sell are sometimes three and four times the price of one home my teammates are selling. This year the trip is roundtrip airfare and all-inclusive trip for two to Bora Bora for ten days nine nights. The trip will be just after I heal, and the babies are old enough for me to travel if I win so I felt what a better push gift to myself than this. I have given my prizes away a few times in the years past to single moms who I saw trying so hard and who have totally sold their behinds off. This year I need this break, but I also know that I can afford to go without the win, it's the bragging rights I care about.

My mother has been feeding me so much I feel like I am going to pop. I miss our brunch meetings as well but man we have tried a little of everything. They feed me then walk me to death, I'm like hey these cankles can only take so much. Today she came up to take me out to lunch and I had to explain that we just ate at the job, and I could not go today. She was insistent that I at least have a smoothie to get all my vitamins and minerals in and just the thought of it made me want to vomit. "Mommy I am so full, let's save that for tomorrow." I said as well walked toward my office only for me to see an edible arrangement on my desk. "Mommy are you serious? You are too much. Oh my God oh my God oh my God!" I started to get louder "Ok baby I hear you I will stop." She said, "No oh my God Mommy my water just broke! It is time call Ta'Ron it is happening!" She helped to keep me calm as much as she could. And said she would drive me. I was about thirty-five weeks, so it is not of the norm to go into labor around this time especially with twins, but I had just had a checkup and was doing good. I just knew that I had at least another two good weeks in me minimum. My mom was good at keeping people calm she was a decorated psychologist so her sweet soothing voice was helpful. She made the necessary calls and got me to the hospital and got me all checked in and my heart was racing like never before. They got me setup and checked me, and I was dilating fast, but the heartbeats of the babies were good as well as my vitals. Ta'Ron came running through the door and said that he had called everyone, and that Cassie was headed to go take Bella to my aunt and then she was heading up here. We definitely didn't want to leave her there alone as I knew my husband would be staying by myside. She was already going to have to adjust to having to shares us which should be interesting enough.

I was in so much pain and every five seconds it seemed as if someone wanted to come check me, aka shove their hands up my privates and feel around, while saying just relax. Finally, I was fully dilated, and the doctor came in and gave me some quick instructions and sort of a short overview of what I should expect. Meanwhile I could literally careless, just get these babies out of here and quick. The most annoying part was having the nurse look at a machine I was connected to and tell me I was about to have a contraction as if I couldn't feel it myself. Labor was not cute and sweet like they portray it in the movies and sitcoms. Looking back, I can see why people say it is a beautiful experience but during the moment I couldn't disagree more. When it was time to push, my mom went to the waiting room with the rest of our friends and family and allowed Ta'Ron and I have this moment alone. I know she really wanted to be in the room but all I wanted was for this pain to be over. The doctors were instructing Ta'Ron to push my legs back and he was trying to follow directions and take pictures and record all at once. The first baby came out and I could hear him cry, it was the most amazing sound I had ever heard, but the celebration was short lived. I could feel more contractions, these much more powerful than any other one I had felt. I just stared pushing, the doctor was telling me to hold on, but I could not control it, and with just a few more pushes she came right on out. She had strong lungs; the sound of her cry was much louder than his. Ta'Ron was jumping up and down and recording as they were cleaning the babies up, checking them out and weighing them. Congratulations on a beautiful baby boy weighing 5.6 pounds and measuring 19 inches long. They laid him on my bare chest, and I just looked at his head full of beautiful hair in shock that I was responsible for giving him life. A few moments later they brought her over. Now for your gorgeous baby girl weighing 5.5 pounds measuring 17 and a half inches long. They laid her next to him on my chest She had the same curly jet-black head full of hair. Looking down at them I became overwhelmed with gratefulness. All the sudden nothing else in the world mattered. I forgot about everything I had endure these last several months and all I felt was pure joy, pure happiness, pure love. My husband was taking pictures and finally said, "Baby you're gonna have to give one up, I can't wait any longer!" He kissed her on the top of her head and instantly reached for Legend and kissed him. Just watching him hold him and the way his eyes lit up was like healing waters to my heart. He was a proud father, and it was such a blessing to have a husband who was so loving and so involved from the beginning. The doctor asked him to hold both of them, so he sat down, and the nurse walked her over to him and took pictures as they cleaned me up and got the room prepared for our family to come in. I looked at all the of them and just smiled. "Baby we are really parents!" I said and I felt a sweet relief just come over my body. Shortly after all of our family and friends started to pour in. And as a proud Dad Ta'Ron said "Please help us welcome Legend and Legacy Hunter into the family!" He started to rattle off all the facts of how much they weighed who came first and how long they were. He was so proud, our parents called first dibs on holding them as we knew they would. The rest of the time was just spent laughing talking and hearing our families saying how much they looked like us when we were born, which were followed by embarrassing childhood stories that we could have probably done without. They were beautiful, healthy, not too small, no reason to be in NICU, or anything. This was a blessing. Ta'Ron and I held hands all day and just enjoyed every moment. People were pouring in and out of the room. Many of them bringing flowers and even more gifts for the kids. And out of nowhere I we hear a familiar voice hiding behind a bouquet of roses "Knock knock, The favorite uncle is here." We all looked up and said in unison "Oh my God!" It was Ronnie.

We all screamed with excitement. We had missed him so much, me probably the most. I avoided talking to him the entire time he took his show on the road because I knew for sure he would have come back and without question and definitely would've handled T and Juan. I was praying that no one told him, and I was positive they didn't. We didn't get to talk that much because they were doing concert tours all over the world and with the time difference it was always hard to catch him. Plus, we all had so much going on we only go to do short video chats. He had sent his gift for the shower and all but because we had so much going on we didn't get to give this part of the friendship the attention that he deserved. He was the absolute best. We were all so proud of him – he took a huge leap of faith and joined a team that traveled abroad with a newly signed group out of Atlanta, and they were killing it. They have been able to add more dates as well as open up for well-known artists while they were promoting their own tour. He was doing what he loved and was making good money while he was at it and still promoting the club for the twins from a far. He was sought out all over the country he was a great promoter and had just started dibbling into producing but this particular group used three of his tracks and took off and so they wanted him on the road for both reasons. "Ronnie oh my God what are you doing here? When did you get in? Oh my God what a great surprise, you gonna make me cry!" I said as I tried to sit up and almost jump out of the hospital bed because I was so excited. "Wait crazy girl lay back down, I am coming to you. I wanted to surprise yal I knew I would be back for about a week, and I got in two days, but I slept all day yesterday. I called your Mom when I was headed back because she was gonna help me surprise all of yal, little did we know the baby was gonna come, well let me say the babies, I still am shocked about that. And you know Uncle Ronnie gotta be here. I am so glad I came in town!" We all were talking at once basically asking the same questions how long he was going to be in town and what his plans were and how things were going. He said that as of now he should be in town at least two weeks and maybe a little longer. "I know yal miss me and I hella miss yal too, but can I see the babies for a minute dang?" He said jokingly as he walked towards the babies.

As I looked around the room, I was getting mushy

and emotional I cannot believe we are parents now. This seems so surreal. Everyone keeps asking how it feels to be a Mommy and I am like; I have no clue I am just a few moments in, and I think I am legit in shock. Ta'Ron on the other hand had the best answers, "I feel amazing, I am on cloud nine, the best feeling in the world, I got a whole family!" just listening to him repeat that every time someone walked in and asked just warmed my heart. I was very happy just shocked tired and really just in awe that I am finally seeing and holding and kissing my two new blessings. Our room was huge and private so that his fans would not try to bombard us. The hospital staff was very professional, but you would see a few of them light up as they came in. The family stayed for hours, and I must have dosed off on them a million times. I would find myself waking up to loud laughter that filled the room. We took so many pictures and people were bringing in food and fruit left and right telling me what I need to eat since I was going to breastfeed. At this point I knew that we were very much going to be taken care of. I just giggled and nodded and half the time I had no clue what they were actually saying. The guests were coming in and out and some had even returned a second time. After a while Hubby told everyone that the babies and I needed rest and they promised to come back in the morning. Once everyone was gone and we were just sitting in the calm and quietness of the room we just gave each other a look and a smile, then he said, "We did it Baby!" and I replied, "Yes we did Baby!" The nurse came in and said she was going to give us a little break and take the babies so we could rest a bit. We told her that was fine but that we wanted them to sleep in our room and she told us just to call her when we were rested and had eaten and by then it would be time to try to latch again and do more skin to skin. Hubby found a movie on TV, but we were both out within minutes. I don't know who went first. We woke back up around the same time as they were coming in asking what we wanted to eat, and all I wanted to do was sleep. We picked something and sat up and laughed and talked as we both kept saying how we could not believe it finally happened.

After eating they brought Legend and Legacy back in, and we went back and forth about who we thought they looked like and if they looked more like me and my family or him and his family. They were a beautiful blend between both of us honestly. They were so small and precious I just could not stop kissing them. The latching was easy for my greedy son, but for my little diva it took at little more time and a few tricks to get her to finally latch. They actually slept well through the night, it was Hubby and I who could not stop waking up checking on them every few minutes. When the morning came the nurse told us as long as the doctor was able to come check on us today that we should be getting out of here today because all three of us were doing well. We had visitors start to poor in again starting about ten o'clock, still bringing more and more stuff. Ronnie was among the first to stop by, he said that he had some running around to do and wanted to drop by before everyone started to come, and he had to share the babies and before he had to leave. I told him that the others were coming about 1030 and he said he would hang around to see all of them as well. "Looking good Sis, I am so proud of yal, yal really doing this life thing. You got my Bro over here with the super glow on his face, and all I can do is respect it!" he said and

Ta'Ron and I just smiled and looked at one another and replied in unison "We try!" The staff continued to come and check on us and reminded me that the twins were going to take pictures today and I asked her to move them to the afternoon which she said was perfect as the doctor would be able to see us shortly after. We had the chance to catch up a little bit more. We teased him calling him "Hollywood" and "Big Money," and other similar names and he just shook his head and replied "yal got it I'm just trying to get it!" I immediately went into nosey sister mode, "Ok you already know what I'm about to ask, so let's get right into it. All of this traveling and big move making, I know you have met somebody's daughter so spill it!" I said. "Baby!" Ta'Ron quickly interrupted, "What? He knows his sister so stop playing and give us the tea." I replied back as I held up my hand with my pinky finger extended like the people in England do for teatime. Ronnie said he actually had been meeting ladies from all over but there was one special lady in particular that he has being staying in contact with that he really liked, but that he was just taking it slow because he wanted to enjoy this new job opportunity and he knows that not a lot of women can deal with their man being on the road a lot. I couldn't deny that fact by any means. "Well, when that time comes just remind her that he has to pass the sister test from me and Cass!" We all laughed and then there was a knock on the door, and it was the crew minus T walking in. We all embraced and started to talk as they all fought over the babies. Ronnie was serious about not giving up Legacy for another few minutes and he had just put down Legend and just picked her up. He just kept telling everyone that they had to wait.

We continued to talk and catch up and talk about the upcoming wedding as Ronnie assured them that no matter where he was, he was going to travel back to participate in the wedding. "Now you know I am not going to miss this wedding, never. Plus, I am the cutest one in the group and all of the ladies will be expecting ya boy to be there anyway" He said as he poked out his chest. "Boy bye!" Cassie replied while admitting that the ladies do ask about him a lot though. Especially since he has not been there to help the twins with the club in a while. Then he started asking who in particular and that sort of thing as the twins chimed in with the details and physical description of these ladies. Then Ronnie asked if any of us had seen or heard from T. He said that he had not answered or returned any of his calls and texts since he has been back, not even when he told him he was back and that concerned him. The silence that filled the room was so thick you could cut it with a knife and our faces had to say way more than our silence. He immediately stood up and asked what was going on and what were we not telling him, asking if he had gotten into any trouble. Devin tried giving generic answers like I heard from him the day before yesterday and then it went back to the eerie silence. Finally, he was fed up the lack of response in the room and said" Ok what are yal not telling me for real?" Just as Devin was about to say something in walked our parents to save the day. Cassie said that they were all going to stop by when we got home and got settled in, and everyone agreed. I was fine with it, but I was praying that this conversation never came up again, or at least T would respond to him, because I know he is not going to tell Ronnie of all people. Ronnie headed out and little by little everyone trinkled behind them until it was just us and our parents. We sat and laughed, and they stayed for the pictures. The twins did so well they were up, and alert and I cannot wait to get all the pictures back, and of course take the ones we already scheduled for the entire family, which I know is going to be nice. The doctor eventually came in and did his final checks on the babies and I and said that we were good to go, and that he would have the nurses bring my dismissal paperwork. I asked our parents if they would load some of our things into their vehicles because it was going to be too much for us to fit in ours with us and 2 car seats. It looked like we had a baby shower all over again. Mrs. Hunter and Mommy started on me about being old school and staying in the house with the kids until my six weeks have passed, especially since covid was just a huge deal and people are still getting it. I just chuckled and nodded in agreement followed by yes ma'am. The men all went downstairs and loaded the cars and pulled them up front while Mrs. Hunter and Mommy helped me with the twins and gathering the rest of my personal items, I was moving pretty good but it sure was good to have some help. After about twenty more minutes the nurse came in to give me my discharge papers and instructions and put me in a wheelchair to push me out to the front as they grabbed the car seats with my beautiful babies wrapped inside. We loaded up and drove home convoy style to the house so they could bring all of our gifts in as well. Home sweet home to start our beautiful new family.

# CHAPTER 20

**E**verything was so different, but we were adjusting really well. I was really proud of us and all of our corny little systems that we put into place, but so far, they were working out pretty well. For our first day and night at home with two new babies I would say we killed it. So far, the babies sleep well even throughout the night just like they did at the hospital. I only had to wake up to feed them because I haven't started pumping yet, but I will very soon. They do not cry a whole lot, really only if they are wet or hungry, which is great, but again it has only been one night at home so let's just pray that we can keep this same momentum. I really could not complain my husband was hands on and great at it, and I knew eventually he would be back on the road and that he was soaking up all of these precious moments. But just seeing him in full "Daddy" mode was such a turn on. At this point the way he is running around here making it happened for the four of us and catering to the babies and I, has me feeling like come on six weeks cuz Daddy doing his thing. When I make those comments, he just laughs and says, "Don't Play!" The twins were resting, and we sat downstairs in each other's arms just talking and chilling and looking through all the pictures we had taken at the hospital. I had no clue he had taken so many. We agreed that we would wait until the professional pictures came back from the hospital and from our upcoming family shoot before sending out the official birth announcements. However, his cousins and teammates were requesting some pictures now and I didn't want him to share any of me looking crazy or any while I was giving birth. I have a new respect for people with multiple children because the labor was no joke and let's just say I am in no rush to do it again. Before we knew it, we had dosed off for a good bit and we were awakened by Legend's cry. He went to get him and bring him downstairs and said Legacy was still sound asleep. After I fed and burped him, we sat there watching Ta'Ron put everything in its proper place, after dragging it over to me to open up and decide where we wanted it. Soon after making a few trips up and down the steps little mama gave out her cry and he brought her down to be fed as well. I got them washed up and dressed twin style of course and we just continued to relax while Daddy took good care of us. My father called asking when I wanted him to go get Bella and bring her back home or if we needed one more night. I missed her so much, but hubby said we needed one more night, so one more night it is.

Cassie called to check in on us and to see what a good time was for her and the crew to come over with food for us tonight. Babe said to say six that way it wasn't too early or too late and would give us some time to get to get things in order a bit. I know he was excited to have them over and I didn't want to ruin it with talk about what if Ronnie asked about T again. I knew we both were thinking it though. Neither one of us had heard from him and there was no need for us to text or call to tell him about the birth as it was still intense between the two of them, and rightfully so. But I know Ronnie and when he gets over tonight and doesn't see T he is going to ask again, oh well I will just go with the flow if does happen. I am not sure what Devin was going to say when he asked yesterday, so maybe he will take the lead again. I laid the babies back down and started helping and pulling out glasses and drinks. Of course, I knew I was not having any since I am breastfeeding, but I know they are going to want to at least toast. They all already promised not to stay too late so that we can rest up and try to establish a routine. I was glad that they were so understanding. I put old school R&B on low and we occasionally danced as we crossed paths throughout different parts of the house. There is something about some good music as you clean up that gets you moving and sets the mood for whatever comes next. You will two-step through the whole house and next thing you know you are done cleaning. Today was no different, our only problem was we have too much stuff so we put it in their individual closets, and I will go through and organize it better later, most is just the overflow of all size diapers and wipes anyway. We took turns taking a bath and getting dressed so that one of us would be available if the babies got fussy or anything. By the time we were dressed and cleaned up and changed the babies the doorbell rang, and they were here.

"Ok Friend where are you going?" I yelled as Cassie walked through the door. She took another step and then she stopped and gave a model twirl. She looked so cute. Everyone had something in their hand again. "Yal are just too much, thank yal for real. Dinner was enough you know the bar stays stocked over here; you didn't need to bring anything else." Ta'Ron told everyone. "You say that now Bro until all that crying start and double time, we are just ahead of the game." Donovan said as he sat a big bag down on the table. "Ok yal in here jamming I see." Devin said as he started grooving and walking towards the babies and everyone started yelling at him that he wasn't slick and better go wash his hands first. "Yal some haters though, let me do me, yal don't like to share my niece and nephew, so I am going to be first tonight cuz yal legit stingy!" he said sarcastically as he washed and dried his hands. Cassie and I had washed our hands to start sitting out the food. They had all picked up a little something from crab dip to chicken wings. We sat down eating and talking in no organized fashion just throughout the kitchen and great room, as they all complained that no one was sharing the kids, and argued that they were smiling at the other, and so on and so forth. I started picking up the plates and taking them back into the kitchen and Cass followed me and said that she had something that she needed to tell me. She said that as she and Donovan was getting the crab legs and crab dip for tonight, they ran into Juan. She said she didn't think that he seen her, but she wanted to let me know that he was back. She warned me that Donovan was going to tell Ta'Ron, and she didn't want me to be caught off guard. I imagined this day over and over in my head. But I didn't have a scary feeling in the pit of my stomach or anything, that I thought I would have. I told her thank you for telling me anyway. I told her I will not ask them to keep that secret but asked that he waited until tomorrow or at least the end of the night so that we could enjoy ourselves. She said that she would definitely tell him that. Devin saw the deck of cards I had sat on the coffee table and got super excited. "I know yal not trying to get whooped tonight." He said as he held up the deck of cards in his hand. The volume in the room went from a five to a twenty and quick, with all the trash talking. Cassie and I let them have it and we went to talk and chill with the twins as they started a game of spades, just like old times. Listening to them brought back so many memories this was something we loved and missed. We talked more about the wedding plans and how things were going for her at school and how great the club was doing that after the wedding they are talking about opening up another location, which is an amazing idea. I told her how proud I was of them, just following their dreams and going for it all. I asked if they had finally picked the wedding colors and she said that they had narrowed it down to just a few options and would be making a final decision within the next few days so they can give everything to the wedding planner. The babies had dosed back off even with all the noise going on, which my Mommy said is the best. She said that if they can sleep through noise they will sleep when its quiet. I decided to keep them down with us just in case. I asked who was winning and Hubby and Ronnie said that the twins were up by two books as of right now, but they weren't going to win this game. As we were laughing and talking the doorbell rang, and Ta'Ron and I looked at one another because we knew we were not expecting anyone else. I grabbed my phone to see who it was on the video doorbell, and I just froze. It was T! By this time Ronnie was saying that it was probably T that he had finally called him back and that he told him to come over. That gut feeling that I had avoided with Cassie's news of seeing Juan, I definitely got with him being here. Cassie was quick on her feet and said, "Girl you're resting I will get the door!" He came in and he and Ronnie hugged and talked trash for a few moments and then he spoke to the rest of us, and we said hello back. Ronnie yelled at him to go wash his hands so that he could eat and see the twins. He washed his hands and made him a plate and sat down at the table to eat so that he could watch the fellas finish up the game.

Hubby was right the twins did not win, they came back and won the game. So of course, there was a lot of loud talking and "Shoulda coulda woulda's going on." "Bro if you done eating you need to wash your hands and look at these beautiful babies before I go get my turn in, cuz everybody knows I am not sharing my time." And again, that awkward silence hit the room just as it did in the hospital, and I just froze. My brain said go put the babies to bed, but just moments before I had said I would leave them down with us. Still, I kept telling myself to take them up, but my body would not move. T washed his hands and they all started to talk into the room where we were sitting on the sofa. The closer he got, the faster my heart would beat. He got near me and said that they were gorgeous but when he reached out his arms to touch them, I lost it. I thought I was going to be able to hold it together, but I just couldn't. I said, "Uh uh!" and Ronnie said "Wait what is going on, why is it all silent and why don't you want him to touch the kids? Is there something going on?" T quickly said that if he would step outside, he would tell him but not in front of the kids. As he uttered those words I broke out into tears and Ronnie grabbed T by his shirt and asked what the issue was. "Why is she crying and not allowing you to see the kids? Tierra, take the babies upstairs and put them to bed and yes, we can all go outside because on my mama if some shady shit is going down I don't wanna tear up the homies house. But I want Tierra around, so I know I'm getting the whole truth, cuz as soon as you got close to his wife and kids, I noticed Ta'Rons fist was balled, and he stood up. But ain't nobody telling me, cuz yal already know what it is. But the cat is out the bag now you may as well lay it on me, cuz I will not let this rest." Ronnie said, as the twins were pulling him off of T. They were all heading outside, and Cassie and I were headed upstairs to put the Legend and Legacy in their cribs. Ta'Ron had done his best to honor me with the know fighting and drama pact we made especially when I broke it first. Listen you are still a rapist, and you will never ever touch my kids, NEVER! I was shaking and as we joined them outside. Ronnie was so mad he was pacing the yard. "I know yal hiding something and trying to protect one another but I want to hear it straight from my Bro, what he did. Please yal I gotta know!" He said and again I started crying and then Ta'Ron charged him and started cussing him out and asking why he come over and why did he even attempt to touch them, and T shook his head and yelled "I don't know" as he cried. I told you as long as you kept your distance, I would do my best, but this can never happen again. Ta'Ron told T. "What was I supposed to tell him when he called, and kept asking me why he hasn't seen me and why I haven't been up there to see the kids? Was I just supposed to say oh I can't come up there because I raped Tierra and for a minute, we thought she may be pregnant by me?" Before he could finish his statement Ronnie fired off on him. He was screaming and crying asking us all if it was true and we shook our heads yes. He was so mad the punched Ta'Ron too! "How yal not gonna tell me about some serious shit like this? We family, that's my sister, you hurt my sister, you lucky to be alive Bro. If they would've told me any of this, they know I would've been on the next thing smoking to handle yo ass!" Ronnie said as he charged T again. I told Ronnie that no one really knew until recently, that I was scared and ashamed and that I didn't know how to tell him or my husband. He brought his tone down but told me he was hurt because he kept asking where T was, and we all never used that opportunity to tell him. He was feeling bad because he invited him over and had no clue so now, he was angry. Ta'Ron told T to leave, and he said fine but decided to tell all on his way out. "Yeah, I will go, but don't act like I am the only one with secrets, Tierra. I wasn't the only man that needed to be tested, you were raped by Juan from school before me, but nobody is out socking him up!" Everyone charged him at this point and Devin shielded him and said to just let him leave. Ta'Ron started yelling that Juan had left town and that it was on site with him as well, and that's when Donovan threw out that they just saw him as they picked up the crabs to come tonight, now Ta'Ron and Donovan were fighting, and as soon as Devin went to go break up that fight Ronnie and T were back fighting again. "Bro why didn't you tell me Ta'Ron said to Donovan." "Cassie made me promise to wait 'til the end of the night I wanted to tell you. Ta'Ron told everybody to leave and that he never wanted to hear from any of them again. Ronnie was still asking questions about Juan and insisting he didn't care how mad Ta'Ron was that he wasn't leaving until he had some answers. Donovan was yelling at

Cassie to get their things so that they could go, and I was begging everyone to calm down so I could explain, and that the only person that had to leave was T. But everyone was so mad they didn't care. Cassie walked by Ta'Ron on her way back outside and told him that he was wrong for hitting Donovan, and he lost it and started cursing at her and told her that she better leave him alone. Now they were all fighting again because Donovan was not just going to stand there and allow him to disrespect his girl. I went and grabbed him and took him inside and Cassie made a comment that pissed me all the way off. She yelled "All of this bullshit all because of you Tierra-Michelle!" and that was it. I swung on her like I never knew her, like she had not been my best friend all of these years. I tried to knock the life out of her, fresh out of the hospital and all. "I am not some random hoe, I was raped, don't you ever come around me and my family again, or you won't live to walk down the aisle! How could you say that to me?" I said as they pulled me off her as I was unleashing the ass whooping, I wanted to give T and Juan all on her. "Leave my house now!" I told everybody. Ronnie was the only one who didn't care that I said leave he came in and wanted me to tell him everything I knew about Juan, he wanted to know the details of what happened and if we were sure the kids were my husbands and I explained that we had the blood test before birth and that they were his. He told Ta'Ron that he didn't care if he never spoke to him again but if he even saw Juan or knew where he was that he better call him and let him know. And just like that everything fell apart. Our lifelong friendship was destroyed in one night by the same man who had destroyed it ten months ago. I was angry at Ta'Ron for hitting Donovan and talking to Cassie so disrespectfully. I told him he was wrong about that but that now it didn't matter because she was the only person, I had shared every intimate detail of this situation with, and for her to say something so foul even in the heat of the moment was a no go for me. He agreed that he crossed the line but was upset that they knew he was here and didn't say anything and I told him that as soon as they got here Cassie told me and I asked her to ask Donovan to wait until the end of the night because we were celebrating the birth of our kids. He said he would apologize to Donovan, Devin, Cassie, and Ronnie. I told him that they were not going to tell him later but only was being respectful to my request to have a great night. I told him that he never should've addressed Cassie at all, and explained how he would have reacted if Donovan had talked to me like that instead. He knew that he was wrong and texted her and Donovan immediately, they did not respond.

The next several weeks were very quiet, Ronnie continued to come by, but he was the only one we had heard from. He would try to bring the others up letting us know that he has been in contact with them, but we never took the bait. He said that he would be heading out to travel again shortly, but that he was still coming back for the wedding and said we all needed to make up and not allow what T did to destroy the other relationships. Ta'Ron told Ronnie that on the same night it happened he already called and that he texted them to apologize and that they were the ones who didn't answer or respond. I told him I blocked Cassie, so I don't know if she had been trying to call me or not. At this point my babies were almost two months and they needed my attention, and I couldn't be stressed and breastfeeding and all of that. I was a victim, and this is the exact reason why I didn't tell anyone when it happened, because I feared that later on, they would use, my trauma my hurt my pain against me as if I could have avoided any of it. If anyone else would have said it I would have beat them down and got over it but because it was from her, she got the beat down and the dismissal. Yes, I still loved her and yes, I wished them to still have the most beautiful wedding ever, but I don't think I could stand beside her on that day knowing that she felt that way about my sexual assault. I felt horrible because I know my husband missed his boys, with the exception of T which no one has seen or heard from since that night. Ronnie promised to have a talk with everyone and try to restore things. I told him that we had promised to help pay for the wedding and we were not going to go back on that promise, but I could not as of today agree to see her let alone be in her life and or wedding.

# CHAPTER 21

Six months old already? There was no way time had gone by that fast. The twins were beautiful and healthy, and we just left the doctor for their six-month checkup. Ta'Ron was back on the road, but I was doing well with the twins on my own and I had plenty of family to still lean on if I needed any help. Bella had finally got use to the babies after six months, she was so jealous and whinny for such a long time, but always very protective of them. Work was going well, and I was back at it selling like crazy. Private daycare has worked out wonders for me. We actually used one of the older ladies from my church who has been doing daycare for decades and then retired. She agreed after talking to my mother to take care of the twins and she did an amazing job with them. I must admit things were different but not in a bad way at all. I was hanging with coworkers and other basketball wives, and I was still really enjoying life and documenting it all with the camera. Hubby had started talking back to the twins little by little, but it was not the same. We paid what we agreed to pay toward the wedding, but I was still not interested in being in it. Donovan would send word through Ta'Ron that Cassie was so sorry and missed me and wanted to make it right, but I still have not be able to unblock her. He asked if I reached out for her bridal shower – I had received the invitation, but I didn't know if she just didn't want to tell the planner we were not talking or what. I promised Hubby, I would unblock her and hear her out if she called. At this point I was healing well. I had finally told my parents about all that I was going through and Mommy referred me to a great colleague of hers for counseling. I was finally at peace, so I wasn't ready to open up pandoras box just yet.

Hubby and I lived on video chat, he hated missing a single day with the kids, we have traveled to two away games but that is a bit much right now with two infants so when he has home games we go and of course he stays home with us then. But he has also started promoting cologne and shoes from the two new major endorsement deals he just signed, and they keep him pretty busy as well doing appearances and commercials and photoshoots, and other publicity things. I do not complain because he definitely is taking great care of us, while also encouraging and pushing me to step out and do more as well. I have started managing properties for other people with my new Property Management company called "Legend's Legacy." It is doing tremendously well, and I begin house flipping in addition to normal real estate, and my first flip sold really quickly and above asking, so I am very excited to see where this goes. I am probably most excited that I was able to get into the studio and start recording music. I haven't been able to find the strength to sing in so long. This is indeed such an amazing feeling. Of course, my original dream was to be this famous singer, now I am more interested in recording the songs that I wrote and shopping them round as demos in hopes that I can have a major artist perform it, and I will feel just as accomplished. I am just starting but I will finish this album of sixteen songs to shop it around. Singing has played an instrumental part in my healing process. I still have days when I just breakdown and cry but not that I was a victim of so many unfortunate circumstances, but that I survived them all, that I overcame them and persevered despite what was thrown at me. One day I will be able to tell my story and encourage other women and most importantly my children, that you can still be great and fulfil your dreams no matter how big the hurdles and mountains are in your path. I think that many times we keep things in because of guilt and or shame and it literally keeps us bound and unable to move forward. I will not lie it is not easy and it is a daily task but because I made up in my mind that they will not win, and I will not be defeated I strive daily. I know that my children literally saved my life, and my goal is to live a life that makes them proud and teaches them to be good to people and to themselves. Getting back in church has been just as helpful as counseling. That mind-body-and soul connection is something serious. I am learning you can't strengthen one and not equally work out the other piece.

The piece that I am struggling with the most is Cassie I finally answered the phone for her, and she started with "We both said some things we shouldn't have." I instantly got pissed, "Um no we didn't, what I am not about to do is hold this phone after six months just to get a half assed apology. You are either sorry or you are not, but you are not going to include me in your short comings. My husband was wrong, and I got onto him, but I didn't disrespect you or air out your shit to embarrass you, nor did I throw any of your tragedies up in your face. I know how to apologize on my own which I am willing to do, but if you are not sincere, please don't ever dial this number again. I love you but I will not hold on to broken or damaged relationships simply because of the number of years we have invested." I said firmly as she started in on what sounded as a weak ass attempt to apologize. She said she realized that sounded terrible once it came out and asked that I give her the opportunity to get it out and explain without me being so stuck on the wording. I agreed and she was right I could be very literal, but honestly, I was hurt, broken, betrayed, by one of the people I loved the most and I honestly feel like I could forgive anyone for anything but to say all of this was my fault as if I asked or deserved to be raped was just unacceptable. She started to cry which made me cry, she asked if we could meet in person and I told her I did not know if I was ready yet, that we would see how this phone call went. I missed her like crazy, but I also knew that if she ever said anything close like that to me again, I was going to snap. She agreed and continued to explain that she was pissed at the time and how that was no excuse and that she honestly doesn't know why she said it, and how Donovan and her mom have been all over her. "I'm getting married, Tierra, married! I cannot have my dream wedding without you being in it! Money aside Donovan and I would much rather have yal back. The boys have been working on their friendship, we are the only ones who haven't even tried." She said as she sobbed. I told her that there were many times that I wanted to reach out and apologize for jumping on her. But that I was afraid I was developing this "let people walk all over me" complex that I wanted no part of. I had been in the victim seat one time too many. I told her how sorry

I was for not allowing her the opportunity to apologize by blocking her but told her that because I just knew we would live like the golden girls to the end, and then this happened, I honestly didn't know if I would be able to get things back like they used to be no matter how much I desired it. She asked how I had been and how the twins were, and that she missed us so much and was so depressed that she has not been able to be in their lives and that I was missing out on something that I also said I would never miss, which was her wedding. "Listen, I am just going to come out and ask and it may be too soon, but here it goes anyway. Will you please be my matron of honor and take your place back in my life as my best friend? I cannot imagine life without you in it, and if anyone would have told me that we would have ever gotten to this point I would have bet all I owned that they were lying. I was wrong, I am so sorry, and I do understand how much it hurt because of what I said and when I said it and because it was me who said it. Tierra, I'm begging you, even if we start out slow, I am cool with that." She continued to pour her heart out and I began to feel like a monster, was I overreacting, was I protecting my peace, now I am super emotional and unsure what to do. I told her exactly how I felt without holding back but I also told her that I would definitely try but that I didn't want to feel rushed. Emotions were high and I honestly didn't know if I said yes because she was crying so hard, and I didn't want to hurt her. I definitely love her and always will or was it that I built all the walls up for her that I never put up for anyone else and now it's hard for even me to knock them down. She asked if we could meet up for dinner tomorrow at the club and I agreed. The timing was perfect as my parents had already asked for the twins tomorrow so, I didn't have to call and ask them, and once I told them that Cassie and I had talked they would've come anyway, they were on me just as much as Ta'Ron to fix things with her. We met at the club, and I hadn't seen her in so long, she had been getting in shape for her wedding dress and sis was snatched in all the right places. I had worked off this baby fat as well, and so the first thing we said when we saw one another was "OK I see you!" and we hugged and cried and sat down to talk. The fellas stopped by the table to speak and to say that Ronnie would be back in a few days, and that he was staying until the wedding. I told them that Ta'Ron was still very excited and that he was being secretive about the plans for the bachelor party. They laughed and said he was supposed to and asked what we were doing for the bachelorette party. We said in unison "None of your business!" Honestly, I had not planned anything because we had not talked. I know that I missed her bridal shower and I know that I will never be able to go back in time, but I guess since we are working on getting back to us, I am going to jump in and do what I do best and plan the most elaborate bachelorette party ever. We caught up for hours and as the more talked and were just honest with one another, it felt better and real and I knew at that moment I had forgiven her and so I just flat out said it and asked for her forgiveness as well. And just like that it was like a weight had been lifted up off me, and she asked if this weekend was too soon to ask to see the kids and I told her no. I made it back to my parents who pretty much were holding the twin's hostage. They decided to tell me they were staying and that they would take them to daycare on their way to work because they were not ready to part with them. I had not ever really been without them while Ta'Ron was gone as well, but I said ok and I knew they had everything they needed in there, so I went home and got some of the best rest I had ever had, just Bella and I like the old days.

The next several days were smooth at work and at home as well as with Cassie and I. The wedding plans were smooth as well she already had a planner and all I had to do is go and get fitted for my dress which I did. When I finally got to the boutique and saw the dress I was in awe. A lot of bridesmaids' dresses were hideous, but these were beautiful, and with everything going on I had just realized I never knew her wedding colors. My dress was a dark deep burgundy- wine colored mermaid style dress that was very shimmery. It was absolutely gorgeous. The other bridesmaids' dresses we coral and our floral bouquets had both colors with some gold accents. It was so beautiful, especially when you see everything all together. When she stepped out in her princess style gown there was not a dry eye in the room, she looked stunning, something right off a magazine cover. "Oh my God Cassie, you are perfect! You are gonna make Donovan cry like a baby!" All the other women agreed, and we kept wiping our eyes. We changed back to our clothes, and I talked to the other ladies about the final touches on the bachelorette party while Cass was finishing up. I could not wait to pull out all of my surprises and her favorite things. I am so glad we moved past this; I hate we lost six months but glad to have her back.

Time was going by way to fast. It is like I blinked, and a week had passed. Ronnie had made it back into town and we were days away from the parties and the wedding.

Ta'Ron will be home tomorrow, and I just knew this was going to be an event to remember, plus after all we had been through as a collective group, this was a great way to celebrate. Cassie had been enjoying time with the kids and took so many pictures anytime they were together. She has one of her nieces and one of her nephews pushing them down the aisle in decked out strollers during the ceremony as honorary flower girl and ring bearer. Legacy loves her dress, she cries every time we take it off of her, looks like we have a little diva in the making. Donovan and the fellas finished finalizing everything with the music and venue and the wedding coordinator was on top of her game. My bestie is getting married. We often joked about her payback time of walking around quoting from the Color Purple movie "I's Married Nah!" she always I said it too much and that she was going to irritate me just as much when she finally had her turn, and here we are literally days away. I went to pick up the bride to be and took her to be pampered and run some last-minute errands. She suggested that we go and get some ice cream after, which I didn't think was a good idea because we looked amazing in those dresses and all we needed was an ice cream sandwich looking belly the day of. But she was in charge, so we got the babies and headed to grab some ice cream. We pulled up and everyone must have had the same idea. We sat outside on the patio and patiently waited and ran our mouths like we always do. As we were laughing hysterically, I heard a voice ask if the babies were mine and when I looked up, to my surprise it was Juan's ass. "Yes, they are and get the hell away from me!" I said as I stood up. Cassie immediately started going off and told him to walk away. He then had the nerve to ask me if there were his and that's when I tried to knock his head off. He apologized and he rubbed his jaw and called me crazy and got in his car and sped off, while yelling out the window "I'm back and you know where to find me!" This man has lost his damn mind. "Find him wear I'm sick of him?" Cassie asked, "Girl hell if I know, I know they still own they house, but you know I ain't looking for his weird ass!" I said as she high fived me for punching him in his mouth. "Sis change of plans to hell with this ice cream I need something stronger now, let's grab a daiquiri and you know we are telling everyone today cuz we ain't keeping no more secrets." Cassie said as she put on her blinged out shades. I was still breast feeding so no drinking for me, but it was a drive through, and you could get nab as well, so I got one just to feel grown.

When we dropped her back off the guys were there and so we called Ta'Ron on video and told them all at once so that there were no secrets and that we didn't have another fight especially days before the wedding. Cassie told them what he yelled out the window, and they were all pissed, before I could say a word, she was telling them what I just told her that they still owned the property to my knowledge. I asked everyone to take it easy, that I felt good handling myself and if I ever seen him again, I promised to file an actual report. I begged everyone to lets only focus on Cass and Donovan and their big day and then we could revisit this. They all promised even Ronnie and Ta'Ron but made sure they knew how serious I was. I told My hubby that I would see him tomorrow when I picked him up from the airport. We made it home and got settled and my phone started to ring like crazy, but I was bathing the twins, so I didn't grab it right away. I put them down for bed and did a few more things around the house before preparing to run my own bath water and checked my phone and this man, Juan had called me all of those times and texted from some new number he obviously has. I started running my bath water and lighting my candles and got setting in my hot bubble bath and called Ta'Ron and he was mad as hell. I told him that we only had the parties tomorrow, the wedding Saturday and we were not going to adjust the spotlight one bit, that I would talk to my dad and go to the station to make a report first thing in the morning once I drop the babies off at daycare. When we hung up, I got dressed and called my dad and told him what had happened, and he instructed me not to block the number only to mute the notifications and to get him to say his name via text without holding a conversation. He said the more evidence we have the better. He told me over and over not to chat with him even a little as those people see that as you want them back, and for me not to try to get him to admit anything just ask who it is get him to text his name and never respond after. I did as I was instructed and called Cassie to tell her, and she said that she was going to meet me there as a witness to what happened when we were trying to get ice cream. I slept very well and woke up and took the kids to daycare and then went to the police station as I promised my husband and father. Making a report is a headache. They treat you like you just randomly woke up and said hey I think I will make a police report today. I had to tell them that my attorney instructed me not to leave without a case number and to call him if I had any issues, for them to take me seriously. Cassie was frustrated and also told them about what he said, and they asked me if I knew the address, I told him I did not, but the job could get it as we sold him the house. And I called and they gave them the information they requested. After getting everything, we needed including the case number, I hugged Cass and told her I was headed to get my man.

I picked up Ta'Ron and as always, he greeted me as if he hadn't seen me in years. I had to run him to try on his tux since he had been on the road just to make sure it still fit well. After handling the wedding stuff, we went and had lunch and headed home for some quality time. We were going to have a crazy busy next two days between tonight's festivities and the wedding tomorrow. His parents were picking up and keeping the kids and bringing them to the wedding tomorrow so that I could focus all of my attention on the beautiful bride. I called and confirmed we were still on schedule for the limo to pick us up from Cassie's tonight and everything was in order. I took full advantage of snuggling up with my baby and just talking. I brought him up to speed and showed him the report I filed. I told him I had to scan it and send it over to my dad's office and I would do that once he headed out and before I got dressed for the evening. Until then it was good just to relax and not worry about anything for a minute. He tried his best to stay off the subject, but every few minutes he would blurt out things like, "He gone get his, and that's a promise. And "Ooh he better thank God that the wedding is tomorrow but once they say I do that's his ass and don't even ask me not to handle it however I handle it." I didn't give much push back I usually tried to flip the subject. The little time we had to spend with each other was great and I didn't want to waste it talking about Juan. He brought me up to speed about road life and said he was really getting the itch to retire. I told him that I back him on whatever he decided, but I made sure he knew that the kids and I were fine and he did not need to stop for us, only if he wanted to. He said he appreciated me having his back and he got up to shower and get dressed. "Damn you lookin' and smellin' like a million bucks Baby! What's yo name, what's the secret?" I said as I rubbed all over him. "I am the secret!" he said back quick on his feet as usual. I told him I was going to get dressed and drive to Cassie's house. She knows we are picking her up, but she doesn't know about the limos. And that when the night was over, we were going to take my car to the hotel, still withholding all the details of our crazy night that I planned for twenty-two women. We kissed and I walked him to the door and then I got dressed. I called Cassie again; she didn't answer but I know her phone is blowing up from everyone calling her which I directed her to tell them to call me instead, but she was too nice and would stay on the phone with them anyway. When she didn't answer this time, I texted her and said "Hey Heffa, I know you see me calling. I am getting dressed and headed to you!" She replied with the laughing emoji and a skeleton. And said "Girl you crazy, love you Bestie – see you in a few for the time of my life, you're the best. Love you!" I told her not to be running late that we had a lot to get in tonight and she just laughed and said "Oh Lord. I'm ready. I have one last run to make, and I am not answering any more calls or texts because it's slowing me down, then I'm going home to get dressed so I will be ready when you get there." I told her that I loved her too and sent out a group text to text to call me only, that Cassie needed to focus so she can be ready. They all agreed, and I got dressed and grabbed the goodie bags I had made and some games full of some crazy shenanigans that I was certain would make this a night to remember.

I pulled up a few minutes earlier than I expected so I double checked a few last-minute things and made a few calls to the locations just making sure everything was going to be perfect for tonight, before going inside. Once I looked up, I could see some of the other ladies pulling up and parking, so I got out of the car and greeted them. Everyone looked amazing, I knew we were about to go crazy tonight. Shante, one of the administrators at the school Cassie works at, was one of the first to arrive. They had gotten closer during the six months that we were not talking. She was always nice though. "Ok Tierra don't hurt nobody tonight!" She said as she saw what I was wearing. "Girl that's you that is going to be making heads spin." I said back to her as she tugged on her skirt. "That's the plan girl, I'm trying to be next." We just started laughing as we walked up to more of the ladies. I excused myself to go get Cassie and make sure she didn't need any help with her final touches. Plus, we had a sash and veil to hook her up with and a few other things. I went up to the door and rang the doorbell and my heart was racing, I could not believe the time was finally here. She didn't come to the door right away, so I figured she was using the bathroom or something. I told them I would wait a few minutes and go back up to the door. More of the ladies piled in and the limos started to pull up. The ladies were really getting excited, but they had no clue the kind of night I had planned. It is gonna start off nice and easy and then get a little intense as the night passes. I called Cassie again and there was no answer, so I went up to the door again and rang the doorbell, no answer, I rang it again while singing crazy songs like Betty Wright's, "Tonight is the Night!" I rang the video doorbell again and finally an answer, "Tierra why in the world are you outside my house ringing the doorbell over and over?" Donovan said. He was answering me from his phone, he and the guys were already out. "I am trying to get yo slow poke wife to be out of the house so we can go, Our chariot awaits us!" I replied as I danced around on the porch. "She didn't come to the door yet?" he said feeling puzzled? I told him no and that she was not answering the phone either but that I would get her. He told me the code to open the garage and get in. I used the code and opened the door and went it and it was quiet, no lights no music not "pre-game" cups laying around or anything. I went upstairs to her room and master bathroom and nothing. She wasn't even home yet. I came down and told the crew and we all started calling and texting her that we were about to kick it without her. I sent the ladies on to the restaurant after waiting a few minutes longer. I knew that if at least some of us were not there they would cancel our reservation. One limo and a few ladies, including Shante stayed back and waited with me. We popped some champagne and danced out by the limo and took pictures, waiting on her to call or pull up. After about 30 minutes I started to worry and I called Ta'Ron, who didn't answer the first few times I called. When he finally picked up, he said that it is loud and that he couldn't hear me. I told him Cassie still wasn't home and wasn't answering her phone and that I sent a few of the ladies ahead but that she wasn't even responding to my text and that I was getting worried. He asked was I able to get in the house and I told him I was but that no one was inside no lights were on or anything. He said to give her a few more minutes and that he would keep an eye on his phone, so he didn't miss my call. He wanted me to tell him when she finally got there. I said ok and I pulled Shante to the side and told her I was worried, that I know Cass of all people did not get cold feet. She reassured me that everything was going to be fine and that maybe that last run she was making took longer than expected. "Yeah, that's true but she would answer for me, she wouldn't want me to be worried about her." I kept saying every few minutes. The limo driver asked how much longer we would be waiting, and I told him just that I wasn't sure. He was polite, we used them frequently and paid and tipped well, so he didn't care, he just wanted an update. At this point I was frantic, and everyone was trying to calm me down. Another thirty minutes or so had passed and no one had heard from her since she said that she was going to stop responding because it was slowing her down. I called Hubby back and told him that we still had not heard from her. He was just as worried and said he would pull Devin to the side and talk to him and Ronnie before getting Donovan all worked up. I told him that I would keep him posted. As the night grew later, I was beyond nervous I tried not to over call the fellas because I knew it would put them all into a panic especially Donovan. But another hour had passed, and we had not even got a text message back. We chatted among ourselves trying to figure out what her last errand could have been, and we were all clueless. I had taken her to be pampered and sent her to get her makeup done, I got her clothes for tonight and there was NOTHING she was responsible for tonight other than showing up and having a great time. One of the girls said she probably picked up some last-minute things for the wedding night since today was the last time she would have time, but that would still not make sense to why she is not answering the phone. I hated to be a worried pest, but I called my husband back and told him we still had heard nothing and that he needed to tell Donovan immediately. He did and he instantly went into a whirlwind of emotions as he even knew it wasn't like her. Luckily, they have a family plan, so he went to find her phone and was able to track it and it was still showing that it was on. They were speaking so fast and all at once I could barely understand them. "Slow down yal, I'm shaking where is she cuz we are locking up the house as we speak and will jump in the limo and head over now." I said as I paced the ground. Ta'Ron said that Donovan said he didn't recognize the area and it was not somewhere he has ever known her to be. "Baby he said she is over by Ansley Park. What is over there? It shows she has been over there for a long time." Before he could finish, I started screaming and told everyone to get in the car immediately if they were going. They were running in heels and asking me what was wrong. "Baby I am headed there now that is where Juan lives, tell Donovan now and meet me there!" I was crying hysterically. This had to be some coincidence the fellas kept saying. The ladies were clueless, of course they have no clue what happened to me and so they just kept telling me she was ok. I programed the address in my GPS. I had just got it from the police report I filed earlier, and she was there and heard it, I was overthinking it I was sure, but I was hoping she didn't go to confront him. When we finally hit the block, we couldn't get close. The streets were blocked with yellow caution tape and police and emergency vehicles were everywhere. I jumped out the limo, kicked off my heels and hauled ass to the scene and I saw that the fellas and Donovan were doing the same thing. Shante tried to keep up, but she just couldn't. As we grew closer, I could see what looked like two bodies on the ground covered up. One in the yard and one in the street next to Cassie's car. Donovan and I could not be stopped. I ran as hard and as fast as I could yelling her name. A police officer stopped us and asked who we were. I tried explaining but I couldn't get any words out. Donovan was being restrained and was screaming and crying asking where the owner of the car was, telling them that he was the husband, and they were getting married tomorrow and she was late to her bachelorette party, so we looked up her location and that's how we got there. He asked us her name and description and then I saw him drop his head. Immediately I knew something horrible had happened. They asked us to stand to the side and promised to come talk to us when they knew more. "What the hell was she doing over her Tierra?" Donovan screamed with the little breath he had left. "I have no clue; I would have never let this happen. She was with me this morning when I made a report so she must have remembered the address from there, she never even joked about pulling up over here." I tried to get it all out, but my chest was tightening, and I could not breathe Ta'Ron as squeezing me as Devin and Ronnie tried to hold Donovan. An older lady from across the street started walking toward us and said she had seen a little of what happened and that she was the one who called the police. She said a Hispanic male came out of the house bleeding chasing this woman and she was getting away and as she almost made it to the car, she was screaming at him saying "I just got her back, I just got her back!" and that they both were shooting but as she almost got to the street he lifted his gun and shot her and then fell out himself, and that to her knowledge they were both dead before the police arrived. At this point we all lost it and I just charged at the scene and pulled the cover off and it was her. I just screamed and hollered, and they had to pry me off of her body and I still refused to let her go, Donovan had passed out and EMT's were working on him, and the fellas were all in an uproar the ladies were crying and screaming. To say it was chaotic was an understatement. I knew her family were all in town of course because the wedding was tomorrow. This has to be a crazy nightmare. There is no way Cassie would have come to confront and try to kill him. I just kept replaying the ladies' words in my mind over and over. "I just got her back!" I knew immediately she was talking about me, that we just mended our friendship, a friendship that he was ultimately responsible for breaking. It was his assault on me that started the domino effect of events that came after. And the statement that she had made that separated us for six months was because he had started it all. Just as we pulled ourselves together, we had to run into him at the ice cream parlor and he had to start texting and calling again. She must've been afraid that his presence back in my life was going interrupt or possibly end our friendship. Cassie was right, all of this was over me. I should've never stopped talking to her for those six months. As soon as I saw the Chaplin start to walk towards us, I knew he was coming over to confirm. Donovan was still out, and Devin was inconsolable. His voice was low and soft, and he said "I am sorry to inform you that

Cassandra Reynolds has passed from what appears to be a gunshot to the back of the head, we will not know everything until the autopsy is complete. I am so sorry for your loss!" Anything that was said after that is a blur. It was at that point that I heard my husband, and the fellas cry a cry I had never heard. The pain in their voices made it worse for me. I felt like my heart was ripped right out of my chest. Donovan was up and alert and when they walked over to tell him he lost it. "No not Boo Baby. We are getting married in the morning, Nah man nah!" He screamed. Reporters were pulling up cameras were flashing and Ta'Ron and Ronnie were about to fight every camera man out there. "I have to ride with her body, I can't leave her, I can't tell her mom, Lord have mercy!" Donovan was a mess. They assured him that they would go to the hotel and tell her mother. My head was spinning, I could not breathe and so they felt that I should go get checked out, I didn't want to leave her. The thought of her being gone was way too much pain to bear. I had never had a heart attack before, but I was sure I was having one now. Shante called the ladies that had went on before us to break the bad news. They authorities assured us they had not released any names so that the press could not leak it before they make it to the hotel, which they were in route now.

As I laid there in the back of the ambulance getting checked out and my husband held my hand, I just saw flashes of all the wonderful times we had together, all the memories since our school days, and that just made me cry even harder. They kept asking me to stay calm but that was nearly impossible. There had been no greater pain I had ever felt, not the pain from Juan, the betrayal of

T, who none of us still have heard from, the birth of the twins, the temporary loss of the best friendship I had ever had. Nothing could compare to the heaviness I felt in this moment, the thought of never talking to her again, the guilt of feeling like it was my fault or that I could have somehow prevented this from happening. I just wanted to curl up into a ball and disappear. My phone was starting to ring off the hook which means they called Mrs. Reynolds, and she has called my parents. I tried to fix my lips to say hello, and as soon as I heard Mommy's voice "Tierra Baby!" I just started screaming and crying all over again. As if that wasn't enough the corner van had pulled up and they were loading her body, I tried unhooking myself and getting back over to her. All I could remember was all the blood that was everywhere and her face, her beautiful face was sagging and almost unrecognizable. "Jesus, Jesus, Jesus!" is all I can remember saying. Watching that van drive off was the worst feeling in the world, seeing everyone's pain especially Donovan was just too much. He came over to the ambulance and tried telling me that he loved me and that it wasn't my fault, but he could barely get his words out and I couldn't stop bawling. He hopped in to ride with me and Ta'Ron so that he could get all the information from the hospital as well concerning him, he was going to be checked out. "This is not your fault baby girl, don't you dare carry this, she loved you so much she was down to protect you to the end, as we all wanted to. We all just promised to wait until after the…." He started crying before he could get the word wedding out. "I am so sorry I don't have the words friend; I am in disbelief." I tried to articulate my feelings and condolences, but I couldn't gather my words enough.

"He better be glad he is already dead; We will get through this!" He screamed at the top of his lungs with the little voice that he did have left. We pulled up to the hospital and they wheeled me in. All I could say was "Damn Cass! Damn!" Our lives will never be the same. Damn Cass!

**Phone:** (316)-993-0219

**Email:** <u>authorlameshia@gmail.com</u>

**Social Media:**  @AuthorLaMeshia

 @mzmelodic

*For booking and calendar information or to purchase
a copy of this book, or other books and merchandise,
please contact us using any of the information
above, and follow us on social media.*

# Dignified Jewels & Accessories
## "Unleash Your Inner Diva!"

 WWW.FACEBOOK.COM/DIGNIFIEDJEWELS

**Email:** *dignifiedjewels@gmail.com*

*We offer a wide variety of- Jewelry and Accessories, Sunglasses, Eyelashes, Scarfs, Hats, Watches, Home Décor, Unique Trinkets, and much more!*